William Shakespeare, Robert R. Raymond

Typical Tales of Fancy, Romance and History From Shakespeare's

Plays

in narrative form, largely in Shakespeare's words, with dialogue passages in the

original dramatic text

William Shakespeare, Robert R. Raymond

Typical Tales of Fancy, Romance and History From Shakespeare's Plays
in narrative form, largely in Shakespeare's words, with dialogue passages in the original dramatic text

ISBN/EAN: 9783337394875

Printed in Europe, USA, Canada, Australia, Japan

Cover: Foto ©Andreas Hilbeck / pixelio.de

More available books at **www.hansebooks.com**

TYPICAL TALES

OF

FANCY, ROMANCE, AND HISTORY

FROM

Shakespeare's Plays:

*IN NARRATIVE FORM, LARGELY IN SHAKESPEARE'S WORDS, WITH
DIALOGUE PASSAGES IN THE ORIGINAL DRAMATIC TEXT.*

EDITED BY

ROBERT R. RAYMOND, A.M.,

LATE PRINCIPAL OF THE BOSTON SCHOOL OF ORATORY; FORMERLY PROFESSOR OF
THE ENGLISH LANGUAGE AND LITERATURE IN THE BROOKLYN
POLYTECHNIC INSTITUTE.

NEW YORK:
FORDS, HOWARD, AND HULBERT.

PREFACE.

HE purpose of this book needs no apology. The period when Shakespeare may be effectively and profitably introduced to the youthful mind arrives earlier in the life of the child than is generally supposed. The phenomenon of the intelligent youngster, stealing away into the family library to revel in the mysterious delights of the " Tempest," or the " Midsummer Night's Dream," or to steep himself in the soul-searching horrors of " Macbeth," is familiar. To such a student of the magic page, all its critical difficulties are as though they were not, — so unconsciously, yet so swiftly and surely, are they disposed of. The prophet-heart of the poet is laid upon the child-heart : the throb is unison : the nascent powers of the young soul spring to life in the contact.

Now, one of the factors in this curious problem is, undoubtedly, the inalienable right of " skipping." What the young mind can assimilate, it appropriates ; the rest is passed over. It is the loss necessarily incurred in this process that the present version — of story and play together — proposes to supply. In other words, it assumes to " skip " *for* the youth, judiciously ; bridging the dreary void of omitted passages with a lively representation of the original, in which the language of the author is to be reproduced only so far as is consistent with the interest of the young reader, — in this case, the prime consideration. Similar service has been attempted also with reference to single obscure expressions, occurring in connections otherwise attractive ; the aim being to

put the reader in possession of the entire work, so far as he is capable
of receiving it. In short, the effort is to do systematically and intelli-
gently what thousands of parents and teachers have long been trying to
do, in order to awaken in the young a love for the Great Master which
should bear its best fruit at a later day. Of all this number perhaps
not one has failed to dream, at some time or other, of some such work
as the one now offered. The wish would necessarily become the father
to the thought. It is in the successful execution of the work that the
main difficulty lies ; and this, in the present case, remains to be tested.

In attempting to carry out the plan suggested by the publishers,
the editor availed himself of the literary taste and intelligence of Mrs.
Louisa T. Craigin, an author well known for her many successful ventures in catering for the youthful mind. To her valuable aid, especially
in the earlier stages of its preparation, the present volume owes much
of its interest.

That this version makes no pretence to critical accuracy, hardly
needs saying. Such a claim would be at war with its very object. Yet,
while not assuming to take account of the nice questions which so legit-
imately occupy the attention of the Shakespearian editors, it is believed
to contain no unwarrantable departure from the texts most generally
approved. No larger latitude of choice between disputed passages has
been used than some of the best authorities habitually indulge in.
Wherever a "conjectural emendation," from a respectable source, has
seemed to furnish a sense more facile to the young reader, it has been
welcomed to the present text, without any very weighty sense of critical
responsibility. Any obscure single word or short phrase in the original
page has been supplanted by a near-enough synonym, when it could be
done without violence to the metre. In all such cases of substitution,
the new word or phrase has been enclosed in brackets. But such changes
as *if* for the obsolete *an ; its* for *his*, when the neuter sense is intended ;
and the definitive use of *would* and *should*, in accordance with the
idioms of our own day instead of the interchangeable usage of Shakespeare's, — being regarded as part of the universally accepted modern-
izing process, — have been adopted without sign or apology. When the
substituted expression could not find place in the text, on account of
rhythmical difficulties, it has been put in a glossary at the bottom of
the page, and referred to by small *figures*. For more extended eluci-
dation — in the few cases where such has been thought indispensable —
recourse has been had to foot-notes, referred to by small *letters*. Pas-

sages confessedly obscure, or requiring very elaborate explanation, have been reduced to the form of narrative, with the original language preserved as nearly as possible. In this connection it will be observed, that while, in the effort to keep the narrative spirited and natural, the sponge has passed freely over such archaisms as might tend to repel the young reader, care has been taken to preserve the "marrys" and "pr'ythees," and similar minute colloquialisms, which, as having a certain "smack of the time," he has generally appeared to appreciate and relish.

The plays here given were selected for the double reason, that they represent three distinct types of Shakespeare's dramas, and that, in different ways, they seemed peculiarly adapted to interest the youthful mind.

A favorable reception of the present volume will be acknowledged by the production of others, which are already in preparation.

R. R. R.

LIST OF ILLUSTRATIONS.

₊ *Together with numerous ornamental and symbolical vignettes,
head and tail pieces, etc.*

CONTENTS.

WILLIAM SHAKESPEARE

BOUT three hundred years ago there lived in England a
poet, whose wonderful works have been more and more prized
from the time when they were written until now ; and to-day
they are the delight and admiration of all the reading people
of Europe and America.   His name was WILLIAM SHAKESPEARE.

He was born on the 23d of April, 1564, in a lovely country town
called Stratford, situated on the banks of the winding and peaceful river
Avon.   His parents were plain, respectable people, and William was
sent to the grammar school of the town, where he made pretty good use
of his time, if we may judge from his after-life and his works, which show
not only the greatness of his genius, but the extent and variety of his
knowledge.   It seems certain that he must have begun very early to
cultivate his mind by study.

When he was only eighteen years of age he married the daughter of
a farmer in a neighboring village, and before he was twenty-two years
old he had a wife and three little children to support. This was probably
the reason that he went up to London about this time to seek his fortune in that great city; though there is a story, which has been handed
down from generation to generation among the good people of Stratford,

TRINITY CHURCH AT STRATFORD, ON THE AVON.

that William, who had been a rather frolicsome boy and was very fond of
hunting, had got into trouble with a rich neighbor for poaching, or shoot-
ing game without permission on his grounds. If this be true, the act
was one which is not for a moment to be defended ; but we ought to
remember that the English law was far more strict on such matters than
ours, and although the youngster made himself liable to severe punish-
ment, his fault was not much greater than that of stealing apples from an
orchard would be in our day. There is happily some ground to doubt the

truth of the story ; but it is sure, that for one reason or another our hero did go up to London in the year 1586, or thereabouts, and did not return to his native village to reside until he became possessed of considerable property.

There are various things told about his adventures in the great metropolis, which do not appear to be well established. It is even said that he earned his first pennies there by holding the horses of gentlemen who had ridden on horseback to attend the theatre. But whether this be true or not, we know that in a very few years he had written several fine poems, which brought him the favor and friendship of some of the first noblemen and gentlemen of London. We know, too, that he became an actor in one of these theatres ; and then began to write plays to be performed in them. These plays became very popular ; for nothing so beautiful, so witty, and so interesting in every way, had been seen on the stage before. Soon they attracted the attention of Queen Elizabeth, who was then on the throne of England ; and it is said both of her and her successor, King James the First, that no amusement delighted them so much as to witness a play of Shakespeare's. They extended their royal patronage to the poet, and he prospered accordingly. He shortly became one of the managers of the Globe Theatre, which was open at the top, and used in summer weather, and also of the Blackfriars Theatre, which was roofed for use in winter.

In this position he continued several years, writing plays for his theatres, and sometimes taking part in the performance of them. There were, in all, thirty-seven of these dramas, some tragedies and some comedies, and of course his works increased in power and beauty as he grew in years and experience. During this time he revisited his native place once every year, and at last, in the year 1612 or 1613, he retired to it, to spend the remainder of his days. He was then about forty-eight years old, and was possessed of a comfortable fortune, gained by his own talents and industry.

Meanwhile his only son had died, and shortly after his arrival in Stratford his eldest daughter married ; but he settled down with what remained of his family, and with a fair prospect of a peaceful and happy

old age. But, though yet in the prime of life, his days were now drawing to a close, and on the 23d of April, 1616, his fifty-second birthday,
he breathed his last. He was buried under the chancel-floor of the
beautiful old Stratford church. His gravestone bears. this curious
inscription : —

Good frend for Iesvs sake forbeare,

To digg the dust encloased heare :

Bleste be y^o man y^t spares thes stones.

And cvrst be he y^t moves my bones.

There has been not a little desire on the part of certain people to look
into this hallowed tomb, and perhaps to inspect the skull that held this
mighty brain, but, as you may well suppose, nobody has been found
hardy enough to brave that fearful curse. So this consecrated resting-
place of the world's greatest poet, together with a rude likeness carved
in stone by some village artist, adorning the wall above it, yet remains to
gratify the curiosity and awaken the reverence of thousands of pilgrims
who visit it from all quarters of the world.

A MIDSUMMER NIGHT'S DREAM.

INTRODUCTION.

MONG the earliest of those dramas which were written by Shakespeare for his theatre. was one which he called " A MIDSUMMER NIGHT'S DREAM."
This title immediately leads us to inquire, Who is the dreamer, — the poet, the characters of the drama, or the spectators ? It is not very easy to reply. First, the whole composition seems to have passed through the mind of the poet like a lovely, fantastic dream, — a procession of shadows thrown by a magic lantern on a screen. Then, much that passes in the play seems only fit to be regarded as a dream by the characters themselves, who are made the sport of fairies. And, finally, it comes before the audience under the notion of a dream. It is a curious composition, full of exquisite poetry and the jolliest fun. In it are mingled a strange variety of personages, — dukes, queens, lords, ladies, young lovers, clownish mechanics, and the dearest little elves, from their royal rulers, who king and queen it with a pretty dignity, to the tricksy sprites that plague poor mortals with their pranks. And then the conduct of some of the persons is so strange and unnatural : their jealousies, their petty passions, and their little meannesses are such as might well have been born in a haunted grove, — the children of magic

and the moonlight.   We might be amused with their fantastic doings as the shifting shadows of a dream, but would never think of trying them by the waking judgments of the cold, gray morning.

The key to the whole matter is given by Puck, the merry hobgoblin of the play, in these words of the epilogue, or conclusion : —

> " If we shadows have offended,
> Think but this — and all is mended :
> That you have but slumbered here,
> While these visions did appear ;
> And this weak and idle theme,
> No more yielding but a dream,
> Gentles, do not reprehend."

We must remember all the way through, then, that the author dreams, — a restless, brilliant, teeming vision, such

> " As youthful poets dream
> On summer eve by haunted stream ; "

and that we are dreaming too, — dreaming with Shakespeare ! Happy mortals we, that we may take him by the hand and fly with him through the wide heaven of his glorious fancy !

It remains to be said, as to the fitness of this title, that though the time of the action is the month of May, which seems to us too early to be called *midsummer*, we must remember that May in those days was reckoned half a month later than now, and was a great deal warmer.   It might have been called the " midsummer's spring," or the beginning of midsummer, as the dawn of the morning is called the " day-spring " in the Bible.   Indeed we shall find this very expression used in the play (p. 30), in words addressed by the Queen to the King of the Fairies.   This was, more than any other, the fairies' time, when (they say), if you knew where to look, you could see the tiny folk dancing in green circles in the moonlight.

The place of the play is said to be " Athens, and a wood near Athens," but, really, it is just *Dream-land*, — an Athens, and a grove, and a company of people, that existed nowhere but in the beautiful fancy of Shakespeare.

No other poet has ever known so well as he how to catch the words and understand the ways of Fairy-land, and explain them to the world of mortals. These words and ways, therefore, it shall be the aim of this little book to give you in the very language of Shakespeare. We will add to this (also in the words of the drama) the doings of the clownish play-actors who are brought into such funny contrast with the fairies. The rest we will tell in clear and simple story, hoping that the day is not far distant when you will read the whole work for yourselves, and then recognize in it the features of an old and beloved friend.

ATHENS.

A MIDSUMMER NIGHT'S DREAM.

I.

ACT I. SCENE 1.

NCE upon a time there lived a mighty hero, Theseus, Duke of Athens. It was he who conquered the Centaurs, a strange and warlike race, half man and half horse; who slew the monster Minotaur, with the body of a man and the head of a bull, that devoured thirty Athenian youths and maidens every year; who sailed with the Argonauts to find the Golden Fleece, which was guarded by a fierce dragon; and engaged in many other famous expeditions, winning great renown for his exploits. At last he had overcome in battle those terrible warrior-women, the Amazons. At the

time our story begins, he had just returned from this final victory, and was about
to marry Hippolyta, the Amazon queen, in his palace at Athens. He says
to her. —

Theseus. Hippolyta, I wooed thee with my sword.

Hippolyta, I wooed thee with my sword,
And won thy love, doing thee injuries ;
But I will wed thee in another key,
With pomp, with triumph, and with revelling.

Great preparations were making
for the wedding, which was to take
place in four days. While the be-
trothed lovers were talking of their
happiness, Egeus, an old Athenian
lord, entered, together with his
daughter Hermia, and two young
Athenians, named Lysander and Demetrius.
The old man approached the Duke,
and said that he came to complain of the
conduct of this daughter. The youth Demetrius had his consent to marry her, but
Lysander had bewitched her with rhymes,
with presents of flowers and sweetmeats,
and with songs sung at her window in the
moonlight, changing her obedience into stub-
born hardness : —

And, my gracious Duke,
Be it so she will not here, before your grace,
Consent to marry with Demetrius,
I beg the ancient privilege of Athens,
As she is mine, I may dispose of her ;
Which shall be either to this gentleman
Or to her death, according to our law *
Immediately provided in that case.

The Duke then reasoned with Hermia : he told her that Demetrius was a worthy
gentleman ; that she ought to obey her father, to whom she owed so much ; and
explained to her the Athenian law. But all in vain. The unhappy Hermia was
quite sure that she would rather die, or live in a convent, than marry Demetrius.

Then Duke Theseus (perhaps to give the lovers a chance to escape) told the
maiden to take a few days to think about it : by the next new moon, which was to

---

* In Solon's time there was a law in Athens giving to a parent power of life and death
over his child. Shakespeare seems to have taken it for granted that the law existed even
before that.

be his wedding-day, she must decide either to die for disobedience, or to wed Demetrius, or to vow upon Diana's altar to live a lonely single life.

Demetrius called upon Lysander to "yield his crazy title" to Hermia's hand; but Lysander appealed to the Duke, saying: " I am in rank and wealth as good as Demetrius, and, what is more, the beauteous Hermia loves me. Demetrius cannot deny that he made love to Helena, old Nedar's daughter, and she, sweet lady, still dotes in idolatry on this wicked, inconstant man."

Theseus seems to have heard something about this before: he bade Egeus and Demetrius follow him, upon some business connected with his coming marriage, and, with a last kind word of warning to Hermia, went out with Hippolyta, leaving the two young lovers alone together.

Lysander tried to comfort the weeping Hermia, but said, rather sadly, —

> Ah me! for aught that I could ever read,
> Could ever hear by tale or history,
> The course of true love never did run smooth.

At last Lysander remembered that he had an aunt, living about twenty miles away from Athens; a widow lady, of great wealth, who loved him as a son. There they could be married without fear of the sharp Athenian law. If Hermia would meet him the next night in the wood, a league outside the town, where once they went a-Maying, he would wait there for her. Hermia brightened at the thought.

> My good Lysander!
> I swear to thee, by Cupid's strongest bow,
> By his best arrow with the golden head,
> In that same place thou hast appointed me,
> To-morrow truly will I meet with thee!

Hardly had these two lovers decided on their plan of escape, when Helena, the lovely and unhappy young lady of whom Lysander had spoken, came in.

Helena had been a schoolmate of Hermia's. The two girls were very fond of

each other. They used to sit side by side, embroidering the same sampler, singing the same songs, and telling each other all their joys and sorrows. They grew up together like twin cherries on a single stem. Both the girls were thought fair throughout all Athens, but they were quite unlike. Helena was tall and dignified ; mild and gentle in manner, timid and affectionate in disposition. Hermia was short and dark ; a very lively, wide-awake little lady, with a warm heart, a hasty temper, and a ready tongue.

The treatment that Helena had received from Demetrius had made her extremely sad, and Hermia and Lysander wished so much to comfort her, that they were glad to meet her just then, so that they might tell her of their new plans.

Hermia was afraid she might pass by without seeing them, because, poor soul, she was so unhappy that her eyes were always full of tears ; so Hermia called gayly to her : —

God speed, fair Helena ! Whither away ?
Helena. Call you me fair ? that fair again unsay.
Demetrius loves your fair:[1] O happy fair !
Your eyes are lode-stars,[2] and your tongue's sweet air
More tunable than lark to shepherd's ear,
When wheat is green, when hawthorn buds appear.
O ! teach me how you look, and with what art
You sway the motion of Demetrius' heart.
Hermia. I frown upon him, yet he loves me still.
Helena. O that your frowns would teach my smiles such skill!
Hermia. The more I hate the more he follows me.
Helena. The more I love the more he hateth *me.*
Hermia. His folly, Helen, is no fault of mine.
Helena. None but your beauty's : would that fault were mine !
Hermia. Take comfort: he no more shall see my face :
Lysander and myself will fly this place ;
And in the wood, where often you and I
Upon faint primrose-beds were wont to lie,
Emptying our bosoms of their counsel sweet,
There my Lysander and myself shall meet ;
And thence from Athens turn away our eyes,
To seek new friends and stranger companies.
Farewell, sweet playfellow !

Then Hermia and Lysander went away in different directions, leaving Helena alone. Now Helena ought to have been very glad to know that Hermia and Lysander were going to be so happy, and that Demetrius would soon be free, and so perhaps come back some day to his old love for her. But, instead of that, she only remembered how unhappy she was herself, and how much she wished to see

---

[1] Fairness.   [2] Polar stars.

Demetrius, and so she formed a strange plan, — a plan which would seem quite unbecoming a maiden, except in a dream. She said to herself, —

> I will go tell him of fair Hermia's flight ;
> Then to the wood will he, to-morrow night.
> Pursue her ; and for this intelligence
> If I have thanks, it is dear recompense :
> But herein mean I to enrich my pain,
> [With him to go] thither, and back again.

With these words Helena went away to find Demetrius.

ROOM IN THE COTTAGE OF QUINCE THE CARPENTER.

II.

THENS was now full of rejoicing over the approaching marriage of Theseus and Queen Hippolyta. All the people wanted to do something in honor of the great occasion and to show their love. Among the rest, a number of rough workingmen — "rude mechanicals, hard-handed men, that worked for bread upon Athenian stalls " — met in a cottage to talk over their plan, which was to act a play before the Duke and his bride " on his wedding-day at night," as they said.

They were a queer company for such a purpose, and comical work they made of it, as you will see. First, there was *Quince*, the carpenter, who seems to have planned and managed the whole affair, perhaps because he was a carpenter and did everything by rule. Next in importance came *Bottom*, the weaver, who was a general favorite, and was thought by his friends, as well as by himself, to be very bright and witty. He was certainly conceited enough ; for he was quite sure no one could do anything so well as he : and he actually wanted to take all the principal parts in the play himself ! *Francis Flute*, the bellows-mender, was a little fellow, with a small, squeaky voice ; which was the reason that he was chosen for the woman's part. *Snug*, the joiner, was a quiet, peaceable man, slow of speech, and

" slower yet of study." *Starveling*, the tailor, was a snip of a chap, who stuttered and stammered whenever he attempted to speak. And at the end of the list stood *Snout*, the tinker, who was timorous and doubtful. He saw the dark side of everything, and when anybody spoke of a difficulty, it seemed to him that there was no possible way of overcoming it.

These poor fellows really wished to do something that would be a credit to themselves and a high compliment to the Duke ; but they were so ignorant that, without knowing or meaning it in the least, they only made themselves ridiculous. The tragedy which they meant should be pathetic and heart-breaking was funny instead ; and the only tears it caused were those that came from laughing.

Having met in the carpenter's cottage as agreed, they looked to Quince as their leader, who thus began : —

Is all our company here ?

Bottom. You were best to call them generally, man by man, according to the [writing].

Quince. Here is the scroll of every man's name, which is thought fit, through all Athens, to play in our interlude before the Duke and Duchess on his wedding-day at night.

Bottom. First, good Peter Quince, say what the play treats on ; then read the names of the actors, and so go on to appoint.

Quince. Marry, our play is — The most lamentable comedy, and most cruel death of Pyramus and Thisbe.

Bottom. A very good piece of work, I assure you, and a merry. — Now, good Peter Quince, call forth your actors by the scroll. Masters, spread yourselves.

Quince. Answer, as I call you. — Nick Bottom, the weaver.

Bottom. Ready. Name what part I am for, and proceed.

Quince. You, Nick Bottom, are set down for Pyramus.

Bottom. What is Pyramus ? a lover, or a tyrant ?

Quince. A lover, that kills himself most gallant for love.

Bottom. That will ask some tears in the true performing of it : if I do it, let the audience look to their eyes ; I will move stones ; I will condole in some measure. To the rest : — yet my chief humor is for a tyrant : I could play Ercles[1] rarely, or a part to tear a cat in, to make all split.

> " The raging rocks,
> And shivering shocks,
> Shall break the locks
> Of prison-gates :
> And Phibbus'[2] car
> Shall shine from far
> And make and mar
> The foolish fates."

This was lofty ! — Now name the rest of the players. — This is Ercles' vein,[3] a tyrant's vein ; a lover is more condoling.

---

[1] Hercules. [2] Phœbus's car, — the sun. [3] Style.

Bottom.   A part to tear a cat in, to make all split.

Quince. Francis Flute, the bellows-mender.

Flute. Here, Peter Quince.

Quince. You must take Thisbe on you.

Flute. What is Thisbe? a wandering knight?

Quince. It is the lady that Pyramus must love.

Flute. Nay, faith, let me not play a woman: I have a beard coming.

Quince. That's all one. You shall play it in a mask, and you may speak as small as you will.*

Bottom. If I may hide my face, let me play Thisbe too. I'll speak in a monstrous little voice, thus, thus: "Ah, Pyramus, my lover dear! thy Thisbe dear, and lady dear!"

Quince. No, no; you must play Pyramus, and, Flute, you Thisbe.

---

* In Shakespeare's time, the female parts were acted by boys or young men, and if the actor's face was not sufficiently smooth, he was permitted to wear a mask. The poet assumes the same customs to have existed in the more ancient times.

Bottom. Well, proceed.

Quince. Robin Starveling, the tailor.

Starveling. Here, Peter Quince.

Quince. Robin Starveling, you must play Thisbe's mother.—Tom Snout, the tinker.

Snout. Here, Peter Quince.

Quince. You, Pyramus's father; myself, Thisbe's father. — Snug, the joiner, you, the lion's part; — and, I hope, here is a play fitted.

Snug. Have you the lion's part written? pray you, if it be, give it me, for I am slow of study.

Quince. You may do it extempore, for it is nothing but roaring.

Bottom. Let me play the lion too. I will roar, that it will do any man's heart good to hear me: I will roar, that I will make the Duke say, "Let him roar again: let him roar again."

Quince. If you should do it too terribly, you would fright the Duchess and the ladies, that they would shriek; and that were enough to hang us all.

All. That would hang us, every mother's son.

Bottom. But I will aggravate my voice so, that I will roar you as gently as any sucking dove: I will roar you as if 't were any nightingale.

Quince. You can play no part but Pyramus; for Pyramus is a sweet-faced man : a [handsome] man, as one shall see in a summer's day; a most lovely, gentlemanlike man; therefore, you must needs play Pyramus.

Bottom. Well, I will undertake it.

Quince. Then, masters, here are your parts; and I am to entreat you, request you, and desire you, to [learn] them by to-morrow night, and

All. That would hang us, every mother's son.

meet me in the palace wood, a mile without the town, by moonlight: there will we rehearse. In the meantime I will draw a bill of properties,[a] such as our play wants. I pray you, fail me not. Take pains; be perfect; adieu. At the duke's oak we meet.

And so the company separated.

---

[a] *Properties*— Articles wanted on the stage for the proper performance of a play. The man who has charge of such things in a theatre is still called the *property-man.*

A WOOD NEAR ATHENS.

III.

HE dream now changes, as dreams will, and the new scene is a fairy-haunted wood near Athens. Oberon, the king, and Titania, the queen of the fairies, had always lived happily together, dancing in the moonlight, hunting the butterflies, sporting amid the flowers, and singing with the nightingales. But a change had come upon them. Titania had stolen from an Indian king a lovely little child, whose mother had been her dear friend, and Oberon had begged for the pretty boy as his page ; but Titania had refused to give him up. This made a mighty quarrel.

Titania and her fairies kept as far away as possible from Oberon and his elves ; for whenever they did meet, the royal couple looked so angrily at each other that all the little people were glad to hide in the acorn cups for fear.

Puck (or Robin Goodfellow, as he was sometimes called) was a mischievous little sprite, always in close attendance on King Oberon, and ready to do his bidding, if need be, in the twinkling of an eye. Puck was full of fun and mischief, and never quite happy unless he was plaguing or misleading somebody. But he seemed to do it more for the sport of the thing than because he had any wicked intention.

Fairies are always most at home in the lovely, shadowy woods, where the grass is the greenest and the flowers are the fairest ; and Titania loved to sport there with her train of little followers. One of these came by chance to a mossy dell, seeking dewdrops (which are the fairies' pearls), just as Puck entered the wood from the other side. Now Puck was on the lookout for a good place for King Oberon's midnight revels, and, spying Titania's elf, he greeted him in fairy fashion, thus : —

Puck. How now, spirit ! whither wander you ?
Fairy. Over hill. over dale,
    Thorough bush, thorough brier,
  Over park, over pale,
    Thorough flood, thorough fire,
  I do wander every where,   ·
  Swifter than the moony sphere ;
  And I serve the fairy queen,
  To dew her [circles on] the green :
  The cowslips tall her pensioners ª be :
  In their gold coats spots you see.
  Those be rubies. fairy favors,
  In those freckles live their savors:
  I must go seek some dew-drops here,
  And hang a pearl in every cowslip's ear.

ª The allusion is to Queen Elizabeth's band of Gentlemen Pensioners, who were chosen from among the handsomest and tallest young men of family and fortune. They were dressed in habits richly garnished with gold lace.

Farewell, thou lob[1] of spirits :[a] I 'll be gone.
Our queen and all her elves come here anon.
Puck. The king doth keep his revels here to-night.
Take heed the queen come not within his sight;
For Oberon is passing fell and wrath,[2]
Because that she, as her attendant, hath
A lovely boy, stolen from an Indian king :
She never had so sweet a changeling ;[b]
And jealous Oberon would have the child
Knight of his train, to trace the forests wild :
But she, perforce, withholds the lovèd boy.
Crowns him with flowers, and makes him all her joy;
And now they never meet in grove, or green,
By fountain clear, or spangled starlight sheen,[3]
But they do square,[4] that all their elves, for fear,
Creep into acorn cups, and hide them there.
Fairy. Either I mistake your shape and making quite,
Or else you are that shrewd and knavish sprite,
Called Robin Goodfellow.[c] Are you not he,
That frights the maidens of the villagery ;
Skims milk, and sometimes labors in the quern,[5]
And bootless makes the breathless housewife churn ;
And sometimes makes the drink to bear no barm :[6]

| [1] Lubber. | [2] Savage and angry. | [3] Bright. |
| [4] Quarrel. | [5] Hand-mill. | [6] Froth ; yeast. |

[a] *Lob of spirits* — Puck was a clumsy fellow in shape, though quick enough in motion. He was so different in appearance from the other fairies, that this spirit recognized him at first sight. Milton, describing Robin Goodfellow in *L' Allegro*, says, —

> "Then lies him down the lubber fiend."

[b] *Changeling* — It was a common superstition that fairies stole beautiful children, leaving elves in their places. In the " Pranks of Puck," ascribed to Ben Jonson, we have these lines : —

> "When larks 'gin sing,
> Away we fling,
> And babes new-born steal as we go :
> An elf instead
> Leave we in bed,
> And wind out laughing, ho, ho, ho ! "

(See the piece, given entire at the end of this play.)

[c] *Robin Goodfellow* — This account of Puck was gathered from the popular notions of the time. Burton, in his *Anatomy of Melancholy*, says : " A bigger kind there is of them [fairies], called with us Hobgoblins and Robin Goodfellows, that would in those superstitious times grind corn for a mess of milk," etc. Harsenet, in his *Declaration of Popish Impostures*, says : " And if that the bowle of curds and creame were not duly set out for Robin Goodfellow, the friar, and Sisse the dairy-maid, why then either the pottage was burnt next day in the pot, or the cheeses would not curdle, or the butter would not come, or the ale in the fat [vat] never would have good head."

Misleads night-wanderers, laughing at their harm?
Those that Hobgoblin call you, and sweet Puck,
You do their work, and they shall have good luck.
Are not you he?
 Puck.   Fairy, thou speak'st aright;
I am that merry wanderer of the night.
I jest to Oberon, and make him smile,
When I a fat and bean-fed horse beguile,
Neighing in likeness of a filly foal:
And sometimes lurk I in a gossip's[1] bowl,
In very likeness of a roasted crab:[2]
And, when she drinks, against her lips I bob,
And on her withered dew-lap[3] pour the ale.
The wisest aunt[a] telling the saddest tale,
Sometime for three-foot stool mistaketh me:
Then slip I from [behind], down topples she.

And [rails or] cries, and falls into a cough;
And then the whole quire[4] hold their hips, and laugh,
And waxen in their mirth, and neeze,[5] and swear
A merrier hour was never wasted there. —
But room, Fairy: here comes Oberon.
 Fairy. And here my mistress. Would that he were gone!

---

[1] Chatting woman. [2] Crab-apple. [3] Neck. [4] Company. [5] Sneeze.
[a] *The wisest aunt* —The most serious old woman.

Enter OBERON, *from one side, with his train, and* TITANIA, *from the other, with hers.*

    Oberon. Ill met by moonlight, proud Titania.
    Titania. What, jealous Oberon! Fairies, skip hence.
I have forsworn his bed and company.

Then, turning to Oberon, Titania chides him for intruding upon her and her
fairies, and interrupting their sports. " You well know," she says, —

    [That] never, since the middle summer's spring,[a]
    Met we on hill, in dale, forest, or mead,
    By pavèd fountain, or by rushy brook,
    Or on the beachèd margin of the sea,
    To dance our ringlets to the whistling wind,
    But with thy brawls thou hast disturbed our sport.
    Therefore the winds, piping to us in vain,
    As in revenge, have sucked up from the sea
    Contagious fogs ; which falling in the land,
    Have every [petty] river made so proud,
    That they have overborne their continents : [1]
    The seasons alter : hoary-headed frosts
    Fall in the fresh lap of the crimson rose ;
    And on old Hyems'[2] thin and icy crown,
    An odorous chaplet of sweet summer buds
    Is, as in mockery, set. The spring, the summer,
    The [fruitful] autumn, angry winter, change
    Their wonted liveries : and the [puzzled] world,
    By their increase, now knows not which is which.
    And this same progeny of evils comes
    From our debate, from our dissension :
    We are their parents and original.
    Oberon. Do you amend it then; it lies in you.
    Why should Titania cross her Oberon ?
    I do but beg a little changeling boy,
    To be my henchman.[3]
    Titania.   Set your heart at rest :
    The fairy land buys not the child of me.
    His mother was a votaress of my order,[b]
    And for her sake I do rear up her boy,
    And for her sake I will not part with him.
    Oberon. How long within this wood intend you stay?
    Titania. Perchance, till after Theseus' wedding-day.
    If you will patiently dance in our round,

---

    [1] Banks.   [2] Winter.   [3] Page
  [a] That is, the *beginning* of midsummer. The word *spring* was often thus used in
Shakespeare's time. See Introduction, p. xiv.
    [b] One who loved and respected fairies.

And see our moonlight revels, go with us ;
If not, shun me, and I will spare your haunts.
Oberon. Give me that boy, and I will go with thee.
Titania. Not for thy fairy kingdom. — Fairies, away !
We shall chide downright, if I longer stay.
[TITANIA, *with her train, goes out.*
Oberon. Well, go thy way : thou shalt not from this grove,
Till I torment thee for this injury. —
My gentle Puck, come hither.

Then Oberon reminds Puck how once, when they were on a high mountain by the sea, they heard the mermaids sing ; and says that at that very time he saw (though Puck could not see) flying between the cold moon and the earth, Cupid, all armed ; he saw the little love-god shoot an arrow smartly from his bow, aimed at a fair virgin queen,[a] and though the arrow was swift enough to pierce a hundred thousand hearts, it missed the queen, who quietly passed on,

" In maiden meditation, fancy-free."

But the mischief-loving little god did something with his shot after all, for Oberon says, —

Yet marked I where the bolt of Cupid fell :
It fell upon a little western flower, —
Before milk-white, now purple with love's wound, —
And maidens call it love-in-idleness.[b]
Fetch me that flower ; the herb I showed thee once :
The juice of it on sleeping eyelids laid,
Will make or man or woman madly dote
Upon the next live creature that it sees.
Fetch me this herb ; and be thou here again,
Ere the leviathan [1] can swim a league.
Puck. I 'd put a girdle round about the earth
In forty minutes. [PUCK *flies away.*
Oberon. Having once this juice,
I 'll watch Titania when she is asleep,
And drop the liquor of it in her eyes :
The next thing then she waking looks upon,
(Be it on lion, bear, or wolf, or bull,
On meddling monkey, or on busy ape,)
She shall pursue it with the soul of love ;

---

[1] Whale.
[a] This is supposed to have been intended by Shakespeare as a compliment to Queen Elizabeth, who was never married.
[b] The flower which we call the pansy.

And ere I take this charm off from her sight,
(As I can take it with another herb,)
I 'll make her render up her page to me.
But who comes here ?   I am invisible,
And I will overhear their conference.   [OBERON *retires.*

    In the meantime Helena has told Demetrius of the plans of Lysander and Hermia, and now Demetrius has come to the wood to find them. Helena pursues him ; and at last they reach the very dell where Oberon still remains, invisible. Demetrius here spoke rudely and unkindly to poor Helena, reproaching her for running after him ; but she took it all patiently because she loved him so much ; and when Demetrius ran away again she continued to follow him, little dreaming that Oberon, the fairy king, had seen and heard all that had passed between them. Oberon was sorry for Helena, and as she disappeared, he said very softly, —

    Fare thee well, nymph : ere he do leave this grove,
    Thou shalt fly him, and he shall seek thy love. —

Re-enter PUCK.

Hast thou the flower there ?   Welcome, wanderer.
    Puck. Ay, there it is.
    Oberon.   I pray thee, give it me.
I know a bank whereon the wild thyme blows,
Where ox-lips, and the nodding violet grows :
Quite over-canopied with lush [1] woodbine,
With sweet musk-roses, and with eglantine :
And where the snake throws her enamelled skin,
Weed [2] wide enough to wrap a fairy in :
There sleeps Titania, some time of the night,
Lulled in this bower with dances and delight;
And with the juice of this I 'll streak her eyes,
And make her full of hateful fantasies.
Take thou some of it, and seek through this grove :
A sweet Athenian lady is in love
With a disdainful youth : anoint his eyes ;
But do it, when the next thing he espies
May be the lady.   Thou shalt know the man
By the Athenian garments he hath on.
Effect it with some care, that he may prove
More fond on her, than she upon her love.
And look thou meet me ere the first cock crow.
    Puck. Fear not, my lord: your servant shall do so.

---

[1] Luscious.   [2] Clothing.

Titania. Come, now a roundel, and a fairy song.

THE FAIRIES' ERRANDS.

IV.

ACT II. SCENE 2.

HE scene now changes, and Titania enters another part of the wood with her fairy train. She calls for a dance around and a fairy song; then sends some of the fairies away on different errands, while she bids others sing her to sleep :—

Come, now a roundel, and a fairy song;
Then, ere the third part of a minute, hence:
Some, to kill cankers in the musk-rose buds :
Some war with rear-mice [1] for their leathern wings,
To make my small elves coats ; and some keep back
The clamorous owl, that nightly hoots, and wonders
At our quaint [2] spirits. Sing me now asleep ;
Then to your offices, and let me rest.

FAIRIES' SONG.

1st Fairy. *You spotted snakes, with double tongue,*
Thorny hedge-hogs, be not seen ;
Newts, and blind-worms, do no wrong,
Come not near our fairy queen :

CHORUS.

Philomel,[3] *with melody,*
Sing in our sweet lullaby ;
Lulla, lulla, lullaby ; lulla, lulla, lullaby :
Never harm,
Nor spell nor charm,
Come our lovely lady nigh ;
So, good night, with lullaby.

II.

2d Fairy. *Weaving spiders, come not here ;*
Hence, you long-legged spinners, hence !
Beetles black, approach not near ;
Worm, nor snail, do no offence.

CHORUS.

Philomel, with melody, etc.

1st Fairy. Hence away ! now all is well.
One, aloof, stand sentinel.

Titania sleeps, and the fairies fly softly away. Then, seeing his queen asleep,
King Oberon entered softly, and touched Titania's eyelids with the magic flower,
saying, as he did so, —

What thou seest, when thou dost wake,
Do it for thy true love take ;
Love, and languish for his sake :
Be it ounce, or cat, or bear,
Pard,[4] or boar with bristled hair,
In thy eye that shall appear
When thou wak'st, it is thy dear.
Wake when some vile thing is near.

---

[1] Bats.　　　[2] Pretty, curious.　　　[3] Nightingale.　　　[4] Leopard.

Oberon. What thou seest, when thou dost wake,
Do it for thy true love take.

Then out he crept, leaving the sweet little fairy queen in an enchanted sleep. At this moment Lysander and Hermia, who had met in the forest according to agreement, came into the same place hand-in-hand. They had been walking a long way on their tiresome night-journey, and were quite weary. Of course they could not see Titania, for though the fairies can see mortals, mortals cannot possibly see fairies. Lysander was sorry that his dear Hermia should be so tired, and he said, —

Fair love, you faint with wandering in the wood,
And, to speak truth, I have forgot our way ;
We'll rest us, Hermia, if you think it good,
And tarry for the comfort of the day.
    Hermia. Be it so, Lysander, find you out a bed ;
For I upon this bank will rest my head.
                Good night, sweet friend :
Thy love ne'er alter till thy sweet life end !
    Lysander. Amen, amen; Sleep give thee all his rest !
    Hermia. With half that wish the wisher's eyes be pressed !

They both fall asleep on the green turf, a little distance apart.

Now who should come along but Master Puck, looking for Demetrius, whom King Oberon had commanded him to find?· His only way of knowing this person was to be by his Athenian dress. But Lysander, being also an Athenian, was dressed of course in the same fashion, and Puck, not having been told that any other Athenian was in the wood, made a great mistake, and took Lysander for Demetrius. So he hastened to touch the eyes of the sleeping Lysander with the flower which was to make him madly love the first live thing he should see when he awoke. Puck had been scolding, as he went, because of his failure to find Demetrius, when suddenly his eye fell on the sleepers, — Lysander on one bank, and Hermia at some distance away. Then he exclaimed, —

Night and silence! who is here?
Weeds of Athens he doth wear :
This is he my master said
Despisèd the Athenian maid ;
And here the maiden, sleeping sound
On the dank and dirty ground.
Pretty soul ! she durst not lie
Nearer this lack-love, this kill-courtesy.
Churl, upon thy eyes I throw
All the power this charm doth owe.[1]
        [*Touching his eyes with the flower.*
When thou wak'st, let love forbid
Sleep his seat on thy eyelid.
So awake when I am gone,
For I must now to Oberon.

Then, quite content, and pleased with his success, Puck hastened back to his royal master.

At this time Demetrius, running through the wood to get away from Helena, came upon this very spot. Helena still followed him, — a queer thing for a

---

[1] Own.

nice and well-behaved young lady to do ! But you are not to forget that all this took place in a dream, and in dreams people never act as they do in the wide-awake world. Demetrius ran faster than Helena, who, out of breath with her fond chase, stopped for a moment, and perceived Lysander on the ground, either dead or asleep. She called him by name, — "Lysander, wake !" Lysander suddenly opened his eyes, and, under the influence of the magic flower, forgot all about Hermia, fell instantly in love with Helena, and began telling her how fair she seemed to him, and how fond he was of her. Helena was much grieved by his words, which she thought were meant in scorn and mockery, because she knew how truly he had loved Hermia ; and she ran away as fast as she could, Lysander pursuing her.

After they were quite out of sight and hearing, Hermia awoke, frightened by a bad dream, and called to Lysander to come and help her. Then, terrified at finding herself alone, she too ran swiftly away into the wood to find her lost lover. Thus had Puck's blunder set everything in confusion, and, one would think, started mischief enough for one night.

But more was to come.

V.

T the very place where we left the Queen of the Fairies lying asleep, the company of clownish actors —Quince, Snug, Bottom, Flute, and Starveling — met to rehearse their play. They thought the quiet greensward in the midst of the forest would be a marvellous convenient place for this purpose : the grass-plot could be their stage, and the hawthorn bushes their dressing-room and place of retreat when they wished to retire from the stage. Of course they did not see Titania, who was sleeping quietly on a bank of flowers.

Since their last meeting, Bottom had been thinking a great deal about the play and the difficult things that must be done to make it go off well. As he was to be the chief actor, he felt very important, and wished his companions to understand that he saw all the hard places, and was wise enough to tell them what to do. So he began at once : —

Peter Quince, —
Quince. What say'st thou, bully Bottom ?
Bottom. There are things in this comedy of " Pyramus and Thisbe," that will never please. First, Pyramus must draw a sword to kill himself, which the ladies cannot abide. How answer you that ?
Snout. By 'r lakin,[a] a parlous [1] fear.
Starveling. I believe we must leave the killing out, when all is done.
Bottom. Not a whit: I have a device to make all well. Write me a prologue,[b] and let the prologue seem to say, we will do no harm with our swords, and that Pyramus is not killed indeed ; and, for the more better assurance, tell them that I, Pyramus, am not Pyramus, but Bottom the weaver. This will put them out of fear.

---

[1] Perilous.

[a] By our ladykin (or little lady), meaning the Virgin Mary.
[b] Bottom has a very confused idea of the nature of a prologue, which is the poetical introduction to a play.

Quince. Well, we will have such a prologue.

Snout. Will not the ladies be afeard of the lion?

Starveling. I fear it, I promise you.

Bottom. Masters, you ought to consider with yourselves: to bring in, God shield us! a lion among ladies, is a most dreadful thing; for there is not a more fearful wild-fowl than your lion living, and we ought to look to it.

Snout. Therefore, another prologue must tell he is not a lion.

Bottom. Nay, you must name his name, and half his face must be seen through the lion's neck; and he himself must speak through, saying thus, or to the same defect : — " Ladies," or, " Fair ladies, I would wish you," or, " I would request you," or, " I would entreat you, not to fear, not to tremble : my life for yours. If you think I come hither as a lion, it were pity of my life : no, I am no such thing: I am a man as other men are : " and there, indeed, let him name his name, and tell them plainly he is Snug. the joiner.

Quince. Well, it shall be so. But there is two hard things: that is, to bring the moonlight into a chamber; for you know, Pyramus and Thisbe meet by moonlight.

Snug. Doth the moon shine that night we play our play?

Bottom. A calendar, a calendar! look in the almanac; find out moonshine, find out moonshine.

Quince. Yes, it doth shine that night.

Bottom. Why, then you may leave a casement of the great chamber window, where we play, open; and the moon may shine in at the casement.

Quince. Ay; or else one must come in with a bush of thorns and a lanthorn, and say, he comes to disfigure, or to present, the person of moonshine. Then, there is another thing : we must have a wall in the great chamber; for Pyramus and Thisbe (says the story) did talk through the chink of a wall.

Snug. You can never bring in a wall. — What say you, Bottom?

Bottom. Some man or other must present wall : and let him have some plaster, or some loam, or some rough-cast about him, to signify wall; and let him hold his fingers thus (*holding up the first and second fingers of his hand, spread wide*), and through that cranny shall Pyramus and Thisbe whisper.

Quince. If that may be, then all is well. Come, sit down, every mother's son, and rehearse your parts. Pyramus, you begin. When you have spoken your speech, enter into that brake; and so every one according to his cue.

Just then Puck chanced to come along. Of course he was invisible. He was sure some fun must be going on; so he thought he would listen, and perhaps take part, if he got a chance. Said he, —

> What hempen home-spuns have we swaggering here,
> So near the cradle of the fairy queen?
> What, a play toward?[1] I'll be an auditor;
> An actor too, perhaps, if I see cause.

And now the play begins : —

---

[1] Preparing.

Quince. Speak, Pyramus. — Thisbe, stand forth.
Pyramus. " Thisbe, the flowers have odious savors sweet," —
Quince. Odors, odors.
Pyramus.   — " odors savors sweet :
        So hath thy breath, my dearest Thisbe, dear. —
        But, hark, a voice ! stay thou but here awhile,
        And by and by I will to thee appear."

Pyramus (that is, Bottom, the weaver) goes out, and mischievous Puck goes after him.   Then says Flute, the tinker, in the character of Thisbe, —

Must I speak now ?
Quince. Ay, marry, must you ; for you must understand, he goes but to see a noise that he heard, and is to come again.
Thisbe.   " Most radiant Pyramus, most lily-white of hue,
        Of color like the red rose on triumphant brier,
        Most brisky juvenal, and eke most lovely Jew,
        As true as truest horse, that yet would never tire,
        I 'll meet thee, Pyramus, at Ninny's tomb."
Quince. Ninus' tomb, man.   Why, you must not speak that yet; that you answer to Pyramus.   You speak all your part at once, cues ᵃ and all. — Pyramus, enter : your cue is past ; it is, "never tire."

At this point in comes Puck leading Bottom, on whose shoulders the rogue, by his fairy power, has placed an ass's head.   Of course Bottom knows nothing about the change in his own looks, and when Thisbe says, —

        "As true as truest horse, that yet would never tire,"

he answers, as Pyramus ought to, —

        " If I were fair, Thisbe, I were only thine."

At the sight of such a frightful creature, with the body of a man and the head of an ass, speaking and taking part in their play, they all shriek with terror.   Quince cries out, —
        O monstrous ! O strange !   We are haunted.
        Pray, masters ! fly, masters ! help !

They all run away, and leave poor Bottom in great distress, both surprised and hurt at their conduct.   Puck is delighted.   He dances, and capers about, and sings, —

        I 'll follow you, I 'll lead you about a round,
          Through bog, through bush, through brake, through brier :
        Sometimes a horse I 'll be, sometimes a hound,
          A hog, a headless bear, sometimes a fire ;

ᵃ *Cue* — A theatrical term, meaning the last words of any speech, set down as a signal to the actor who is to speak next.

> And neigh, and bark, and grunt, and roar, and burn,
> Like horse, hound, hog, bear, fire, at every turn.*

And off he goes after the poor frightened clowns.

After they had all disappeared Bottom said, —

Why do they all run away? I see their knavery. This is to make an ass of me, to fright me, if they could; but I will not stir from this place, do what they can. I will walk up and down here, and I will sing, that they shall hear I am not afraid.

[*Sings.*

> *The ousel-cock,*[1] *so black of hue,*
> *With orange-tawny bill,*
> *The throstle*[2] *with his note so true,*
> *The wren with little quill.*

At the sound of this noise, which Bottom was pleased to call singing, Queen Titania, who had been sleeping near by, suddenly awoke. Her eyes, you remember, had been touched by the magic flower, and she could not see anything as it really was. To her sight, Bottom, the rough and clumsy Bottom, with the ass's head on his shoulders, was more beautiful than her own King Oberon, and his roaring was sweeter than the song of the nightingale.

---

[1] Blackbird.   [2] Thrush.
* See the ballad of the "Pranks of Robin Goodfellow," p. 71.

Titania. What angel wakes me from my flowery bed ?
I pray thee, gentle mortal, sing again :
Mine ear is much enamored of thy note,
So is mine eye enthrallèd to thy shape ;
And thy fair virtue's force perforce doth move me,
On the first view, to say, to swear, I love thee.

Bottom. Methinks, mistress, you should have little reason for that : and yet, to
say the truth, reason and love keep little company together now-a-days.

Titania. Thou art as wise as thou art beautiful.

Bottom. Not so, neither ; but if I had wit enough to get out of this wood, I have
enough to serve mine own turn.

Titania. Out of this wood do not desire to go :
Thou shalt remain here, whether thou wilt or no.
I am a spirit of no common rate;
The summer still doth tend upon my state,
And I do love thee : therefore, go with me ;
I 'll give thee fairies to attend on thee :
And they shall fetch thee jewels from the deep,
And sing while thou on pressèd flowers dost sleep :
And I will purge thy mortal grossness so,
That thou shalt like an airy spirit go. —
Peas-blossom ! Cobweb ! Moth ! and Mustard-seed !

At this summons four queer-looking little fairies come dancing in. As Titania
calls them by name, they fold their tiny wings and answer, —

1 *Fairy.* Ready.
2 *Fairy.*   And I.
3 *Fairy.*   And I.
4 *Fairy.*   Where shall we go ?
Titania. ' Be kind and courteous to this gentleman :
Hop in his walks, and gambol in his eyes ;
Feed him with apricocks [1] and dewberries,[2]
With purple grapes, green figs, and mulberries.
Their honey bags steal from the humble-bees,[3]
And for night tapers crop their waxen thighs,
And light them at the fiery glow-worm's eyes,
To have my love to bed, and to arise :
And pluck the wings from painted butterflies,
To fan the moon-beams from his sleeping eyes.
Nod to him, elves, and do him courtesies.

1 *Fairy.* Hail, mortal.
2 *Fairy.* Hail !
3 *Fairy.* Hail !
4 *Fairy.* Hail !

---

[1] Apricots.   [2] Blackberries.
[3] The same as our bumble-bee ; called *humble-bee* from the humming noise it makes.

Bottom. I cry your worship's mercy, heartily. — I beseech your worship's name.
Cobweb. Cobweb.
Bottom. I shall desire of you more acquaintance, good master Cobweb. If I cut my finger, I shall make bold with you. — Your name, honest gentleman?
Peas-blossom. Peas-blossom.
Bottom. I pray you, commend me to mistress Squash,* your mother, and to master Peascod, your father. Good master Peas-blossom, I shall desire of you more acquaint-ance too. — Your name, I beseech you, sir?

---

* The allusions to the *squash* in Shakespeare are not to the American squash; the word means any young unripe pod. *Peascod* is what we call *pea-pod*.

Mustard-seed. Mustard-seed.

Bottom. Good master Mustard-seed, I know your patience well : that same cowardly, giant-like ox-beef hath devoured many a gentleman of your house. I promise you, your kindred hath made my eyes water ere now. I desire of you more acquaintance, good master Mustard-seed.

Titania. Come, wait upon him : lead him to my bower.

And so this funny procession — poor donkey-headed Nick, lumbering along, escorted by these droll little children of the air — makes its way toward the leafy chamber of the Fairy Queen.

VI.

HILE this was going on, Oberon, in another part of the wood, was seeking his servant Puck, quite anxious to know what had happened to Titania, and also whether the charm had been successful with Demetrius.

> *Oberon.* I wonder if Titania be awaked ;
> Then, what it was that next came in her eye,
> Which she must dote on in extremity.
>   *Enter* PUCK.
> Here comes my messenger. — How now, mad spirit?
> What night-rule [1] now about this haunted grove ?
> *Puck.* My mistress with a monster is in love!

Then Puck goes on to tell Oberon what he had done to the clumsy clown, Nick Bottom, and how the others had been so frightened by this that they ran away and left Bottom, with the donkey's head on him, standing near Titania's " close and consecrated bower,"—

> When, in that moment (so it came to pass),
> Titania waked. and straightway loved an ass.
> *Oberon.* This falls out better than I could devise.
> But hast thou yet [smeared] the Athenian's eyes
> With the love-juice, as I did bid thee do?
> *Puck.* I took him sleeping (that is finished too),
> And the Athenian woman by his side.

---

[1] Revelry.

But, meanwhile, Demetrius, having at last got clear of Helena, happened to meet Hermia looking for her lost Lysander, and, in spite of her distress and fear, began to tell again the unwelcome story of his love. Hermia really feared that Demetrius had murdered Lysander, who she was sure would never have stolen away from her while sleeping. She used bitter, angry words, and bade Demetrius take his hated presence from her sight : —

"See me no more, whether he be
    dead or no ! "

With these words she left him. Demetrius, thinking it useless to follow her in this fierce mood, lay down to rest.

In this enchanted wood every one seems to have easily fallen asleep, and Demetrius immediately dropped into a slumber, as the others had done. But Oberon, being near, had seen Demetrius and Hermia together, and came forward quite vexed with Puck, saying, —

What hast thou done ? thou hast mistaken quite,
And laid the love-juice on some true-love's sight :
About the wood go swifter than the wind,
And Helena of Athens look thou find :
All fancy-sick [1] she is, and pale of cheer [2]
With sighs of love, that cost the fresh blood dear.
By some illusion see thou bring her here :
I 'll charm his eyes against she do appear.
    Puck. I go, I go ; look how I go ;
Swifter than arrow from the Tartar's bow.

Puck hastened away. Oberon touched the eyes of the sleeping Demetrius, saying, as he did so, —

Flower of this purple dye,
Hit with Cupid's archery,
Sink in apple of his eye.
When his love he doth espy,

---

[1] Love-sick.   [2] Countenance.

Let her shine as gloriously
As the Venus of the sky. —
When thou wak'st, if she be by,
Beg of her for remedy.
Re-enter PUCK.

Puck. Captain of our fairy band,
Helena is here at hand,
And the youth, mistook by me,
Pleading for a lover's fee.
Shall we their fond pageant see ?
Lord, what fools these mortals be !
Oberon. Stand aside : the noise they make
Will cause Demetrius to awake.
Puck. Then will two at once woo one ;
That must needs be sport alone ;
And those things do best please me.
That befall preposterously.[1]

And so Oberon and Puck stand aside, to see the waking of the bewitched
Demetrius.

Lysander had been pursuing Helena with his love ever since he came under
the influence of Oberon's flower. Helena was grieved that he should mock her :
she could not believe him to be in earnest. They entered together, without seeing
Puck and Oberon (who were always invisible), or Demetrius, who still lay asleep.
While they were yet speaking, Demetrius awoke. Seeing Helena, and being now
under the flower-enchantment, his old love for her returned, and he was as
ready now to quarrel with Lysander on her account as he had been before
on Hermia's. They were talking angrily when Hermia entered. Having found
at last her loved Lysander, she ran to him with joy, and asked him eagerly
why he had left her so. He, still under the influence of the fairy spell, replied
that it was because he hated her. The last time they had been all four together, the two young men had both been in love with Hermia, and now both
were pursuing Helena with their vows. Poor Helena was more puzzled than ever,
and was convinced that her old friend and playmate, Hermia, had joined with the
two young men to make sport of her. " You also are grown unkind, O cruel,
ungrateful Hermia," she exclaimed ;

Is all the counsel that we two have shared,
The sister-vows, the hours that we have spent,
When we have chid the hasty-footed time
For parting us, — O ! and is all forgot ?'
All school-day friendship, childhood innocence ?
We, Hermia, like two artificial [2] gods,

---

[1] Absurdly.   [2] Artistic ; skillful.

Have with our needles created both one flower,
Both on one sampler, sitting on one cushion,
Both warbling of one song, both in one key,
As if our hands, our sides, voices, and minds,
Had been incorporate.[1] So we grew together,
Like to a double cherry, seeming parted,
But yet an union in partition ;
Two loving berries moulded on one stem,
So, with two seeming bodies, but one heart.
And will you rend our ancient love asunder,
To join with men in scorning your poor friend ?
What though I be not so in grace as you,
So hung upon with love, so fortunate,
But miserable most to love unloved,
This you should pity, rather than despise.
    Hermia. I understand not what you mean by this.

All this time Lysander and Demetrius were quarrelling. Hermia tried to separate them, but Lysander was extremely rude to her, and a great many unkind
things were said. At last Demetrius and Lysander rushed furiously away into the
forest, with drawn swords, to find a place to fight. Helena and Hermia also went
away, in different directions, both of them unhappy, and puzzled to understand
how it had all happened. After they had disappeared, Oberon came forward and
scolded Puck : —
    This is thy negligence : still thou mistak'st,
    Or else commit'st thy knaveries wilfully.
        Puck. Believe me, king of shadows, I mistook.
    Did you not tell me I should know the man
    By the Athenian garments he had on ?
    And so far blameless proves my enterprise,
    That I have 'nointed an Athenian's eyes ;
    And so far am I glad it so did sort,[2]
    As this their jangling I esteem a sport.
        Oberon. Thou seest these lovers seek a place to fight :
    Hie, therefore, Robin, overcast the night ;
    And lead these testy rivals so astray,
    That one come not within another's way,
    Till o'er their brows death-counterfeiting sleep,
    With leaden legs and batty wings, doth creep.
    Then crush this herb into Lysander's eye ;
                            [*Giving him another flower.*
    Whose liquor hath this virtuous property,
    To take from thence all error with its might,
    And make his eyeballs roll with wonted sight.

---

[1] United in one.   [2] Happen.

When they next wake, all this derision
Shall seem a dream, and fruitless vision :
And back to Athens shall the lovers wend,
With league, whose date till death shall never end.
Whilst I in this affair do thee employ,
I 'll to my queen, and beg her Indian boy :
And then I will her charmèd eye release
From monster's view, and all things shall be peace.

   Puck. My fairy lord, this must be done with haste,
For night's swift dragons cut the clouds full fast,
And yonder shines Aurora's harbinger.

   Oberon.   Make no delay :
We may effect this business yet ere day.

Then Oberon goes off to Titania. Puck, in great glee, laughs and sings, —

   Up and down, up and down ;
   I will lead them up and down :
   I am feared in field and town ;
   Goblin, lead them up and down.
Here comes one.

And at this moment Lysander enters. Puck calls out to him in the voice of
Demetrius, daring him to follow to more open ground that they may fight, and off
rushes Lysander after the voice. Then Puck turns about and in the same way
fools Demetrius, who is not far behind ; and he keeps up this merry farce until he
has tired them both out, and leaves them at last fast asleep on the turf where they
have thrown themselves, one after the other, and each unconscious that the other
is so near.

Soon after this Helena came wearily along. In the dusky shadow of the
wood, seeing no one, she too lay down and slept. And shortly Hermia, sore-
footed and weeping, bedabbled with the dew and torn with briers, crawled to
the self-same spot, and, equally under the spell of the place, lay down, and soon
was soundly slumbering like the rest. Puck danced joyfully around them, saying
or singing, —

On the ground sleep sound :
I 'll apply to your eye,
Gentle lover, remedy.
          [*Anointing* LYSANDER'S *eyes with the second flower.*
When thou wak'st, see thou tak'st
True delight in the sight
Of thy former lady's eye:
And the country proverb known,
That every man should take his own,
In your waking shall be shown :
    Jack shall have Jill ;
    Nought shall go ill ;
The man shall have his mare again,
And all shall be well.

Then he bounded away into the forest, leaving Helena and Hermia, Demetrius and Lysander, all fast asleep on the ground.

VII.

BUT of all the mischievous pranks of Puck, the most absurd was that which he had played on Bottom, the weaver, to whom he had given the donkey's head ; and Puck himself could not have wished a more ridiculous effect from the magic flower with which Titania's eyes had been bewitched. than the caresses which she bestowed upon this monstrous creature, who was to her view the loveliest of his sex. There she sat, in all her beauty, in her forest bower, and while her attendants waited upon the ill-matched couple. she held in her lap the long-eared head. and wreathed the hairy brows with flowers.

All the while Oberon stood behind, unseen. He had recently met Titania in the wood, and her new love had made her so meek that she had borne all his taunts with patience, and even yielded to him the Indian boy. So now he pitied her, and resolved to deliver her from the spell of the magic flower.

Titania says to her shaggy darling, —

> Come, sit thee down upon this flowery bed,
> While I thy amiable cheeks do coy,[1]
> And stick musk-roses in thy sleek smooth head,
> And kiss thy fair large ears, my gentle joy.

Bottom. Where's Peas-blossom ?
Peas-blossom. Ready.
Bottom. Scratch my head. Peas-blossom. — Where's monsieur Cobweb ?
Cobweb. Ready.

---

[1] Stroke.

Bottom. Monsieur Cobweb ; good monsieur, get your weapons in your hand, and kill me a red-hipped humble-bee on the top of a thistle ; and, good monsieur, bring me the honey-bag. Do not fret yourself too much in the action, monsieur ; and, good monsieur, have a care the honey-bag break not: I would be loath to have you over-flowed with a honey-bag, signior. — Where 's monsieur Mustard-seed ?

Mustard-seed. Ready.

Bottom. Give me your neif,[1] monsieur Mustard-seed. Pray you, leave your cour-tesy,[2] good monsieur.

Mustard-seed. What 's your will ?

Bottom. Nothing, good monsieur, but to help Cavalero Peas-blossom to scratch. I must to the barber's, monsieur ; for, methinks, I am marvellous hairy about the face, and I am such a tender ass, if my hair do but tickle me, I must scratch.

Titania. What, wilt thou hear some music, my sweet love ?

Bottom. I have a reasonable good ear in music : let 's have the tongs and the bones.[a]   [*Rural music.*

Titania. Or, say, sweet love, what thou desirest to eat.

Bottom. Truly, a peck of provender : I could munch your good dry oats. Me-thinks, I have a great desire to a bottle [b] of hay : good hay, sweet hay, hath no fellow.

Titania.   I have a venturous fairy that shall seek
        The squirrel's hoard, and fetch thee thence new nuts.

Bottom. I had rather have a handful or two of dried peas. But, I pray you, let none of your people stir me: I have an exposition of sleep come upon me.

Titania.   Fairies, be gone, and be a while away.   [*Fairies go away.*
        Sleep thou, and I will wind thee in my arms.
        So doth the woodbine the sweet honeysuckle
        Gently entwist: the female ivy so
        Enrings the barky fingers of the elm.
        O, how I love thee! how I dote on thee!

Hardly had they fallen asleep in this loving attitude when in comes Puck, his jolly face all lighted up with glee, as he fairly jumps for joy at the mischief worked by the little flower. King Oberon saw Puck, and went forward to meet him, saying, —

        Welcome, good Robin! Seest thou this sweet sight?
        Her dotage now I do begin to pity ;
        For meeting her of late behind the wood,
        Seeking sweet savors for this hateful fool,
        I did upbraid her, and fall out with her ;
        For she his hairy temples then had rounded

---

        1 Fist.   2 Bowing.

a *The tongs and the bones* were rustic music, common in Shakespeare's time. The tongs was a rough instrument, struck by a key, and making a ringing sound like a triangle ; the bones were "clappers," such as are used by boys at the present day.

b *A bottle of hay* was a truss, or bundle, of hay ; a word yet in use in the northern part of England.

Titania. O, how I love thee! how I dote on thee!

With coronet of fresh and fragrant flowers;
And that same dew, which sometime on the buds
Was wont to swell like round and orient pearls,
Stood now within the pretty flowerets' eyes,
Like tears that did their own disgrace bewail.
When I had at my pleasure taunted her,
And she in mild terms begged my patience,

I then did ask of her her changeling child,
Which straight she gave me ; and her fairy sent
To bear him to my bower in fairy land,
And now I have the boy, I will undo
This hateful imperfection of her eyes :
And, gentle Puck, take this transformèd scalp
From off the head of this Athenian swain,
That he, awaking when the other do,
May all to Athens back again repair,
And think no more of this night's accidents,
But as the fierce vexation of a dream.
But first I will release the fairy queen.
    Be, as thou wast wont to be ;
           [*Anointing her eyes with the last flower.*
    See, as thou wast wont to see ;
    Dian's bud o'er Cupid's flower
    Hath such force and blessed power.
Now, my Titania ! wake you, my sweet queen.
    Titania (waking). My Oberon ! what visions have I seen !
Methought I was enamored of an ass.
    Oberon. There lies your love.
    Titania.   How came these things to pass ?
O, how mine eyes do loathe his visage now !

So all was right again between the fairy king and queen. Presently Oberon, looking about the pretty dell where Puck's quick wit and activity had brought together the two furious young men, the two unhappy damsels, and Bottom the weaver, all lying asleep in that charmed fairy circle in the wood, spoke out and commanded silence for a while. Then he asked Titania to call for "music such as charmeth sleep," which should "strike more dead than common sleep" the senses of all the five. Calling to Puck, he cried, —

    Robin, take off this head.

Puck sprang forward, and with his elfish power changed poor old Bottom back again to his natural form, saying, as he did it, —

    Now, when thou wak'st, with thine own fool's eyes peep.

"Sound, music !" cried King Oberon ; and as the soft music began, weaving a magic spell of slumber over the sleeping five, he called to Titania, —

    Come my queen, take hands with me,
    And rock the ground whereon these sleepers be.

Then they danced round the sleepers until they heard the note of the morning lark, when they followed the shadows of the night, and vanished away.

All was now quiet in the shady forest, and the four lovers were so sound asleep that they did not hear the hunting-horns in the distance, and were quite unconscious of the approach of Duke Theseus and Queen Hippolyta, with their train of noblemen and huntsmen, who had come forth at the dawn of day to chase the dappled deer.

Theseus had been telling Hippolyta about his fine hunting-dogs of Spartan breed, and he asked her to come up on the mountain-top, and hear the beautiful music of their baying and the echo answering it. Suddenly he espied the lovers on the ground, and asked Egeus who they were. The old lord recognizes his daughter there asleep, and then Lysander, Demetrius, and Helena, and he wonders how they should be out thus in the woods together at such a time ; but the Duke thinks they probably came out for an early Maying party, and orders that the huntsmen shall wake them with their horns.   At the sound of the horns so near them, they all start up, and, seeing Theseus and his splendid party, hardly know whether they are awake or asleep.

The Duke greeted them kindly, and heard their story.   When he found that Lysander and Hermia were still true to each other, and that Helena had again won Demetrius's love, he told Egeus that he would overrule his wishes, and the lovers should be married in the temple at the same time with Hippolyta and himself. Then the Duke and his train, the courtiers, and the huntsmen went away, leaving the four lovers happy indeed, but so bewildered that they could not feel quite sure they were not still dreaming.   After reasoning about it among themselves, and calling to mind the Duke's very words, they decided that they were really awake,

and followed as they had been commanded, agreeing to tell their dreams to one another on the way.

No one was left now in the dell but Bottom ; and he too presently awoke, just as the others went out, with rather confused ideas as to where and what he was.   He remembered that he had been playing Pyramus, and thought it must be time for his cue, or signal to go upon the stage.   As he became more thoroughly awakened, he recalled something strange, which, after puzzling over it for a while, he was quite certain must have been a dream.   As he first started up, on waking, he said, —

When my cue comes, call me, and I will answer : — my next is, " Most fair Pyramus."—— Hey, ho !— Peter Quince ! Flute ! Snout ! Starveling ! God 's my life !ᵃ stolen hence, and left me asleep.   I have had a most rare vision.   I have had a

---

ᵃ *God 's my life !* — One of the curious exclamations common in Shakespeare's time.   In another of his plays (" Much Ado about Nothing ") one of his characters says, "God 's my life ! where 's the sexton ? "

dream, — past the wit of man to say what dream it was : man is but an ass, if he go about to expound this dream. Methought I was — there is no man can tell what. Methought I was, and methought I had, — but man is but a patched[a] fool. if he will offer to say what methought I had. The eye of man hath not heard, the ear of man hath not seen, man's hand is not able to taste, his tongue to conceive, nor his heart to report, what my dream was. I will get Peter Quince to write a ballad of this dream : it shall be called Bottom's Dream, because it hath no bottom. and I will sing it in the latter end of our play, before the duke : peradventure, to make it the more gracious, I shall sing it after death.[b]

Then Bottom hastened away to find his companions.

We can imagine how our actors felt when they had just lost their principal performer, as they thought, forever. Quince, Flute, Snout, and Starveling were in a room in Quince's house, talking about this strange thing that had happened to Pyramus Bottom. Nothing had been heard of him anywhere, not even at his own house. They thought he must have been "transported," — by which they meant *translated*, or carried bodily to some other world. They were sure that no one else in all Athens could play Pyramus, and so their play was spoiled. Such a . pity ! Just then Snug came in, all out of breath with the news, and shouted : " Masters, the Duke is coming from the temple, and there is two or three lords and ladies more married. If our sport had gone forward, we had all been made men," — that is, their fortunes would have been made. The rest joined in the wail : —

Flute. O, sweet bully Bottom ! Thus hath he lost sixpence a-day during his life ; he could not have 'scaped sixpence a-day : if the Duke had not given him sixpence a-day for playing Pyramus, I 'll be hanged ; he would have deserved it : sixpence a-day in Pyramus, or nothing.

While they were thus lamenting the loss of the play, and the strange disappearance of Nick Bottom, that worthy came blustering in, crying out, —

Where are these lads ? where are these hearts ?
Quince. Bottom ! — O most courageous day ! O most happy hour !
Bottom. Masters, I am to discourse wonders : but ask me not what, for, if I tell you, I am no true Athenian.
Quince. Let us hear, sweet Bottom.
Bottom. [No]; not a word of me. All that I will tell you is, that the Duke hath dined. Get your apparel together ; good strings[c] to your beards, new ribbons to your pumps : meet presently at the palace ; every man look o'er his part ; for, the short and the long is, our play is [presented]. In any case let Thisbe have clean linen, and let

---

[a] This probably refers to the many-colored dress worn by the professional fools or jesters in those days.
[b] That is, after his death as Pyramus, in the play.
[c] *Strings* — to tie on the false beards.

not him that plays the lion pare his nails, for they shall hang out for the lion's claws. And, most dear actors, eat no onions, nor garlic, for we are to utter sweet breath, and I do not doubt but to hear them say, it is a sweet comedy.   No more words: away! go : away !

And, too delighted at Bottom's reappearance to stop for the further satisfying of their curiosity, they all went out noisily to prepare for the play.

VIII.

ND now the wedding-day had come, and the ducal party was assembled in an apartment of the palace. They found it hard to believe the story of the lovers' adventures in the wood. "'T is strange, my Theseus," said Hippolyta, "that these lovers speak of;" and Theseus replied, —

> More strange than true. I never may believe
> These antique fables, nor these fairy toys.
> Here come the lovers, full of joy and mirth.

The two happy pairs now arrive as the Duke's guests, and Philostrate, the manager of the revels, hands to the Duke a list of the entertainments, from which he may choose the evening's sport, to "beguile the lazy time." The Duke noticed the odd title of the clowns' play. "What's this?" said he, —

> *A tedious brief scene of young Py-*
> *ramus*
> *And his love Thisbe; very tragical*
> *mirth.*

> Merry and tragical! Tedious and
> brief!
> That is, hot ice, and wondrous
> [swarthy] snow.
> How shall we find the concord of
> this discord?
> What are they that do play it?
>   *Philostrate.* Hard-handed men, that work in Athens here,
> Which never labored in their minds till now;

And now have toiled their unbreathed [1] memories
With this same play, against your nuptial.
 Theseus. I will hear that play :
For never any thing can be amiss,
When simpleness and duty tender it.
Go, bring them in ; — and take your places, ladies.

Then Philostrate goes out to bring in the performers.

After the company are all seated, there is a great flourish of trumpets, and Philostrate introduces the Prologue, in the person of Peter Quince, the carpenter. He recites his piece, which is meant to tell the story of the play ; but he goes on without any stops for punctuation ; or rather he stops always in the wrong place, so that it makes very droll nonsense like this : —

Prologue. " If we offend, it is with our good will.
 That you should think, we come not to offend,
But with good-will. To show our simple skill,
 That is the true beginning of our end.
Consider, then, we come but in despite.
 We do not come as minding to content you,
Our true intent is. All for your delight.
 We are not here. That you should here repent you.
The actors are at hand ; and, by their show,
 You shall know all that you are like to know." [a]

At this all the ladies and gentlemen of the court laughed and joked among themselves over the queer jumble of words.

Now came the "dumb show." [b]

Pyramus and Thisbe, Wall, Moonshine, and Lion come in and show themselves, while a man, called the Presenter, introduces them to the audience, and talks about them thus : —

 "Gentles, perchance, you wonder at this show :
 But wonder on, till truth make all things plain.

---

[1] Unpractised.

[a] This speech, pointed as it ought to have been, would read as follows : —

> " If we offend, it is with our good will
> That you should think we come not to offend;
> But with good will to show our simple skill :
> That is the true beginning of our end.
> Consider then. We come ; but in despite
> We do not come. As minding to content you,
> Our true intent is all for your delight.
> We are not here that you should here repent you.
> The actors are at hand ; and by their show
> You shall know all that you are like to know."

[b] It was the custom in the theatres of Shakespeare's time (and he has imagined it to have been in ancient Athens also) for all the characters of a play to appear in a row upon the stage, saying nothing, but simply standing to be looked at, while the Presenter introduced them by name to the audience.

This man is Pyramus, if you would know;
This beauteous lady Thisbe is, certain.
This man, with loam and rough-cast, doth present
Wall, that vile wall which did these lovers sunder;
And through wall's chink, poor souls, they are content
To whisper, at the which let no man wonder.
This man, with lantern, dog, and bush of thorn,
Presenteth Moonshine; for, if you will know,
By moonshine did these lovers think no scorn
To meet at Ninus' tomb, there, there to woo.
This grisly beast, which by name lion hight,[1]
The trusty Thisbe, coming first by night,
Did scare away, or rather did affright:
And, as she fled, her mantle she did fall,
Which Lion vile with bloody mouth did stain.
Anon comes Pyramus, sweet youth and tall,
And finds his gentle Thisbe's mantle slain:
Whereat, with blade, with bloody blameful blade,
He bravely broached his boiling bloody breast,
And Thisbe, tarrying in mulberry shade,
His dagger drew, and died. For all the rest,
Let Lion, Moonshine, Wall, and lovers twain,
At large discourse, while here they do remain."

Then they all marched out in a row, and Duke Theseus said, with a laugh, "I wonder, if the lion be to speak."

"No wonder, my lord," answered Demetrius; "one lion may, when many asses do."

Next, Snout the tinker, with a rough coat, covered with loam and mortar, and carrying some stones, comes forward and explains what he is to do : —

Wall. " In this same interlude, it doth befall,
That I, one Snout by name, present a wall;
And such a wall, as I would have you think,
That had in it a cranny, hole, or chink,
Through which the lovers, Pyramus and Thisbe,
Did whisper often very secretly.
This loam, this rough-cast, and this stone, doth show
That I am that same wall: the truth is so;
And this the cranny is, right and sinister,[2]
Through which the fearful lovers are to whisper."

Here the Duke leaned over and asked Demetrius, "Would you desire lime and hair to speak better?"

"It is the wittiest partition that ever I heard discourse, my lord," answered the young Athenian.

---

[1] Called.   [2] Right and left.

" Pyramus draws near the wall," said Theseus : " silence ! "

So Pyramus comes in upon the stage, and, approaching the wall, in a tragic manner begins the play : —

"O grim-looked night !   O night with hue so black !
 O night, which ever art, when day is not !
O night ! O night ! alack, alack, alack !
 I fear my Thisbe's promise is forgot. —
And thou, O wall ! O sweet, O lovely wall !
 That stand'st between her father's ground and mine ;
Thou wall, O wall ! O sweet and lovely wall !
 Show me thy chink to blink through with mine eyne.[1]
                    [*Wall holds up his fingers.*

---

[1] Eyes.

Thanks, courteous wall: Jove shield thee well for this !
But what see I ?   No Thisbe do I see.
O wicked wall ! through whom I see no bliss ;
Curst be thy stones for thus deceiving me ! "

This seemed comical enough to Theseus, who said, "The wall, methinks, being sensible, should curse again."

Bottom was so afraid the company would not understand the play, that he forgot he was acting, and, turning around to the Duke, right in the middle of his part, he broke out, —

No, in truth, sir, he should not. — " Deceiving me," is Thisbe's cue : she is to enter now, and I am to spy her through the wall.   You shall see, it will fall pat as I told you. — Yonder she comes.

Enter THISBE.

Thisbe.   " O wall, full often hast thou heard my moans,
              For parting my fair Pyramus and me :
              My cherry lips have often kissed thy stones ;
              Thy stones with lime and hair knit up in thee."
Pyramus.   " I see a voice : now will I to the chink,
              To spy if I can hear my Thisbe's face.
              Thisbe ! "
Thisbe.   " My love! thou art my love, I think."
Pyramus.   " Think what thou wilt, I am thy lover's grace ;
              And, like Limander,* am I trusty still."
Thisbe.   " And I like Helen, till the fates me kill."
Pyramus.   " Not Shafalus to Procrus was so true."
Thisbe.   " As Shafalus to Procrus, I to you."
Pyramus.   " O ! kiss me through the hole of this vile wall."
Thisbe.   " I kiss the wall's hole, not your lips at all."
Pyramus.   " Wilt thou at Ninny's tomb meet me straightway ? "
Thisbe.   " 'Tide life, 'tide death, I come without delay."
Wall.   " Thus have I, Wall, my part dischargèd so ;
              And, being done, thus Wall away doth go."
                                    [*Wall,* PYRAMUS, *and* THISBE *go out.*

" Dear, dear ! " exclaimed Hippolyta, " this is the silliest stuff I ever heard."
" O," answered Theseus, " the best things of this kind are but shadows, and need to be made better by one's imagination.   But here come two noble beasts in, a moon and a lion."

Snug the joiner enters, with a lion's skin over his shoulders, his own head sticking out under the lion's head.   Then, in the sleepiest voice, he drones out : —

---

* A bundle of blunders : *Limander* and *Helen* for Hero and Leander ; *Shafalus* and *Procrus* for Cephalus and Procris, — loving couples of the olden time, famous in history.

"You, ladies, you, whose gentle hearts do fear
   The smallest monstrous mouse that creeps on floor,
May now, perchance, both quake and tremble here,
   When lion rough in wildest rage doth roar.
Then know that I, one Snug the joiner, am
   No lion fell, nor else no lion's dam :
For, if I should as lion come in strife
   Into this place, 't were pity of my life."

"A very gentle beast, and of a good conscience," said Theseus.

"This lion is a very fox for valor," said Lysander.

"True ; and a goose for discretion," rejoined Theseus ; "but let us listen to the moon."

Moonshine has a lantern in one hand, a thorn-bush in the other, and a wretched little dog at his heels.

This part was probably taken by Starveling, the tailor, whose stammering utterance was made worse by his forgetting his part, and being frightened almost out of his wits.   After a gasp or two of terror, he began : —

"This lantern doth the hornèd moon present, —
This lantern doth the hornèd moon present ;
Myself the man in the moon do seem to be."

Here the Duke smiled and said, "The man should be put into the lantern : how is he else the man in the moon ? "

"He dares not come there for the candle," answered Demetrius ; "for, you see, it is already in snuff."

"I am aweary of this moon," whispered Hippolyta softly ; "I wish he would change ! "

"It appears by his small light of discretion," said the Duke, "that he is in the wane; but yet, in all reason, we must stay the time."

"Proceed, moon," said Lysander impatiently; and poor Starveling began again, but, despairing of his part, spoke out in his own proper person: —

"All that I have to say, is, to tell you that the lantern is the moon; I, the man in the moon; this thorn-bush, my thorn-bush; and this dog, my dog."

Enter THISBE.

Thisbe. "This is old Ninny's tomb. Where is my love?"

Lion. "Oh —"   [*The Lion roars. —* THISBE *runs off.*

"Well roared, lion," cried Demetrius.

"Well run, Thisbe," laughed the Duke.

"Well shone, moon," said Hippolyta. "Truly, the moon shines with a good grace."   [*The Lion tears* THISBE'S *mantle, and goes out.*

"Well moused, lion," added Theseus. "And now comes Pyramus."

Enter PYRAMUS.

Pyramus. "Sweet moon, I thank thee for thy sunny beams;
I thank thee, moon, for shining now so bright,
For, by thy gracious, golden, glittering gleams,
I trust to taste of truest Thisbe's sight.
       But stay; — O spite!   [*Seeing* THISBE'S *mantle.*
       But mark, poor knight,
    What dreadful dole is here!
    Eyes, do you see?
    How can it be?
    O dainty duck! O dear!
    Thy mantle good,
    What! stained with blood?
    Approach, ye furies fell!
    O fates! come, come;
    Cut thread and thrum; *
    Quail, crush, conclude, and quell![1]

"O, wherefore, nature, didst thou lions frame,
Since lion vile hath here defloured my dear?
Which is — no, no — which *was*, the fairest dame,
That lived, that loved, that liked, that looked with cheer.
    Come, tears, confound;
    Out, sword, and wound
    The pap of Pyramus:

---

[1] Kill.

* An expression borrowed from weaving.

                    Ay, that left pap,
                    Where heart doth hop : —
                    Thus die I, thus, thus, thus !   [*Stabs himself three times.*
                    Now am I dead,
                    Now am I fled ;
                    My soul is in the sky :
                    Tongue, lose thy light !
                    Moon, take thy flight !
                    Now die, die, die, die, die."   [*Dies.*

After the death of Pyramus, Moonshine went out, leaving the place dark ;
and Hippolyta said, " How chance Moonshine is gone before Thisbe comes back
to find her lover ? "

" She will find him by starlight," answered Theseus.   " Here she comes, and
her passion ends the play."

" Methinks she should n't use a long one for such a Pyramus," rejoined Hippolyta ; " I hope she will be brief."

" She hath spied him already with those sweet eyes," said Lysander ; and
Thisbe enters, and, seeing Pyramus lying on the ground, cries out : —

                    " Asleep, my love ?
                    What, dead, my dove ?
                    O Pyramus ! arise :
                    Speak, speak !   Quite dumb ?
                    Dead, dead ?   A tomb
                    Must cover thy sweet eyes.
                    These lily lips,
                    This cherry nose,
                    These yellow cowslip cheeks,
                    Are gone, are gone.
                    Lovers, make moan :
                    His eyes were green as leeks.
                    O ! sisters three,
                    Come, come to me,
                    With hands as pale as milk ;
                    Lay them in gore,
                    Since you have shore
                    With shears his thread of silk.
                    Tongue, not a word : —
                    Come, trusty sword ;
                    Come, blade, my breast imbrue :
                    And farewell, friends ! —
                    Thus Thisbe ends :
                    Adieu, adieu, adieu."
                        [*Stabs herself with* PYRAMUS'S *sword and dies.*

" Moonshine and Lion are left to bury the dead," then said the Duke.
" Ay, and Wall too," added Demetrius.

"No, I assure you," put in Bottom, as he awkwardly arose from his position as dead Pyramus on the floor; "the wall is down that parted their fathers. Will it please you to see the epilogue, or to hear a Bergomask * dance between two of our company?"

"No epilogue, I pray you," said the Duke; "for your play needs no excuse. Never excuse, for when the players are all dead, there need none to be blamed. Come, your Bergomask: let your epilogue alone."

So they dance their clog-dance, till at last the Duke rises, and gives the signal for retiring : —

> The iron tongue of midnight hath told twelve. —
> Lovers, to bed : 't is almost fairy time.
> I fear we shall out-sleep the coming morn,
> As much as we this night have overwatched.
> Sweet friends, to bed.

And so the merry wedding-party broke up, and the company separated.

When the mirth and revelry were at an end, and all had retired for the night, Puck entered the now silent palace with a broom over his shoulder. The fairy people are very dainty and nice, and cannot bear to see the least speck of dirt. Puck's office seems to have been to sweep the corners clean, if, by any mischance or neglect of the maids, a bit of dust were left behind the door. As he begins his work, he says, —

> Now the hungry lion roars,
> And the wolf behowls the moon;
> Whilst the heavy ploughman snores,
> All with weary task fordone.[1]

---

[1] Tired out.

* A rustic dance, imitated from one performed by the people of Bergomasco, a province of Venice, who were ridiculed by the old buffoons for their rude and awkward manners.

And we fairies, that do run
  By the triple Hecate's team,[*]
  From the presence of the sun,
  Following darkness like a dream,
  Now are frolic : not a mouse
  Shall disturb this hallowed house :
  I am sent with broom before,
  To sweep the dust behind the door.

Now that the place is in fit order for the Fairy Queen, she enters with Oberon and all their train. Oberon gives them directions, bidding them dance and sing : —

Through the house give glimmering light,
  By the dead and drowsy fire ;
Every elf, and fairy sprite,
  Hop as light as bird from brier ;
And this ditty after me
Sing, and dance it trippingly.
Titania. First, rehearse your song by rote,
To each word a warbling note :
Hand in hand with fairy grace
Will we sing, and bless this place.

After the fairy dance and song, Oberon sends the elves and fays to bless the palace of Theseus. They are to touch each chamber and each bed with the consecrated field-dew, so that every one in the household may be happy, and all their children fair and wise and good.

No one knows what the fairy song was, for it has been lost ; but this was a part of Oberon's instruction to the fairies : —

Now, until the break of day,
Through this house each fairy stray,
And each several chamber bless,
Through this palace with sweet peace ;
And the owner of it, blest,
Ever shall in safety rest.
Trip away ; make no stay ;
Meet me all by break of day.

The fairies danced gayly away to do their master's bidding, while Oberon and Titania, hand in hand, went upon their own special errand, to bless the chamber of Theseus and Hippolyta, leaving Puck quite alone.

---

[*] *Triple Hecate's team* — that is, the chariot of the moon, or Diana. Hecate was a heathen divinity, called Luna in heaven, Diana on earth, and Hecate, or Proserpine, in hell. Hence her name of "the triple goddess," and she is sometimes represented with three bodies. She was supposed to preside over magic and enchantments, and appears in "Macbeth" as the queen of the witches.

Mischievous Puck now comes forward, and, by way of offering excuse for all the queer actions and entanglements of lovers and fairies and clowns and dukes and queens, makes this little farewell speech ; in which (you will readily understand) all his talk about " 'scaping the serpent's tongue," and asking for the " hands " of his audience, means merely that he hopes they will not hiss, but rather clap and applaud the actors : —

> If we shadows have offended,
> Think but this, and all is mended,
> That you have but slumbered here,
> While these visions did appear ;
> And this weak and idle theme,
> No more yielding but a dream,
> Gentles, do not reprehend :
> If you pardon, we will mend.
> And, as I'm an honest Puck,
> If we have unearnèd luck
> Now to 'scape the serpent's tongue
> We will make amends ere long ;
> Else the Puck a liar call :
> So, good night unto you all.
> Give me your hands, if we be friends,
> And Robin shall restore amends.

THE PRANKS OF

ROBIN GOODFELLOW.

ATTRIBUTED TO BEN JONSON.

FROM Oberon in fairy land,
   The king of ghosts and shadows there,
Mad Robin I, at his command,
   Am sent to view the night-sports here.
      What revel rout
      Is kept about,
In every corner where I go,
   I will o'er see,
   And merry be,
And make good sport, with ho, ho, ho!

More swift than lightning can I fly
   About this airy welkin soon,
And, in a minute's space, descry
   Each thing that 's done below the moon.
      There's not a hag
      Or ghost shall wag,

Or cry, 'ware goblins ! where I go ;
  But Robin I
  Their feats will spy,
And send them home with ho, ho, ho !

Whene'er such wanderers I meet,
  As from their night sports they trudge home,
With counterfeiting voice I greet,
  And call them on with me to roam

Through woods, through lakes ;
Through bogs, through brakes ;
Or else, unseen, with them I go,
  All in the nick
  To play some trick
And frolic it, with ho, ho, ho !

Sometimes I meet them like a man,
  Sometimes an ox, sometimes a hound ;
And to a horse I turn me can,
  To trip and trot about them round.
    But if to ride
    My back they stride,

More swift than wind away I go ;
  O'er hedge and lands,
  Through pools and ponds,
I hurry, laughing, ho, ho, ho !

When lads and lasses merry be,
  With possets and with junkets fine ;
Unseen of all the company,
  I eat their cakes and sip their wine !
    And, to make sport,
    I puff and snort,
And out the candles I do blow :
    The maids I kiss,
    They shriek — who 's this ?
I answer nought but ho, ho, ho !

And now and then, the maids to please,
  At midnight I card up their wool ;
And while they sleep and take their ease,
  With wheel to threads their flax I pull.
    I grind at mill
    Their malt up still ;
I dress their hemp ; I spin their tow ;
    If any wake
    And would me take,
I wend me laughing, ho, ho, ho !

When any need to borrow aught,
  We lend them what they do require :
And for the use demand we nought ;
  Our own is all we do desire.
    If to repay
    They do delay,
Abroad amongst them then I go,
    And night by night
    I them affright,
With pinchings, dreams, and ho, ho, ho !

When lazy queans have nought to do,
  But study how to cog and lie;
To make debate and mischief too
  'Twixt one another secretly:
    I mark their gloze
    And it disclose
To them whom they have wrongèd so:
    When I have done,
    I get me gone,
And leave them scolding, ho, ho, ho!

When men do traps and engines set
  In loopholes, where the vermin creep,
Who from their folds and houses get
  Their ducks and geese and lambs and sheep,
    I spy the gin,
    And enter in,
And seem a vermin taken so;
    But when they there
    Approach me near,
I leap out laughing, ho, ho, ho!

By wells and rills, in meadows green,
  We nightly dance our heyday guise;
And to our fairy king and queen
  We chant our moonlight minstrelsies.

    When larks 'gin sing,
    Away we fling;
And babes new-born steal as we go;
    And elf in bed
    We leave instead,
And wend us laughing, ho, ho, ho!

From hag-bred Merlin's time have I
Thus nightly revelled to and fro ;
And for my pranks men call me by
The name of Robin Goodfellow.
Fiends, ghosts and sprites,
Who haunt the nights,
The hags and goblins do me know :
And beldames old
My feats have told,
So vale,[1] vale ; ho, ho, ho !

---

[1] Farewell.

AS YOU LIKE IT.

INTRODUCTION.

HAKESPEARE had been in London about fourteen years. During that time he had done a prodigious amount of work. Besides several exquisite poems, which had brought him great credit and made him intimate with the noble society of the capital, he had produced some seventeen or eighteen tragedies and comedies — all, either wholly·or in part, the work of his own hand. It was in the year 1600 — the beginning of a new century — and he was thirty-six years old, when there came from his pen what has been truly styled "the very sweetest and happiest of all his comedies." It was called "As You Like It," for reasons which you will understand when you have read it, — as you will now have an opportunity to do.

The author had been writing a number of plays founded on English history, and his mind had been crowded with mighty themes, — of kings and courts and camps, — and we may well believe that it was strained and weary. So, by way of recreation perhaps, he painted this lovely picture of life in the woods. For it would almost seem that, in writing it, Shakespeare himself had escaped from his cares into the forest of Arden, and there, stretched out "under the greenwood tree," was joining in the merry strains of his own princely foresters, —

> "Who doth ambition shun,
> And loves to live in the sun,
> Come hither, come hither, come hither."

And there is not one of us that would not be glad to accept the invitation, — nay, who does not feel, as he reads, that he has already accepted it, and is chasing the wild deer, or roaming the shady forest, with the sunlight darting through the boughs, the breeze bathing his forehead, and the stream murmuring in his ears.

OLD ADAM AND ORLANDO.

AS YOU LIKE IT.

I.

Acr I. Scene 1.

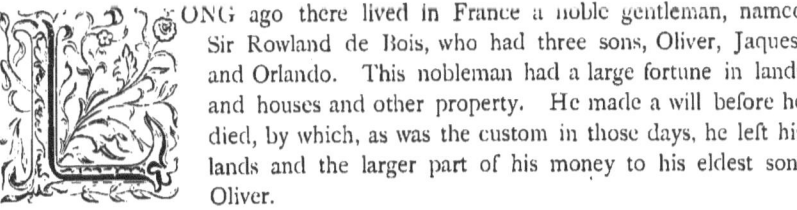

ONG ago there lived in France a noble gentleman, named Sir Rowland de Bois, who had three sons, Oliver, Jaques, and Orlando. This nobleman had a large fortune in lands and houses and other property. He made a will before he died, by which, as was the custom in those days, he left his lands and the larger part of his money to his eldest son, Oliver.

Sir Rowland did not mean, however, to be unjust to Jaques and Orlando; for, besides his blessing and a thousand crowns which he left to Orlando, he charged Oliver to see that both his brothers were educated as was befitting gentlemen of their high birth.

Oliver gave little heed to his father's wish, so far as Orlando was concerned.
Jaques he sent to school, whence came golden reports of his talent and industry,
while poor Orlando (being the youngest, and the least able to resent the injustice)
was kept at home in idleness, and as far as possible in ignorance.   Oliver never
showed any affection for Orlando : he made him eat with the servants, dressed
him shabbily, and in every way kept him from the education and position to which,
as the son of a gentleman of rank and wealth, he was entitled.

It is difficult to understand why Oliver should have treated his own brother so
badly, unless it was because he was envious of Orlando's good qualities, and the
affection he had won from all who knew him.   It was hard for Oliver to find a
reason in his own heart for hating Orlando as he did, for he says : " My soul, I
know not why, hates nothing more than him.   Yet he 's gentle ; never schooled,
and yet learned ; noble, beloved by every one, and most of all by those who know
him best."

Knowing that Orlando was a fine strong fellow, and very fond of wrestling, this
wicked brother determined to persuade him into a wrestling-match with a celebrated prize-fighter, named Charles, in the employment of the duke of that country ; not doubting that this burly champion could be induced to hurt him badly,
or even to kill him.

There was one, however, in Oliver's household who loved Orlando dearly.
This was an old servant of his father's, named Adam,[a] who had lived in the family
for more than sixty years.   Orlando could always go to him when discouraged
and unhappy, sure that Adam would comfort him and make things brighter and
cheerier, if only by his kindly sympathy and warm love.

One day, Orlando felt more unhappy than usual, and, finding Adam in the
orchard, he again repeated the story of his wrongs, and his determination to break
away from his wretched life.· Just then, seeing Oliver approaching the place
where they stood, Orlando bade Adam go away a short distance and listen, so as
to learn for himself how harsh and unkind a brother could be.

Oliver, richly dressed in the fashion of the day, came into the orchard, and in
an extremely rude and disagreeable manner addressed Orlando, whose clothes
were those of a peasant, saying, —

" Now, sir, what are you doing here? "

---

[a] This beautiful character is rendered doubly interesting to us by a curious tradition that
Shakespeare himself played it upon the stage.   The poet had a brother Gilbert, who sur-
vived him more than forty years, and who, when a very infirm old man, with faculties few and
feeble, being asked if he had ever seen his brother play, answered that he remembered
him in one of his own comedies, " wherein, being to personate a decrepit old man, he wore
a long beard, and appeared so weak and drooping that he was forced to be carried by
another person to a table, at which he was seated among some company who were eating,
and one of them sung a song."   This could have been none other than the good old Adam.
(See p. 111.)

ORLANDO'S VICTORY OVER CHARLES, THE DUKE'S WRESTLER.

" Nothing," replied Orlando ; " I am not taught to do anything, but am left to spoil with idleness."

" Well then, be better employed, confound you ! " retorted the elder brother.

" What shall I do? Feed your hogs, and eat husks with them? I believe I have n't spent the prodigal son's portion yet, that I should be brought so low as that."

" Know you where you are, sir? "

" O, sir, very well : here, in your orchard."

" Know you before whom, sir? "

" Ay, better than he I am before knows *me*. I know you are my elder brother, but you should also know me as being of the same blood as yourself. I have as much of our father in me as you ; though I confess your coming before me has brought you nearer to his estate."

This taunt stung Oliver to the quick, and calling his brother " boy " and " villain," he rushed forward as if about to strike him. But in this he made a great mistake, for Orlando was much the stronger of the two, and he seized Oliver by the throat, and was about to give him a hearty shaking, when the old servant interfered, saying, —

Sweet masters, be patient : for your father's remembrance, be at accord.

Oliver. Let me go, I say.

Orlando. I will not, till I please : you shall hear me. My father charged you in his will to give me good education : you have trained me like a peasant, obscuring and hiding from me all gentleman-like qualities : the spirit of my father grows strong in me, and I will no longer endure it : therefore, allow me such exercises as may become a gentleman, or give me the poor [portion] my father left me by testament : with that I will go buy my fortunes.

Oliver. And what wilt thou do ? Beg. when that is spent? Well, sir, get you in : I will not long be troubled with you : you shall have some part of your will. I pray you, leave me.

Orlando. I will no further offend you than becomes me for my good.

Oliver. Get you with him, you old dog.

Adam. Is " old dog " my reward ? Most true. I have lost my teeth in your service. — God be with my old master! *he* would not have spoke such a word.

As Orlando and Adam went away, Oliver said half aloud : " Is it even so? begin you to grow upon me? I will take you down, my fine fellow, and yet give no thousand crowns either."

Then he called to one of his servants and bade him find Charles, the Duke's wrestler. Charles was even then at the door, on an errand of his own, and entered without delay. Oliver asked for the news ; but Charles had only old news to tell, part of which Oliver probably already knew.

" You see, sir," said Charles, " it is old news that the new duke has banished his elder brother, the old duke ; three or four loving lords have gone into exile with the old duke, while the new duke has seized their lands and revenue: so he is quite content to have them stay away."

"Is Rosalind, the duke's daughter, banished with her father?"

"O, no, for the new duke's daughter, her cousin, loves her so much she would die without her. She is at the court. They say her father is in the Forest of Arden,[a] and many merry men with him. There they live like the old Robin Hood[b] of England, and pass the time carelessly as they did in the golden world of long ago."

"Do you wrestle to-morrow before the new duke?"

"Marry, I do, sir; and I came to acquaint you with a matter. I have heard that your younger brother, Orlando, means to try a fall with me. I should be sorry to hurt him, for he is but young and tender; but to-morrow I wrestle for my credit, and he who escapes from me with a broken limb will be happy. I beg you to keep him from his purpose; if not, the harm and disgrace are his doing, not any will of mine."

"Charles," replied Orlando, "I thank thee for thy love, and will reward it. I knew of my brother's purpose, and have quietly tried to dissuade him from it, but he is the stubbornest young fellow in France. Use thy discretion. I had as lief thou didst break his neck as his finger. But this I will tell thee by way of warning: if thou hurtest him only slightly, he will try to do thee some secret harm by poison or treachery, for — almost with tears I speak it — there is not one so young and so villainous this day living. This I tell thee of my own brother, with sorrow and shame."

Charles thanked the wicked brother for the advice which seemed so kindly meant, and went away, promising to pay Orlando well on the morrow for his evil intentions. Oliver had accomplished one part of his purpose in stirring up Charles. His hatred for Orlando seemed to grow stronger with every thought of him and his charming ways, and of the love he won from all sorts of people. "I hope soon to see an end of him," he said. "This wrestler shall clear all: nothing remains but to kindle Orlando into an angry feeling against Charles; which now I'll go about."

---

[a] This was the forest of Ardennes, in French Flanders, lying near the river Meuse, and between Charlemont and Rocroy.

[b] Robin Hood, the noble outlaw, is generally known to young readers. He lived in Sherwood Forest, Nottinghamshire, in the time of Richard I. Something about him and his modes of life can be found in the old Percy Ballads, and in Walter Scott's novel, *Ivanhoe*.

II.

ACT I. SCENE 2.

HILE such hard thoughts and wicked purposes were filling the heart of one brother against another, a happier scene was passing on the lawn in front of the Duke's palace.

Rosalind, the daughter of the banished Duke, and Celia, her cousin, — who seemed to love each other more with each new day, — were strolling through the pleasure-grounds around the palace. Rosalind appeared less cheerful than usual, and Celia, who could not bear to see a shadow on the face of one she loved so dearly, said, —

"I pray thee, Rosalind, my sweet coz, be merry!"

"Dear Celia, I seem merrier than I really am, even now. Can I forget my banished father?"

"But, Rosalind, if thou lovedst me as much as I love thee, thou wouldst take my father for thine. I know I would take thy father, if mine were banished."

"Well, cousin, I will forget the condition of my estate to rejoice in yours."

"When my father dies, I will give back to thee all he has taken away from thy father. Therefore, sweet Rose, dear Rose, be merry."

"From henceforth I will, coz," gayly answered Rosalind, "and what is more, I will invent merry sports. What think you of falling in love? Would not that be amusing?"

"Marry, I pr'ythee, do, to make sport: but love no man in good earnest!"

The two young princesses laughed merrily at the bare thought of either of them falling in love "in good earnest," little dreaming how soon both would try seriously the experiment which they had suggested in sport.

In the midst of their jesting and light-hearted laughter, Touchstone, the court fool, entered, apparently looking for them. In those days sovereigns and nobles kept so-called fools or jesters, to amuse the household with nonsense and wit. They were allowed to say and do almost anything they chose, although, if they went too far in their joking, they might be punished or dismissed. The fool's dress was a fantastic affair ; that of the clown in a modern circus will give you a pretty good idea of it. A cap, orna-

mented with a cock's comb and asses' ears ; a wide collar ; bells hung on the cap and clothing; and " motley " colors, — one leg or arm of one color, one of another color, and so on, — were among the means by which the fool provoked laughter. He also carried a mock sceptre, or " bauble."

There was a great variety in court fools. Some of them were misshapen dwarfs, and half crazy; others were men who concealed much wit and wisdom under the pretence of folly. Touchstone was of the latter kind. With all his solemn absurdities, he managed to utter a great deal of good sense.

When the ladies saw him coming, Celia called to him, —

How now, wit ? Whither wander you ?
Touchstone. Mistress, you must come away to your father.
Celia. Were you made the messenger ?
Touchstone. No, by mine honor ; but I was bid to come for you.
Rosalind. Where learned you that oath, fool ?
Touchstone. Of a certain knight, that swore by his honor they were good pancakes, and swore by his honor the mustard was naught:[1] now, I 'll stand to it, the pancakes were naught, and the mustard was good, and yet was not the knight forsworn.
Celia. How prove you that, in the great heap of your knowledge ?
Rosalind. Ay, marry: now unmuzzle your wisdom.
Touchstone. Stand you both forth now ; stroke your chins, and swear by your beards that I am a knave.

So the princesses stand up and merrily stroke their smooth faces with their hands ; and Celia says, —

By our beards, if we had them, thou art.
Touchstone. By my knavery, if I had it, then I were ; but if you swear by that that is not, you are not forsworn : no more was this knight, swearing by his honor, for

---

[1] Bad.

he never had any ; or if he had, he had sworn it away before ever he saw those pan-cakes, or that mustard.

Celia. You 'll be whipped for [criticising] one of these days.[n]   But here comes Monsieur Le Beau.

Monsieur Le Beau was a gentleman of the court, who entered at this moment, much excited.

" Fair ladies," he exclaimed, " here has been some good sport in wrestling that you have lost sight of."

" Yet tell us the manner of it," Rosalind replied.

" I will tell you the beginning ; and, if it please your ladyship, you may see the end, for the best is yet to do ; and here, where you are, they are coming to per-form it."

" Well, tell us the beginning."

Le Beau. There comes an old man and his three sons.   The eldest of the three wrestled with Charles, the Duke's wrestler ; which Charles in a moment threw him, and broke three of his ribs, that there is little hope of life in him : so he served the second, and so the third.   Yonder they lie, the poor old man, their father, making such pitiful dole over them, that all the beholders take his part with weeping.

Rosalind. Alas !

Touchstone. But what is the sport, monsieur, that the ladies have lost ?

Le Beau. Why, this that I speak of.

Touchstone. Thus men may grow wiser every day !   It is the first time that ever I heard breaking of ribs was sport for ladies !

Rosalind. Shall we see this wrestling, cousin ?

Le Beau. You must, if you stay here : for here is the place appointed for the wrestling, and they are ready to perform it.

Celia. Yonder, sure, they are coming : let us now stay and see it.

With a great flourish of trumpets, Duke Frederick and his lords entered the open courtyard : with them also came Orlando, and Charles, the court wrestler, by the side of whose giant frame Orlando looked even younger and more slender than before.

While the attendants arranged a place for the wrestlers, and Orlando made ready for the contest by laying aside his doublet (or outer coat), Celia and Rosa-lind, who had come near to see the sport, felt their hearts moved with pity to think that one so young in years and so gentle in bearing as Orlando should wrestle with such a man as Charles.   Even Duke Frederick said he wished that the men were more equally matched, and endeavored to dissuade Orlando from his purpose ; but the youngster would not yield.   Then the Duke called Celia and Rosalind to try, saying, " Speak to him, ladies ; see if you can move him."

---

* Although a very large liberty was given to the "allowed fools," nevertheless they were sometimes whipped for using their tongues too freely.

"Call him hither, good Monsieur Le Beau," said Celia.

"Do so," said the Duke ; " I will step aside."

Le Beau having told Orlando that the princesses wished to speak with him, that young gentleman gallantly and courteously drew near, not at all displeased to find two lovely young ladies taking an interest in his welfare.

"Young man," said Rosalind, "have you challenged Charles the wrestler?"

Orlando. No, fair princess ; he is the general challenger : I come but in, as others do, to try with him the strength of my youth.

Celia. Young gentleman, your spirits are too bold for your years. You have seen cruel proof of this man's strength. We pray you, for your own sake, to embrace your own safety, and give over this attempt.

Rosalind. Do, young sir : your reputation shall not therefore [suffer]. We will make it our suit to the Duke, that the wrestling may not go forward.

Orlando. I beseech you, punish me not with your hard thoughts. I confess me much guilty, to deny so fair and excellent ladies anything. But let your fair eyes, and gentle wishes, go with me to my trial : wherein if I be [conquered], there is but one shamed that was never [in favor] ; if killed, but one dead that is willing to be so. I shall do my friends no wrong, for I have none to lament me ; the world no injury, for in it I have nothing ; only in the world I fill up a place, which may be better supplied when I have made it empty.

Rosalind. The little strength that I have, I would it were with you.

Celia. And mine, to eke out hers.

Rosalind. Fare you well. Pray Heaven I be deceived in you !

Celia. Your heart's desires be with you !

Charles. Come ; where is this young gallant, that is so desirous to lie with his mother earth ?

Orlando. Ready, sir ; but his will hath in it a more modest working.

Duke Frederick. You shall try but one fall.

Charles. No, I warrant your Grace, you shall not entreat him to a second, that have so mightily persuaded him from a first.

Orlando. If you mean to mock me after, you should not have mocked me before ; but come [on].

And now the wrestling began. The young princesses looked on with the deepest interest ; especially Rosalind, who from the first felt drawn to the handsome youth, the more because he was unfortunate and alone in the world, like herself ; and she pitied him so very much that it may almost be said she was in love with him already. As for Orlando, the kindness shown to him by these noble ladies seemed to increase his courage and strength, and with one mighty effort he lifted the big champion in his arms and threw him, stunned and apparently lifeless, to the ground. The attendants came and bore the helpless wrestler away ; and the Duke, turning to the flushed and panting young victor, said, —

What is thy name, young man ?

Orlando. Orlando, my liege : the youngest son of Sir Rowland de Bois.

Duke Frederick. I would thou hadst been son to some man else.
The world esteemed thy father honorable,
But I did find him still mine enemy:
Thou wouldst have better pleased me with this deed,
Hadst thou descended from another house.[1]
But fare thee well; thou art a gallant youth ;
I would thou hadst told me of another father.

Duke Frederick's heart was divided between admiration for the bravery and gallantry of Orlando and dislike for Sir Rowland de Bois, Orlando's father. He felt hardly comfortable in the presence of one who, while deserving of praise, was yet a source of annoyance simply because of his parentage. So he turned and departed from the courtyard with his train, leaving Rosalind, Celia, and Orlando together.

Orlando, with great dignity, called after the retiring Duke, " I am more proud to be Sir Rowland's son, his youngest son, than if I were adopted heir to Frederick."

Celia was indignant at her father's cool words, and, turning to Rosalind, said in a regretful way, " Were I my father, coz, would I do this? "

Rosalind eagerly declared, —

My father loved Sir Rowland as his soul,
And all the world was of my father's mind.
Had I before known this young man his son,
I would have given him tears unto entreaties,
Ere he should thus have ventured.
    Celia.   Gentle cousin,   .
Let us go thank him, and encourage him :
My father's rough and [hateful] disposition
Sticks me at heart. — [*To Orlando*] Sir, you have well deserved.

Then Rosalind, taking a heavy gold chain from her neck, put it about Orlando's neck with these words : —
                    Gentleman,
Wear this for me, one out of suits [2] with fortune,
That could give more, but that her hand lacks means. —
Shall we go, coz?
    Celia. Ay. — Fare you well, fair gentleman.
    Orlando [*with eyes cast down and speaking to himself*]. Can I not say, I thank
      you ? My better parts
Are all thrown down, and that which here stands up
Is but a lifeless block.
    Rosalind [*to Celia*]. He calls us back.[3] My pride fell with my fortunes —

---

          [1] Family.   [2] Out of favor.
    [3] Orlando had *not* called them back: Rosalind was deceived by her own fancy, and by her desire to talk with Orlando more.

I 'll ask him what he [wants]. — Did you call, sir? —
Sir, you have wrestled well, and overthrown
More than your enemies.
    Celia.   Will you go, coz?
    Rosalind. [I 'm coming.] — Fare you well.

The two young ladies departed, but Rosalind cast many a lingering look back-
ward to where Orlando stood, like one almost stupefied.

At last, when they were quite gone, he seemed to rouse himself, and slowly said : "What is it that hangs these weights upon my tongue? I cannot speak to her, yet she urged me to speak. O poor Orlando ! thou art overthrown ; either Charles or something weaker masters thee ! "

I think you and I can guess what was the matter with both Rosalind and Orlando.

At this point Le Beau, who was evidently a kindly person, came hastily in, and urged Orlando to leave the place with speed ; because, in spite of all that he had done deserving praise, the Duke was of a temper so moody and uncertain that he would be sure to seek some cause for blame.

Orlando thanked him for his kindness, and begged to know which of the two lovely young ladies who watched the wrestling was the daughter of the Duke.

Le Beau answered : " You would not think either of them could be the Duke's daughter, to judge by their manners ; but the shorter of the two, Celia, is really his daughter. The other is her cousin Rosalind, daughter of the banished Duke, and much beloved for her many virtues, wherein she resembles her father." But these very virtues (he added), together with the pity the people felt for her, had excited the Duke's displeasure, and sooner or later it would break forth on her.

Orlando again thanked Le Beau, bade him farewell, and, with his heart full of happy thoughts about Rosalind, went from the abode of the tyrant Duke toward that of a tyrant brother.

III.

HE two cousins, Celia and Rosalind, had lived together in Duke Frederick's palace ever since the banishment of Rosalind's father. They had played together as children; studied together; slept, walked, and talked together. Every secret was shared between them. If Celia was sad, Rosalind, who was light-hearted by nature, would have some cheery word or merry sport, to beguile her of her sorrow.

It was not often that Rosalind needed comfort, but now, for once, it was she who was dull and out of spirits; and as they entered one of the apartments of the palace in their usual affectionate way, she was silent and sad, and so little like her usual self that Celia jested with her and teased her, in a kindly way.

"Why, cousin; why, Rosalind," she said, — "not a word?"

"Not one to throw at a dog," answered Rosalind, with a heavy sigh.

"My dear Rosalind, this will never do. Come, come; wrestle with thy affections."

"That I cannot do," answered Rosalind; "they take the part of a better wrestler than myself."

"Is it possible," said Celia, "on such a sudden, you should fall into so strong a liking with old Sir Rowland's youngest son?"

"The Duke my father loved his father dearly," Rosalind innocently replied.

"Is that any reason," answered Celia, laughing, "that you should love his son dearly? If that is so, then I should hate him, for my father hated his father dearly.[a] Yet I hate not Orlando."

"No, faith, hate him not, for my sake. Let me love him for deserving well, and do you love him because I do. Look, here comes the Duke, your father, and evidently very angry."

Duke Frederick entered with a heavy frown upon his face and a severe look in his eyes. He spoke harshly to Rosalind, and bade her leave the court without delay, threatening her with death if after ten days she should be found within twenty miles of the palace.

"I do beseech your Grace," said Rosalind, —

> Let me the knowledge of my fault bear with me:
> Never so much as in a thought unborn
> Did I offend your Highness.
> *Duke Frederick.* Let it suffice thee, that I trust thee not.
> *Rosalind.* Yet your mistrust cannot make me a traitor.
> Tell me whereon the likelihood depends.
> *Duke Frederick.* Thou art thy father's daughter; there 's enough.
> *Rosalind.* So was I when your Highness took his dukedom;
> So was I when your Highness banished him.
> Treason is not inherited, my lord :
> Or, if we did derive it from our friends,
> What 's that to me? my father was no traitor.
> *Celia.* Dear sovereign, hear me speak.
> *Duke Frederick.* Ay, Celia : we stayed her for your sake ;
> Else had she with her father ranged along.
> *Celia.* I did not then entreat to have her stay :
> It was your pleasure, and your own remorse.[1]
> I was too young that time to value her ;
> But now I know her. If she be a traitor,
> Why, so am I ; we still have slept together,
> Rose at an instant, learned, played, eat together ;
> And wheresoe'er we went, like Juno's swans,
> Still we went coupled, and inseparable.
> *Duke Frederick.* She is too subtle for thee ; and her smoothness,
> Her very silence, and her patience,
> Speak to the people, and they pity her.
> Thou art a fool ; she robs thee of thy name ;
> And thou wilt show more bright, and seem more virtuous,
> When she is gone. Then, open not thy lips :

---

[1] Compassion.

[a] In Shakespeare's time people talked of *hating* dearly almost as much as they did of *loving* dearly.

Firm and irrevocable is my doom
Which I have passed upon her. She is banished.
Celia. Pronounce that sentence, then, on me, my liege.
I cannot live out of her company.
Duke Frederick. You are a fool. — You, niece, provide yourself :
If you out-stay the time, upon mine honor,
And in the greatness of my word, you die.

After sternly uttering these words, Duke Frederick departed with his attendants.

Celia. O my poor Rosalind! whither wilt thou go?
Wilt thou change fathers? I will give thee mine.
I charge thee, be not thou more grieved than I am.
Rosalind. I have more cause.
Celia. Thou hast not, cousin.
Pr'ythee, be cheerful: know'st thou not, the Duke
Hath banished me, his daughter?
Rosalind. That he hath not.
Celia. No? hath not? Rosalind lacks, then, the love,
Which teacheth me that thou and I are one.
Shall we be sundered? shall we part, sweet girl?
No: let my father seek another heir.
Therefore, devise with me how we may fly,
Whither to go, and what to bear with us :
And do not seek to take the charge upon you,
To bear your griefs yourself, and leave me out.
Say what thou canst, I 'll go along with thee.
Rosalind. Why, whither shall we go?
Celia. To seek my uncle
In the Forest of Arden.
Rosalind. Alas, what danger will it be to us,
Maids as we are, to travel forth so far !
Beauty provoketh thieves sooner than gold.
Celia. I 'll put myself in poor and mean attire,
And with a kind of umber ⁿ smirch my face.
The like do you: so shall we pass along,
And never stir assailants.
Rosalind. Were it not better,
Because that I am more than common tall,
That I did [dress exactly] like a man?
A gallant curtle-axe ¹ upon my thigh,
A boar-spear in my hand ; and in my heart —
Lie there what hidden woman's fear there will —

---

¹ Cutlass.
ⁿ *Umber* is a yellowish earth, which is found in Umbria, Italy, and made into a kind of
dusky paint.

We 'll have a [swaggering] and a martial outside,
As many other mannish cowards have.
Celia. What shall I call thee when thou art a man ?
Rosalind. I 'll have no worse a name than Jove's own page,
And therefore look you call me Ganymede.*
But what will you be called ?
Celia. Something that hath a reference to my state :
No longer Celia, but Aliena.ᵇ
Rosalind. But, cousin, what if we [contrived] to steal
The clownish fool out of your father's court?
Would he not be a comfort to our travel ?
Celia. He 'll go along o'er the wide world with me ;
Leave me alone to woo him.   Let 's away,
And get our jewels and our wealth together,
Devise the fittest time and safest way
To hide us from pursuit that will be made
After my flight.   Now go we in content
To liberty, and not to banishment.

---

* *Ganymede*, in the old Greek mythology, was a beautiful youth who was carried away on an eagle to Olympus, to be cup-bearer to Jove, the king of the gods.

ᵇ The metre requires this name to be pronounced in four syllables, with the accent on the second : *A-lé-e-na*.

IV.

DUKE FREDERICK, the father of Celia, as we have seen, had no right to the kingdom which he called his; it really belonged to his elder brother, the father of Rosalind. But those old times were troublous and uncertain. One might be a king to-day and a banished outlaw to-morrow; for *might made right*, and he who could win a kingdom and hold it cared very little about the rightful owner.

Duke Frederick, then, having a powerful army, had seized his brother's dukedom and palace, and banished that brother and his followers. But he had kept, as a companion for Celia, the pretty Rosalind, who was quite as good and lovely as she had appeared in Le Beau's description.

The banished Duke seemed to take his misfortunes like a philosopher, and with his co-mates and brothers in exile had made a home in the Forest of Arden, where they might indeed feel the churlish chiding of the winter's wind, but not the cruel falseness of the envious court. The blasts might bite and blow upon his body, but, even while shrinking with cold, he would only wrap his mantle the closer round his shivering form, and laughingly remark that these at least were not like flattering courtiers, but frankly reminded him that he was a man like other men.

The Duke was so enchanted with the freedom of his new life, that he began to be rather glad of the trouble and sorrow which had brought him there, and used to say, —

> Sweet are the uses of adversity,
> Which, like the toad,* ugly and venomous,
> Wears yet a precious jewel in his head;
> And this our life, [remote] from public haunt,
> Finds tongues in trees, books in the running brooks,
> Sermons in stones, and good in every thing.

---

* The ancients had a *toad-stone*, so called only from its resemblance in color to that reptile. From this curious epithet arose, in later times, the fable that the toad had in its head a stone endued with wondrous virtues.

DEER IN THE FOREST OF ARDEN.

One day, Amiens, one of the lords who had gone into exile with the Duke, complimented his master upon this cheerful contentment, and then accepted the proposal of his Grace to join in a hunting party.

The Forest of Arden was full of beautiful deer, that really seemed to have more right to their native home, the forest, than these hunters had. Even the Duke sometimes felt doubtful about killing them, and Jaques, the melancholy Jaques, — a queer, odd man, who, having become tired of the world, had joined this company more to get rid of worldly society than for any other reason, — insisted that the Duke was as much of an usurper in their domain as his brother, Duke Frederick, had been in seizing the dukedom.

" Indeed, my lord," said one of the merry hunters, —

> The melancholy Jaques grieves at that;
> And, in that kind, swears you do more usurp
> Than doth your brother that hath banished you.
> To-day, my lord of Amiens and myself
> Did steal behind him, as he lay along
> Under an oak, whose antique root peeps out
> Upon the brook that brawls along this wood ;
> To the which place a poor [secluded] stag,
> That from the hunter's aim had taken a hurt,
> Did come to languish : and, indeed, my lord,
> The wretched animal heaved forth such groans,
> That their discharge did stretch his leathern coat
> Almost to bursting ; and the big round tears
> Coursed one another down his innocent nose
> In piteous chase : and thus the hairy fool,
> Much markèd of the melancholy Jaques,
> Stood on the extremest verge of the swift brook,
> [Increasing] it with tears.*
>
> *Duke Senior.*   But what said Jaques ?

" O," answered the hunter who had secretly watched him, " he pitied the deer for wasting his tears by weeping into the stream that was already full of water : which he said was like wealthy men leaving money in their wills to people who had too much already. When the sleek-coated friends of the poor animal had left him alone, Jaques said it was the way of the world : the miserable were always abandoned : if a man were poor and in trouble, his rich and comfortable friends passed him without a thought : and there we left him weeping and talking about the poor sobbing deer."

The Duke rather liked to see Jaques in these queer moods, for he was always more entertaining then ; so he hastened away, in company with Amiens and the other lords, to seek this singular man.

---

* The poet Drayton says, in a note on a certain passage in one of his own poems, " The hart weepeth at his dying ; his tears are held precious in medicine."

V.

Y this time Duke Frederick had discovered his daughter's absence, and, as we might well suppose, was furious. No one could tell him anything more than this : her ladies-in-waiting had seen her go to bed as usual, but in the morning she was gone. One of the noblemen of the court added, that the clown Touchstone was also missing, and, in his opinion, the young ladies were to be found in the company of the handsome young wrestler who had got the better of Charles in the wrestling-match. One thing was certain, they had been heard to admire and praise him very warmly, and it was believed in the court that, wherever they were gone, that youth was surely in their company.

Duke Frederick was doubly angry at this. He could not like Orlando, who was the son of his old enemy, Sir Rowland de Bois, and the thought that his own daughter Celia might be in such company was more than he could bear.

In these days of telegraphs and railroads it is an easy matter to hunt up runaways, but then it was a far more difficult affair. The great forests were full of delightful hiding-places, and unless Duke Frederick had some one to help him who was as earnest to find the fugitives as himself, it might be long before any tidings would reach the court. But the Duke suddenly bethought him of the brother with whom Orlando lived, and he despatched messengers to the house of Oliver, with orders to bring the young wrestler into his presence. " If he be absent," he added, " bring his brother to me ; I will make *him* answerable. Do it quickly, and let not search and inquiry cease, until these foolish runaways be arrested and brought back again."

As Orlando was returning from the scene of his triumph to Oliver's house, thinking very likely of all that had happened the day before, — of his victory over the burly prize-fighter ; the lovely princesses, and their kind words ; Rosalind's kinder looks and bright smiles ; her gift of the golden chain, now hanging about his neck, which made it certain that all was not merely a happy dream, — he heard a step, and, suddenly raising his head, he demanded, "Who 's there?"

It was old Adam, who had come out on purpose to meet him, and warn him of a great danger.

"What! my young master!" he exclaimed. "O, my gentle master, what are you doing here? Why do people love you? Wherefore are you so gentle, strong, and valiant? Why were you so foolish as to overcome the Duke's big, bony wrestler?"

"Why, what 's the matter, Adam?" answered Orlando.

"O unhappy youth," said Adam; "come not within these doors! Your brother hates you. He has heard of your success, and means to burn your lodging, and you in it, this very night. You must not enter it."

"Why, whither, Adam, wouldst thou have me go?"

"No matter whither, so you come not here."

"What, wouldst thou have me beg my bread, or with a base sword force a thievish living on the common road? That I will never do. I would rather stay here, subject to my unnatural, bloody brother."

> *Adam.* But do not so. I have five hundred crowns,
> The thrifty hire I saved under your father,
> Which I did store, to be my foster-nurse
> When service should in my old limbs lie lame,
> And unregarded age in corners thrown.
> Take that: and He that doth the ravens feed,
> Yea, providently caters for the sparrow,
> Be comfort to my age! Here is the gold:
> All this I give you. Let me be your servant:
> Though I look old, yet I am strong and lusty;
> For in my youth I never did apply
> Hot and rebellious liquors in my blood;
> Therefore my age is as a lusty winter,
> Frosty, but kindly. Let me go with you:
> I 'll do the service of a younger man
> In all your business and necessities.

"O good old man, how different is thy faithful service from that of those who only serve for their own selfish ends!" exclaimed Orlando; —

But, poor old man, thou prun'st a rotten tree,
That cannot so much as a blossom yield,
In lieu of [1] all thy pains and husbandry.
But come thy ways: we 'll go along together,
And ere we have thy youthful wages spent,
We 'll light upon some settled low content.
    Adam. Master, go on, and I will follow thee
To the last gasp with truth and loyalty.
From seventeen years, till now almost fourscore,
Here livèd I, but now live here no more.

Then Orlando and Adam set forth together, the old man leaning on the young one, who carried his bundle, and cheered and comforted him, as they went out into the world to seek their fortune.

---

[1] In return for.

VI.

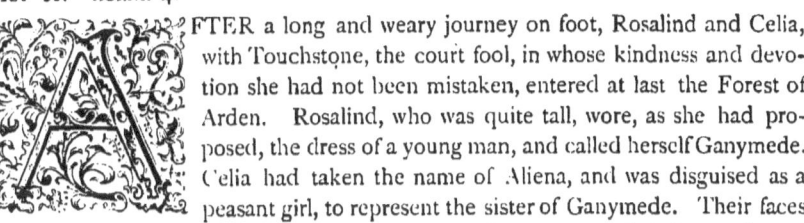 FTER a long and weary journey on foot, Rosalind and Celia, with Touchstone, the court fool, in whose kindness and devotion she had not been mistaken, entered at last the Forest of Arden. Rosalind, who was quite tall, wore, as she had proposed, the dress of a young man, and called herself Ganymede. Celia had taken the name of Aliena, and was disguised as a peasant girl, to represent the sister of Ganymede. Their faces were colored like those of gypsies or sun-browned peasants, and their transformation was so complete that their own fathers would not have recognized them.

They were all weary and footsore, and Rosalind declared that if it were not for her man's dress she could find it in her heart to cry like a woman. But she only laughed instead, saying : "But I must comfort the weaker vessel, as doublet and hose [a] ought to show itself courageous to petticoat. Therefore, courage, good Aliena ! "

Celia. I pray you, bear with me : I can go no farther.

Touchstone. For my part, I had rather bear with you, than bear you : yet I should bear no cross,[b] if I did bear you, for, I think, you have no money in your purse.

Rosalind. Well, this is the Forest of Arden.

Touchstone. Ay, now am I in Arden ; the more fool I : when I was at home I was in a better place, but travellers must be content.

Rosalind. Ay, be so, good Touchstone. — Look you ; who comes here ? a young man, and an old, in [earnest] talk.

These were Corin, an old, gray-haired shepherd, and Silvius, a youthful shepherd. They were talking so earnestly that they saw no one, as they walked in the shadow of the great trees.

---

[a] *Doublet and hose* is about equivalent to coat and pantaloons of modern times.
[b] In Shakespeare's time certain English coins had a cross stamped on them, and hence were called *crosses.*

Silvius was telling Corin about his love for a pretty shepherdess named Phebe, who was not so kind to him as he would like to have her. So affected

was he with his own story that the mere mention of her name seemed more than he could bear, and he ran away to hide his feelings.

Poor Rosalind, hearing Silvius talk so warmly of his love for Phebe, finds that love has hurt her as badly as it has the shepherd, and she says sadly, —

Alas, poor shepherd! searching of thy wound,
I have by hard adventure found mine own.

Touchstone. And I mine. I re-member, when I was in love I broke my sword upon a stone, and bid him take that for coming a-night to Jane Smile : and I remember the kissing of her [clothes-pounder], and the cow's dugs that her pretty chapped hands had milked : and I remember the wooing of a peascod instead of her ; from whom I took two cods, and, giving her them again, said with weeping tears, "Wear these for my sake." [*] We, that are true lovers, run into strange capers.

Rosalind.   Love, love ! this shepherd's passion
Is much upon my fashion.

Touchstone. And mine ; but it grows something stale with me.

Celia, who by this time finds herself hungry as well as tired, thinks it would be much better to get some food and a resting-place than to waste so much time talking nonsense. She is afraid Corin will follow Silvius, and she exclaims, —

I pray you, one of you question yond' man,
If he for gold will give us any food :
I faint almost to death.
    Touchstone. Hallo, you clown !
    Rosalind.   Peace, fool : he 's not thy kinsman.
    Corin. Who calls ?
    Touchstone. Your betters, sir.
    Corin. Else are they very wretched.

---

[*] Touchstone takes two pods from the dish of his kitchen love, as she is shelling peas, and gives them to her again for ear-ornaments.

Rosalind. Peace, I say. —
Good even to you, friend.
Corin. And to you, gentle sir ; and to you all.
Rosalind. I pr'ythee, shepherd, if that love or gold
Can in this desert place buy entertainment,
Bring us where we may rest ourselves and feed.
Here 's a young maid with travel much oppressed,
And faints for succor.
Corin. Fair sir, I pity her,
And wish, for her sake more than for mine own,
My fortunes were more able to relieve her ;
But I am shepherd to another man,
And do not shear the fleeces that I graze :
My master is of churlish disposition,
And little [cares] to find the way to heaven
By doing deeds of hospitality.
Besides, his cote,¹ his flocks, and [pasture-fields],
Are now on sale : and at our sheepcote now,
By reason of his absence, there is nothing
That you will feed on : but what is, come see,
And in my voice ᵃ most welcome shall you be.
Rosalind. What is he that shall buy his flock and pasture ?
Corin. That young swain that you saw here but [just now],
That little cares for buying anything.
Rosalind. I pray thee, if it stand with honesty,
Buy thou the cottage, pasture, and the flock,
And thou shalt have to pay for it of us.
Celia. And we will mend thy wages. I like this place,
And willingly could [spend] my time in it.
Corin. Assuredly, the thing is to be sold.
Go with me : if you like, upon report,
The soil, the profit, and this kind of life,
I will your very faithful feeder be,
And buy it with your gold [immediately].

So Rosalind and Celia went with Corin to see the cottage, well pleased at the prospect of even so humble a home as a shepherd's hut in the grand old forest.

---

¹ Cottage.
ᵃ That is, as far as my voice has any power.

VII.

N an open glade in another part of the forest, the hunters and lords had prepared a banquet under the trees for their exiled Duke. While they were waiting for him, Amiens, to pass the time, sang a merry song, Jaques and the rest joining in the chorus.

SONG.

Under the greenwood tree,
Who loves to lie with me,
And tune his merry note
Unto the sweet bird's throat,
Come hither, come hither, come hither :
Here shall he see
No enemy
But winter and rough weather.

Jaques. More, more! I pr'ythee, more.

Amiens. It will make you melancholy, Monsieur Jaques.

Jaques. I thank it. More! I pr'ythee, more. I can suck melancholy out of a song, as a weasel sucks eggs. More! I pr'ythee, more.

Amiens. My voice is [rough] ; I know I cannot please you.

Jaques. I do not desire you to please me ; I do desire you to sing. Come, sing ; and you that will not, hold your tongues.

Amiens. Well, I 'll end the song. — Sirs, [set the table, meanwhile] ; the Duke will drink under this tree. — He hath been all this day to look [for] you.

Jaques. And I have been all this day to avoid him. He is too disputable for my company : I think of as many matters as he, but I give Heaven thanks, and make no boast of them. Come, warble ; come.

So they sing another verse of the song : —

Who doth ambition shun,
And loves to live in the sun,

Seeking the food he eats,
And pleased with what he gets,
Come hither, come hither, come hither :
Here shall he see
No enemy
But winter and rough weather.

And then Jaques says that he will go somewhere and sleep, while the rest go to seek the Duke, and bring him to the picnic feast.

In the mean time, in still another part of the forest, Orlando and Adam were having a hard time. The journey had been long and tedious. They had brought no food with them, and poor old Adam, who had dragged wearily along for many hours, supported by Orlando's strong arm and loving heart, at last gave way entirely, and sank down upon the ground, murmuring feebly, —

Dear master, I can go no further : O, I die for food ! Here lie I down, and measure out my grave. Farewell, kind master.

Orlando. Why, how now, Adam ! no greater heart in thee ? Live a little ; comfort a little ; cheer thyself a little. If this uncouth forest yield anything savage,* I will either be food for it, or bring it for food to thee. For my sake be comforted ; hold death awhile at the arm's end. I will be here with thee presently, and if I bring thee not something to eat, I will give thee leave to die. Well [done] ! thou look'st cheerily ; and I 'll be with thee quickly. — Yet thou liest in the bleak air : come, I will bear thee to some shelter, and thou shalt not die for lack of a dinner, if there live anything in this desert. Cheerily, good Adam !

Orlando folded the old man's scant cloak around his trembling form, and having made him as comfortable as was possible there in the heart of the forest, said a few kind and cheering words, and departed.

While the young man was ranging the woods in search of some place which might offer shelter and food, the merry party of nobles had gathered again where their banquet was spread. The Duke missed Jaques, and, unwilling to have the feast begin without him, sent one of the lords to seek him. At the same moment they saw him approaching in the distance, laughing to himself, as it were, over some merry thought.

Now the thing that had so pleased Jaques was this. He had met Touchstone lying under the trees in his funny parti-colored fool's-dress, and his cap and bells (for Touchstone had not disguised himself, but wore the very clothes that belonged to his office in the court), and it seemed to Jaques the drollest sight in the world, to meet far away in the forest a Court Fool, a thing the most out of place that it was possible to conceive.

" Why, how now, Monsieur ! " cried the Duke, as he drew nearer ; " what does this mean ? You seem to be merry ! "

---

* That is, any *wild game.*

Jaques. A fool, a fool! — I met a fool i' the forest.
As I do live by food, I met a fool;
Who laid him down and basked him in the sun,
And railed on Lady Fortune in good terms,
In good set terms, — and yet a motley fool.
" Good-morrow, fool," quoth I : " No, sir," quoth he,
" Call me not fool, till heaven hath sent me fortune." *
And then he drew a dial ¹ from his [pouch],
And looking on it with lack-lustre eye,
Says very wisely, " It is ten o'clock :
Thus may we see," quoth he, " how the world wags :
'T is but an hour ago since it was nine,
And after one hour more 't will be eleven ;
And so from hour to hour we ripe and ripe,
And then from hour to hour we rot and rot ;
And thereby hangs a tale." When I did hear
The motley fool thus moral on the time,
My lungs began to crow like chanticleer,
That fools should be so deep-contemplative ;
And I did laugh, [without cessation],
An hour by his dial.
                              O, that I were a fool !
I am ambitious for a motley coat.
     Duke Senior. Thou shalt have one.
     Jaques.   It is my only suit.
But who comes here?

Jaques might well exclaim, for, as he spoke, Orlando rushed madly into the midst of the idle group, his sword drawn, and his face haggard with fatigue and hunger. With a threatening gesture, he shouted, —

     Forbear, and eat no more !
     Jaques.   Why, I have eat none yet.
     Orlando. Nor shalt not, till necessity be served.
     Jaques. Of what kind should this cock come of ?
     Duke Senior. Art thou thus boldened, man, by thy distress,
Or else a rude despiser of good manners,
That in civility thou seem'st so empty ?
     Orlando. You touched my vein at first : the thorny point
Of bare distress hath ta'en from me the show
Of smooth civility ; yet am I inland bred,ᵇ

---

¹ Watch.

* That is, " Call me not fool till I have got rich ; " alluding to the old proverb, " Fortune favors fools," or, as is sometimes said now-a-days, " It takes a fool to make money."

ᵇ *Inland bred* — remote from the sea-shore, where the people were mostly coarse and ill-bred.

And know some nurture.[1] But forbear, I say:
He dies, that touches any of this fruit,
Till I and my affairs are answerèd.
    Jaques. If you will not be answerèd with reason,
I must die.
    Duke Senior. What would you have? Your gentleness shall force,
More than your force move us to gentleness.
    Orlando. I almost die for food, and let me have it.

---

[1] Culture, breeding.

Duke Senior. Sit down and feed, and welcome to our table.
Orlando. Speak you so gently? Pardon me, I pray you.
I thought that all things had been savage here,
And therefore put I on the countenance
Of stern commandment. But whate'er you are,
That, in this desert inaccessible,
Under the shade of melancholy boughs,
Lose and neglect the creeping hours of time,
If ever you have looked on better days,
If ever been where bells have knolled to church,
If ever sat at any good man's feast,
If ever from your eyelids wiped a tear,
And know what 't is to pity and be pitied,
Let gentleness my strong enforcement be.
In the which hope I blush, and hide my sword.   [*Sheathes his sword.*
     Duke Senior. True is it that we have seen better days,
And have with holy bell been knolled to church,
And sat at good men's feasts, and wiped our eyes
Of drops that sacred pity hath engendered ;
And therefore sit you down in gentleness,
And take, upon command, what help we have,
That to your wanting may be ministered.
     Orlando. Then, but forbear your food a little while,
While, like a doe, I go to find my fawn,
And give it food. There is an old poor man,
Who after me hath many a weary step
Limped in pure love : till he be first sufficed, —
Oppressed with two weak evils, age and hunger, —
I will not touch a bit.
     Duke Senior.   Go find him out,
And we will nothing waste till you return.
     Orlando. I thank ye ; and be blessed for your good comfort !

When Orlando found how kindly he was received, he was ashamed of his violence, and, apologizing to the company, he hastened away to bring poor old Adam
where food and drink and comfort awaited him.
     Then the Duke turned to Jaques, saying, —

Thou seest, we are not all alone unhappy :
This wide and universal theatre
Presents more woful pageants than the scene
Wherein we play.
     Jaques [*after a little reflection*]. All the world 's a stage,
And all the men and women merely players :
They have their exits and their entrances,
And one man in his time plays many parts,
His acts being seven ages. At first, the infant,

Mewling and puking in the nurse's arms.
Then, the whining school-boy, with his satchel,
And shining morning face, creeping like snail
Unwillingly to school. And then, the lover,
Sighing like furnace, with a woful ballad
Made to his mistress' eyebrow. Then, a soldier,
Full of strange oaths, and bearded like the pard,[1]
Jealous in honor, sudden and quick in quarrel,
Seeking the bubble reputation
Even in the cannon's mouth. And then, the justice,
In fair round belly, with good capon lined,
With eyes severe, and beard of formal cut,
Full of wise saws and modern instances ;[a]
And so he plays his part. The sixth age shifts
Into the lean and slippered pantaloon,[b]
With spectacles on nose, and pouch on side ;
His youthful hose, well saved, a world too wide
For his shrunk shank, and his big manly voice,
Turning again toward childish treble, pipes
And whistles in its sound. Last scene of all,
That ends this strange eventful history,
Is second childishness, and mere oblivion ;
Sans[a] teeth, sans eyes, sans taste, sans everything.

As Jaques ended his long speech, Orlando entered, bearing old Adam in his arms. The Duke welcomed them both heartily, and bade Orlando take all he desired for himself and the old man, politely saying that he would not ask them any questions about their misfortunes until they were rested and refreshed.

Amiens, at the request of the Duke, sang again for their entertainment, all the others joining in the chorus as before.

SONG.

Blow, blow, thou winter wind,
Thou art not so unkind
    As man's ingratitude ;
    Thy tooth is not so keen,
    Because thou art foreseen,
        Although thy breath be rude.
Heigh, ho ! sing, heigh, ho ! unto the green holly :
Most friendship is feigning, most loving mere folly :
    Then, heigh, ho ! the holly !
        This life is most jolly.

---

[1] Leopard.   [a] Without.
[a] Solemn sayings and worn-out anecdotes.
[b] The *pantaloon* was a common character in old Italian plays, and has come down to us in the pantomime, together with harlequin, columbine, and the clown. He was always a thin old man in slippers.

Freeze, freeze, thou bitter sky,
That dost not bite so nigh
*   As benefits forgot :*
Though thou the waters warp, *
Thy sting is not so sharp
*   As friend remembered not.*
    Heigh, ho ! *sing,* etc.

This song, you see, was quite appropriate to the situation of many of the persons of our story, who were preferring the rough but merry forest-life to the deceit and cruelty found in cities and courts.

After seeing that Adam's needs were supplied, Orlando hastened to tell the Duke about himself.

It was a great pleasure to the good Duke to learn that Orlando was the son of his old friend Sir Rowland de Bois. He greeted the youth again most cordially, and said to Adam : "Good old man, thou art right welcome, as thy master is. Come to my cave, and tell me all : I would know everything." And the gracious Duke — no longer in a court, but a gentleman still, even in the rough, wild forest — raised the old man by the hand, and, directing one of the lords to lend the needed support, led the way to his retreat.

---

* To *warp* is to weave (into a covering of ice). *Old Saxon Proverb*, "Winter shall warp water."

VIII.

EANWHILE, at the palace, Duke Frederick was angry enough when all the search and questioning failed to bring back his daughter Celia, or even any news of her.   He found some comfort, however, in scolding and threatening Oliver.   The latter certainly had reason for feeling guilty and unhappy when he remembered his cruelty to Orlando; but he really knew nothing about the runaways, and said so quite earnestly.

The Duke would not believe him, for he was sure they were with Orlando, and Oliver of course must know where to find his brother.

"Thou hast not seen him?" said the Duke angrily.   "Sir, sir, that cannot be; if I were not a merciful man, I should take my revenge on thee!   Look to it; find out thy brother, wherever he may be, and bring him here alive or dead within the year.   Thy lands and all thy possessions are forfeit; and we shall keep them until thy brother's own lips shall prove thee innocent."

Oliver was not ashamed to hate Orlando, and to have cruelly driven him out into the world; but to be accused by the Duke of being in league with him to steal away the pretty young princesses was too much, and he angrily exclaimed: "I would your Highness knew my heart in this!   I never loved my brother in my life!"

"More villain thou!" retorted the Duke.

If Oliver really fancied the Duke would like him the better for hating his brother, he soon found his mistake; for the Duke only told the officers to make the more haste to turn him out of doors, and to seize his house and lands as quickly as possible.

In the great Forest of Arden many different things were going on at once. The Duke and his lords were living gayly, — enjoying their hunting, feasting, and singing, and having little care for the world outside.   Rosalind and Celia (or Ganymede and Aliena) lived happily in the little cottage purchased from the shepherd, with Touchstone to serve them and divert them with his nonsense. Orlando had little to do but to think of his love for Rosalind, now that Adam was comfortably cared for among the kindly foresters.

Orlando seems to have been a poet, as lovers often fancy themselves to be, with much less reason. He spent a great deal of time in writing verses in praise of Rosalind, and although it is likely he did not care whether others read them or not, he got a kind of comfort in merely expressing his feelings in these verses, and hanging them here and there on the trees of the forest. It made him happy also to carve the name of Rosalind on the bark of the trees with his hunting-knife. One day he had just finished some verses, and as he fastened them on a tree, he said to himself (for there certainly was no one to hear him), —

> Hang there, my verse, in witness of my love :
> And thou, thrice-crownèd queen of night,[a] survey
> With thy chaste eye, from thy pale sphere above,
> Thy huntress' name, that my full life doth sway.
> O Rosalind ! these trees shall be my books,
> And in their barks my thoughts I 'll character.
> That every eye, which in this forest looks,
> Shall see thy virtue witnessed everywhere.
> Run, run, Orlando : carve on every tree
> The fair, the chaste, and unexpressive [b] she.

After Orlando had left one tree that he might in the same way adorn another, Corin, the old shepherd, came along with Touchstone. Strolling to an open space where Corin's sheep could graze, they seated themselves under the huge trees and went on with their conversation. Now, in spite of his motley dress and fool's cap and bells, Touchstone liked to seem wise, and to give good advice on every occasion. And Corin was quite ready to minister to this self-importance, for he had the deepest respect for the superior knowledge of the gentleman from the Court, and, in his eyes, Touchstone's gay attire seemed like the uniform of some illustrious officer. When Corin humbly inquired, " And how like you this shepherd's life, Master Touchstone ? " Touchstone answered with an air of profound wisdom, —

Truly, shepherd, in respect of itself, it is a good life ; but in respect that it is a shepherd's life, it is [bad]. In respect that it is solitary, I like it very well ; but in respect that it is private, it is a very vile life. Now, in respect it is in the fields, it pleaseth me well; but in respect it is not in the Court, it is tedious. As it is a spare life, look you, it fits my humor well ; but as there is no more plenty in it, it goes much against my stomach. Hast any philosophy in thee, shepherd ?

---

[a] *Thrice-crowned queen of night* — the moon (see note on p. 68). *Thy huntress' name* — Diana. Orlando calls Rosalind by the name of this virtuous goddess.

[b] Inexpressibly lovely.

CORIN AND TOUCHSTONE.

Corin. No more, but that I know the more one sickens, the worse at ease he is; and that he that wants money, means, and content, is without three good friends; that the property of rain is to wet, and fire to burn; that good pasture makes fat sheep, and that a great cause of the night is lack of the sun; that he that hath learned no wit by nature nor art, may complain [that he lacks] good breeding, or comes of a very dull kindred.

Touchstone. Such a one is a natural philosopher. Wast ever in Court, shepherd?
Corin. No, truly.

"Then," said Touchstone, "thy case is hopeless; for if thou wast never at Court, thou never saw'st good manners; if thy manners are not good, they are wicked, and wickedness is sin. Thou art in a dangerous condition, shepherd."

"Not a whit, Touchstone," said Corin. "Those manners that are good at Court are ridiculous in the country. You say courtiers kiss their hands when they salute one another, which would not be cleanly among shepherds, for our hands are not clean; besides, our hands are hard as well as greasy."

"Shallow reasons, O most shallow man," replied Touchstone. "Thou art green; there's no hope for thee."

"Your wit is too courtly for me, Master Touchstone," answered Corin. "I'll stop. I am a true laborer: I earn what I eat, get that I wear; owe no man hate, envy no man's happiness; am glad of other men's good, content with my own harm; and my greatest pride is to see my ewes graze and my lambs suck. But here comes young Master Ganymede, my new mistress's brother."

Rosalind came gayly along, reading aloud from a paper she carried in her hand: —

From the east to western Ind,
No jewel is like Rosalind.
Her worth, being mounted on the wind,
Through all the world bears Rosalind.
All the pictures, fairest lined,[1]
Are but black to Rosalind.
Let no face be kept in mind,
But the fair of Rosalind.

This amused Touchstone, and he said mockingly, "I'll rhyme you so eight years together, dinners, and suppers, and sleeping hours excepted: it is the right butter-women's [trot] to market."

Rosalind. Out, fool!
Touchstone. For a taste: —

"If a hart do lack a hind,
Let him seek out Rosalind.
If the cat will after kind,
So, be sure, will Rosalind.

---

[1] Drawn.

They that reap must sheaf and bind;
Then to cart with Rosalind.
Sweetest nut hath sourest rind;
Such a nut is Rosalind.
He that sweetest rose will find,
[Rumty tumty] Rosalind."

This is the very false gallop of
verses : why do you infect* yourself
with them?

Rosalind. Peace, you dull fool! I
found them on a tree.

Touchstone. Truly, the tree yields
bad fruit.

While Touchstone and Rosalind
were talking, Celia appeared, with a
paper in her hand also, which she
read aloud as she walked. This
proved to be another poem in
praise of Rosalind, evidently by the
same unknown hand, and, like the
first, torn from the trunk of a tree, to which it had been fastened. Through many
lines it dwelt upon the beauty and the virtues of this wonderful lady, comparing
her with all the famous women that had ever appeared in history. So full of
earnest words was it that Rosalind, coming forward to her cousin, laughed, and
likened it to preaching.

" O most gentle pulpiter ! " she exclaimed, " with what tedious homily of love
have you wearied your parishioners, without ever saying, *Have patience, good
people !*"

As the two cousins merrily looked over the paper together, Touchstone and
Corin drew near with a natural curiosity. But Celia had picked up some knowledge about the authorship of these verses, which she wished to impart to Rosalind
privately, so she turned good-naturedly to the men, and said, —

" How now? back, friends. — Shepherd, go off a little : — go with him, sirrah."

" Come, shepherd," said Touchstone, " let us make an honorable retreat ;
though not with bag and baggage, yet with scrip and scrippage."

After they were gone, Celia turned to her cousin, and asked, —

Didst thou hear these verses ?

Rosalind. O, yes, I heard them all, and more too ; for some of them had in them
more feet than the verses would bear.

Celia. That's no matter: the feet might bear the verses.

---

* Touchstone speaks as if such poetry were like a contagious disease — to be avoided.

Rosalind. Ay, but the feet were lame, and could not bear themselves without the verse, and therefore stood lamely in the verse.

Celia. But didst thou hear without wondering how thy name should be hanged and carved upon these trees?

Rosalind. I was seven of the nine days out of the wonder, before you came: for look here what I found on a palm-tree. [*Showing another paper.*]

Celia. [Can you guess] who hath done this?

Rosalind. Is it a man?

Celia [*nodding her head*]. — And a chain, that you once wore, about his neck. Change you color?

Rosalind. I pr'ythee, who?

Celia. O lord, lord! it is a hard matter for friends to meet: but mountains may be removed with earthquakes, and so [they may] encounter.

Rosalind. Nay, but who is it?

Celia [*teasing her*]. Is it possible?

Rosalind. Nay, I pr'ythee now with most petitionary vehemence, tell me who it is.

Celia [*still teasing*]. O, wonderful, wonderful, and most wonderful wonderful! and yet again wonderful, and after that, out of all whooping!

Rosalind. My good [perplexer]! dost thou think, though I am caparisoned ¹ like a man, I have a doublet and hose in my disposition? I pr'ythee tell me who it is quickly: and speak apace.

Celia. It is young Orlando, that tripped up the wrestler's heels and your heart, both in an instant.

Rosalind. Orlando?

Celia. Orlando.

Rosalind. Alas the day! what shall I do with my doublet and hose? — What did he when thou saw'st him? What said he? How looked he? What [does] he here? Did he ask for me? Where remains he? How parted he with thee, and when shalt thou see him again? Answer me in one word.

Celia. You must borrow me Gargantua's ª mouth first: 't is a word too great for any mouth of this age's size.

Rosalind. But doth he know that I am in this forest, and in man's apparel? Looks he as freshly as he did the day he wrestled?

Celia. I found him under a tree, like a dropped acorn. There he lay stretched along, like a wounded knight. He was furnished like a hunter.

Rosalind. O, ominous! he comes to kill my heart!

Celia. I would sing my song without a [chorus]: thou [puttest] me out of tune.

Rosalind. Do you not know I am a woman? When I think, I must speak. Sweet, say on.

Meanwhile Orlando and Jaques had been holding a sharp discussion as they sauntered idly through the woods, — a habit which had become quite common

---

¹ Dressed.

ª A famous giant, who crammed into his mouth five pilgrims at once.

with Orlando since he had joined the party of the banished Duke. While the cousins were talking thus earnestly about Orlando, they saw him coming. The young ladies did not wish to be discovered just then, so they withdrew still farther into the shadow of the woods. Jaques and Orlando went on with their sharp exchange of words and wit.

Celia. Soft ! Comes he not here ?
Rosalind. 'T is he : slink by, and note him.   [*They retire.*

Enter ORLANDO *and* JAQUES, *talking as they enter.*

Jaques. I thank you for your company ; but, good faith, I had as lief have been myself alone.
Orlando. And so had I; but yet, for fashion sake, I thank you too for your society.
Jaques. Good bye, you : let's meet as little as we can.
Orlando. I do desire we may be better strangers.
Jaques. I pray you, mar no more trees with writing love-songs in their barks.
Orlando. I pray you, mar no more of my verses with reading them [badly].
Jaques. Rosalind is your love's name ?
Orlando. Yes, just.
Jaques. I do not like her name.
Orlando. There was no thought of pleasing you, when she was christened.
Jaques. What stature is she of ?
Orlando. Just as high as my heart.
Jaques. You are full of pretty answers. — Will you sit down with me ? and we two will rail against our mistress the world, and all our misery.
Orlando. I will chide no breather in the world, but myself, against whom I know most faults.
Jaques. The worst fault you have is to be in love.
Orlando. 'T is a fault I will not change for your best virtue. I am weary of you.
Jaques. By my troth, I was seeking for a fool when I found you.
Orlando. He is drowned in the brook : look but in. and you shall see him.
Jaques. I'll tarry no longer with you. Farewell, good Signior Love.
Orlando. I am glad of your departure. Adieu, good Monsieur Melancholy.

Orlando was not sorry to have the sour, melancholy Jaques disappear, and you may be sure Rosalind and Celia were delighted to have a chance of speaking to their handsome young acquaintance. Rosalind had no fear of being discovered in her disguise ; so she determined to play the part of a pert, saucy boy. She came swaggering up to Orlando, with a jaunty, careless air, and speaking to him as if he had been a woodsman, said, —
Do you hear, forester ?
Orlando. Very well : what would you ?
Rosalind. I pray you, what is 't o'clock ?
Orlando. You should ask me. what time o' day : there 's no clock in the forest.
Rosalind. Then, there is no true lover in the forest; else sighing every minute, and groaning every hour, would detect the lazy foot of time as well as a clock.

Orlando. Where dwell you, pretty youth ?

Rosalind. With this shepherdess, my sister ; here in the skirts of the forest, like fringe upon a petticoat.

Orlando. Are you native of this place ?

Rosalind. As the coney, that you see dwell where she is [born].

Orlando. Your accent is something finer than you could purchase in so [secluded] a dwelling.

Rosalind. I have been told so of many : but, indeed, an old religious uncle of mine taught me to speak, who was in his youth an inland man ;[a] one that knew court [life] too well, for there he fell in love. I have heard him read many lectures against it ; and I thank God I am not a woman, to be touched with so many giddy offences as he hath generally taxed their whole sex with.

Orlando. Can you remember any of the principal evils that he laid to the charge of women ?

Rosalind. There were none principal : they were all like one another, as halfpence are ; every one fault seeming monstrous, till his fellow fault came to match it.

Orlando. I pr'ythee, recount some of them.

Rosalind. No ; I will not cast away my physic, but on those that are sick. There is a man haunts the forest, that abuses our young plants with carving *Rosalind* on their barks ;. hangs odes upon hawthorns, and elegies on brambles ; all, forsooth, deifying the name of Rosalind : if I could meet that fancy-monger, I would give him some good counsel, for he seems to have the [very ague] of love upon him.

Orlando. I am he that is so love-shaked. I pray you, tell me your remedy.

Rosalind. There is none of my uncle's marks upon you : he taught me how to know a man in love : in which cage of rushes, I am sure, you are not prisoner.

Orlando. What were his marks ?

Rosalind. A lean cheek, which you have not ; a [dark] and sunken eye, which you have not ; an [unsociable] spirit, which you have not ; a beard neglected, which you have not : — but I pardon you for that, for [what you have] in beard is simply a younger brother's revenue.[b] — Then, your hose should be ungartered, your bonnet unbanded, your sleeve unbuttoned, your shoe untied, and everything about you [showing] a care-

---

[a] An *inland man* was probably one, who having lived away from the coast, where the society was ruder, might be supposed to possess some refinement.

[b] *A younger brother's revenue,* according to English law, is generally very little. Here, while Rosalind playfully taunts Orlando on the lightness of his beard, she hits also on his private history and fortunes, of which he never suspects she can know anything.

less desolation. But you are no such man ; you are rather [a dandy in your dress] ; as loving yourself, than seeming the lover of any other.

Orlando. Fair youth, I would I could make thee believe I love.

Rosalind. Me believe it ? you may as soon make her that you love believe it ; which, I warrant, she is apter to do than to confess she does ; that is one of the points in which women [always] give the lie to their consciences. But, in [real truth], are you he that hangs the verses on the trees, wherein Rosalind is so admired ?

Orlando. I swear to thee, youth, by the white hand of Rosalind, I am that he, that unfortunate he.

Rosalind. But are you so much in love as your rhymes speak ?

Orlando. Neither rhyme nor reason can express how much.

Rosalind. Love is merely a madness, and, I tell you, deserves as well a dark house and a whip, as madmen do ; ª and the reason why they are not so punished and cured is, that the lunacy is so ordinary that the whippers are in love too. Yet I profess curing it by counsel.

Orlando. Did you ever cure any so ?

Rosalind. Yes, one ; and in this manner. He was to imagine me his love, his mistress, and I set him every day to woo me : at which time would I, being but a moonish youth, grieve, be [soft], changeable, longing, and liking ; proud, shallow, inconstant, full of tears, full of smiles ; for every passion something, and for no passion truly anything ; would now like him, now loathe him ; now weep for him, then spit at him : that I drove my suitor from his mad humor of love. And thus I cured him ; and this way will I take upon me to wash your liver ᵇ as clean as a sound sheep's heart, that there shall not be one spot of love in it.

Orlando. I would not be cured, youth.

Rosalind. I would cure you, if you would but call me Rosalind, and come every day to my cote, and woo me.

Orlando. Now, by the faith of my love, I will. Tell me where it is.

Rosalind. Go with me to it, and I 'll show it you ; and, by the way, you shall tell me where in the forest you live. Will you go ?

Orlando. With all my heart, good youth.

Rosalind. Nay, you must call me Rosalind. — Come, sister, will you go ?

Orlando was rather pleased with the idea of even playing at making love to his beautiful Rosalind, and without delay followed Ganymede and Aliena to the cottage.

As they walked off together, Touchstone made his appearance with a young woman ; and Jaques, who always liked to watch other people and give his advice about what they should or should not do, was not far off.

Not to be out of the fashion, Touchstone also had found in the Forest of Arden a lady-love in the person of Audrey, a goat-tender ; an honest, kindly soul, ignorant of anything beyond her daily task ; homely, awkward, and silly enough to

---

ª This was the way in which lunatics were usually treated in Shakespeare's time.

ᵇ The liver used to be regarded as the seat of love.

think Touchstone the wisest and handsomest man in the world. Touchstone had promised to marry her, and told her that Sir Oliver Mar-text, the vicar of the next village, would meet them in the forest at that very place and marry them.   In fact, just then Sir Oliver arrived.

Audrey made no objection, but Jaques, who had overheard the conversation, told Touchstone that it was a disgrace for a man of his breeding to be married under a bush like a beggar.   Touchstone was ready to listen to reason, and quite willing to go to church and be married properly.   Jaques offered to give away the bride, so the queer wedding-party went off together in search of the nearest chapel.

IX.

N another part of the wood, at the door of a rude but pretty cottage, were sitting our two young ladies, one in lad's clothes, with her head bowed in her hands, the other looking at her with a roguish expression of countenance, as though she had just been giving her boy-sister a good-natured scolding. Here was serious trouble. Orlando had promised to call at an appointed time; it was now a whole hour later, and he had not made his appearance! Can we wonder that Rosalind was in tears? In vain were the remonstrances of the amused Celia. She only retorted, —

Never talk to me; I will weep.

Celia. Do, I pr'ythee; but yet have the grace to consider that tears do not become a man.

Rosalind. But have I not cause to weep?

Celia. As good cause as one would desire; therefore weep.

Rosalind. His very hair is of the dissembling color.

Celia. Something browner than Judas's.[a]

Rosalind. ▸ In faith, his hair is of an excellent color.

Celia. An excellent color : chestnut was ever the only color.

Rosalind. But why did he swear he would come this morning, and comes not?

Celia. Nay, certainly, there is no truth in him.

Rosalind. Do you think so?

Celia. Yes; I think he is not a pick-purse nor a horse-stealer; but, for his [truth] in love, I do think him as [hollow] as a covered goblet or a worm-eaten nut.

Rosalind. Not true in love?

Celia. Yes, when he is *in;* but I think he is not in.

Rosalind. You have heard him swear downright he was.

Celia. Was is not *is :* besides, the oath of a lover is no stronger than the word of a tapster. He attends here in the forest on the Duke your father.

---

* Judas was represented in old paintings and tapestry with *reddish* hair and beard.

Rosalind. I met the Duke yesterday, and had much [talk] with him : he asked me of what parentage I was ; I told him, of as good as he ; so he laughed, and let me go. But what talk we of fathers, when there is such a man as Orlando ?

Celia. O, that 's a brave man ! he writes brave verses, speaks brave words, swears brave oaths, and breaks them bravely : but all 's brave that youth mounts and folly guides. — Who comes here ?

It was old Corin, the feeder, who said, as he entered, " Mistress and master, you have often inquired about young Silvius and the shepherdess he is in love with. . As you seem to take an interest in the youth, I will lead you, if you like, where you may see how true love may be treated by scorn and proud disdain." So they all repaired to a shady nook in the forest, where, themselves unseen, they could witness an interview between the lovelorn shepherd and the black-eyed, red-cheeked Phebe.

"Sweet Phebe, do not scorn me," pleaded the poor fellow ; " say that you love me not, but say not so in bitterness."

" O, for shame, for shame," said the scornful maiden, " to pretend that mine eyes have pierced thee ! Now I do frown on thee with all my heart ; and if mine eyes can wound, why dost thou not fall down ? "

" Ah, Phebe dear," said Silvius, " if ever in the future you feel the power of love, then you will know how keen, although invisible, are the wounds that are made by its arrows."

" When that time comes," she answered, " I will not ask thy pity ; and until it comes, I certainly shall not pity thee."

This unfeeling speech was too much for Rosalind to bear : she broke from her hiding-place, and rated the saucy maiden soundly.

"And who are you, I pray you ? " she began ; " and who might be your mother, that you thus insult the wretched ? I see no such wondrous beauty in you that you should presume to be so proud and pitiless." But just here she remarked the fixed gaze and heightened color of the shepherdess, and knew in a moment that the silly little thing had fallen in love with the handsome youth who was so severely scolding her. " Why, what means this ? " continued Rosalind ; " why look you so upon me ? "

"Sweet youth," said Phebe, " I pray you, chide me so a year together : I had rather hear you chide than this man woo."

" I pray you, do not fall in love with *me*," retorted Rosalind.

'T is not your inky brows, your black-silk hair,
Your bugle eyeballs, nor your cheek of cream,
That can entame my spirits to your worship. —
You foolish shepherd, wherefore do you follow her ?
You are a thousand times a properer man
Than she a woman. —
But, mistress, know yourself : down on your knees,

And thank Heaven, fasting, for a good man's love :
For I must tell you friendly in your ear, —
Sell when you can : you are not for all markets :
[Beg] the man's [pardon]; love him.
     — Shepherd, ply her hard.—
Come, sister : to our flock.

Then, with Celia, she departed, accompanied by Corin, and left Silvius and Phebe together.

But now a change seemed to have come over the spirit of the shepherdess, and when her unhappy lover timidly approached her again, she turned to him with a softened look, and said gently, " I am sorry for thee, Silvius." And immediately after she inquired, " Know'st thou the youth that spoke to me just now ? " When Silvius gave her the information she sought, she began thus to praise and to find fault with Ganymede in the same breath : —

  Phebe. Think not I love him, though I ask for him :
'T is but a peevish boy : — yet he talks well ; —
But what care I for words ? yet words do well,
When he that speaks them pleases those that hear.
It is a pretty youth : — not very pretty : —
But, sure. he 's proud ; and yet his pride becomes him :
He 'll make a proper man : the best thing in him
Is his complexion ; and faster than his tongue
Did make offence, his eye did heal it up.
He is not tall ; yet for his years he 's tall :
There was a pretty redness in his lip,
A little riper and more lusty red
Than that mixed in his cheek.
There be some women [now] would have gone near
To fall in love with him ; but, for my part,
I love him not, nor hate him not : and yet
I have more cause to hate him than to love him :
What [business] had he to chide at me ?
He said mine eyes were black, and my hair black :
And, now I [do remember], scorned at me :
I marvel why I answered not again.
I 'll write to him a very taunting letter,
And thou shalt bear it ; wilt thou, Silvius ?
  Silvius. Phebe, with all my heart.
  Phebe.   I 'll write it straight ;
I will be bitter with him and passing short.
Go with me, Silvius.

And she went off, planning a very different letter from the one she had proposed, and poor Silvius trotted after, like a tame spaniel, to do her bidding.

X.

NE day Rosalind, still in the garb of Ganymede, while walking with Celia in the wood, met Jaques, and answered his greeting with a merry air; for the surly fellow had taken a liking to the pretty youth, and chatted quite gayly for a serious, worldly-wise philosopher. Rosalind joked him about his melancholy, and he told her of his travels, and assured her it was his experience that made him sad. "Then," said Rosalind, "I 'd rather have a fool to make me merry than experience to make me sad; and to travel for it too!"

While they were thus engaged, Orlando entered. Of course Rosalind, who was a very wide-awake young lady, saw him the moment he came in sight, but she was vexed with him because he had not kept his promise about meeting her, and so she did not even look at him till she had finished a long speech to Jaques.

Orlando greeted the supposed Ganymede pleasantly, as still playing that the lad was his sweetheart. "Good day and happiness, dear Rosalind," he said. But Rosalind gave him no answer, pretending not to hear him.

Jaques had at least learned by his experience to know a young lover when he saw one, and wisely took his leave, so that Rosalind now had no excuse for being either deaf or blind; she was really glad to see Orlando, and not in the least surprised, but she pretended to be astonished to find him so near her, and exclaimed, —

Why, how now, Orlando! where have you been all this while? You a lover? — If you serve me such another trick, never come in my sight more.

Orlando. My fair Rosalind, I come within an hour of my promise.

Rosalind. Break an hour's promise in love? He that will divide a minute into a thousand parts, and break but a part of the thousandth part of a minute in the affairs of love, I 'll warrant him heart-whole.

Orlando. Pardon me, dear Rosalind.

Rosalind. Nay, if you be so tardy, come no more in my sight; I had as lief be wooed by a snail.

Orlando. By a snail?

Rosalind. Ay, by a snail; for though he comes slowly, he carries his house on his head; a better [fortune], I think, than you can [bring] a woman. Come, woo me, woo me; for now I am in a holiday humor, and like enough to consent : — What would you say to me now, if I were your very very Rosalind? — Am not I your Rosalind?

Orlando. I take some joy to say you are, because I would be talking of her.

Rosalind. Well, in her person, I say — I will not have you.

Orlando. Then, in mine own person, I die.

Rosalind [*laughing merrily*]. No, faith, die by attorney.* The poor world is almost six thousand years old, and in all this time there was not any man died in his own person; that is, in a love-cause. Men have died from time to time, and worms have eaten them, but not for love.

Orlando. I would not have my right Rosalind of this mind; for, I protest, her frown might kill me.

Rosalind. By this hand, it will not kill a fly. But come, now I will be your Rosalind in a more [favorable] disposition; and ask me what you will, I will grant it.

Orlando. Then love me, Rosalind.

Rosalind. Yes, faith will I, Fridays, and Saturdays, and all.

Orlando. And wilt thou have me?

Rosalind. Ay, and twenty such.

Orlando. What sayest thou?

Rosalind. Are you not good?

Orlando. I hope so.

Rosalind. Why, then, can one desire too much of a good thing? — Come, sister [*turning to* CELIA], you shall be the priest, and marry us. — Give me your hand, Orlando : — What do you say, sister?

Orlando. Pray thee, marry us.

Celia. I cannot say the words.

Rosalind. You must begin, --- "Will you, Orlando," —

Celia. [O, yes.] — Will you, Orlando, have to wife this Rosalind?

Orlando. I will.

Rosalind. Ay, but when?

Orlando. Why now; as fast as she can marry us.

Rosalind. Then you must say, — "I take thee, Rosalind, for wife."

Orlando. I take thee, Rosalind, for wife.

---

* An *attorney* is one who takes the turn or place of another; especially one who is appointed by another to act for him in business matters, or in a cause at law.

Rosalind. I might ask you for your [license]; but [never mind], — I do take thee, Orlando, for my husband.

Rosalind. Now tell me how long you would have her, after you have possessed her.

Orlando. Forever and a day.

Rosalind. Say a day, without the ever. No, no, Orlando ; men are April when they woo, December when they wed : maids are May when they are maids, but the sky changes when they are wives. I will be more jealous of thee than a Barbary cock-pigeon over his hen ; more clamorous than a parrot against rain ; more new-fangled than an ape ; more giddy in my desires than a monkey : I will weep for nothing, like Diana in the fountain, and I will do that when you are disposed to be merry ; I will laugh like a hyena, and that when thou art inclined to sleep.

Orlando. But will my Rosalind do so ?

Rosalind. By my life, she will do as I do.

Orlando. O, but she is wise.

Rosalind. Or else she could not have the wit to do this : the wiser, the way-warder. [Bar] the doors upon a woman's wit, and it will out at the casement ; shut that, and 't will out at the key-hole ; stop that, 't will fly with the smoke out at the chimney.

But Orlando now remembered that he had a duty to perform, and, stopping in the midst of their pretty play of wits, he said, —

For these two hours, Rosalind, I will leave thee.

Rosalind. Alas, dear love, I cannot lack thee two hours.

Orlando. I must attend the Duke at dinner ; by two o'clock I will be with thee again.

Rosalind [*pretending to weep*]. Ay, go your ways, go your ways ; — I knew what you would prove ; my friends told me as much, and I thought no less : — that flatter-ing tongue of yours won me : — 't is but one cast away, and so, — come death. [*Burst-ing into laughter.*] — Two o'clock is your hour ?

Orlando. Ay, sweet Rosalind.

Rosalind. By my troth, and in good earnest, and by all pretty oaths that are not dangerous, if you break one jot of your promise, or come one minute behind the hour, I will never believe you more, I will think you a hollow lover, and the most unworthy of her you call Rosalind, that may be chosen out of the gross band of the unfaithful. Therefore beware my censure and keep your promise.

Orlando promised again and again to keep his word, and return to her as faithfully as if she were indeed his very Rosalind.

When the youth was quite out of hearing, Celia told Rosalind that it was not fair to misrepresent her sex by talking such nonsense.

"O coz, coz, coz," replied Rosalind, "if thou didst know how many fathoms deep I am in love, — my affection is as deep as the bay of Portugal ! I tell thee, Aliena, I cannot live out of the sight of Orlando ! I 'll go find a shade, and sigh till he come."

"And I 'll go sleep," said Celia ; and the cousins went each her own way for an hour or two, until it should be time for Orlando's return.

XI.

WO o'clock came, but it brought no Orlando. Celia was inclined to tease Rosalind, and said that perhaps Orlando had taken his bow and arrows, and gone forth to — sleep ! Just then Silvius, the young shepherd, Phebe's lover, entered, bearing in his hand the letter which Phebe had written to Ganymede. Approaching Rosalind, he said, —

My errand is to you, fair youth.
My gentle Phebe bid me give you this.
I know not the conténts; but, as I guess
By the stern brow, and waspish action,
Which she did use as she was writing it,
It bears an angry tenor. Pardon me,
I am but as a guiltless messenger.

Phebe had really written a very foolish love-letter to Ganymede. Rosalind read parts of it aloud, pretending that it was abusive and full of harshness and mockery, but in fact it was full of the most extravagant praises and declarations of love from Phebe to Ganymede, so that poor Silvius could not fail to see that his mistress had used him to carry her love-letter to another man. Rosalind told Silvius he was foolish to love such a cruel, heartless shepherdess, and do such errands for her, but if he really insisted on loving such a woman, he might say this to her : " If she love me, I charge her to love thee ; if she will not, I will never have her unless thou entreat for her. Go now, without another word," she added, " for here comes some one."

As Silvius went off, a man presented himself, who proved to be Orlando's elder brother Oliver, — he who had been so cruel and hard, and who had driven Orlando to exile himself in this forest.

"Good morrow, fair ones," said he, courteously, and went on to inquire if they could direct him to a certain sheep-cote, fenced about with olive-trees, somewhere in the outskirts of the forest. They told him how to find it : it was their own cottage. He then recognized that they were the brother and sister who lived in the house, and whom he was seeking ; and as they admitted the fact, he said, —

Orlando doth commend him to you both ;
And to that youth he calls his Rosalind
He sends this bloody napkin. — Are you he ?
   Rosalind. I am : what must we understand by this ?
   Oliver. When last the young Orlando parted from you,
He left a promise to return again
Within an hour ; and, pacing through the forest,
Lo, what befell ! he threw his eye aside,
And, mark, what object did present itself :
Under an oak, whose boughs were mossed with age,
And high top bald with dry antiquity,
A wretched ragged man, o'ergrown with hair,
Lay sleeping on his back : about his neck
A green and gilded snake had wreathed itself,
Who with her head, nimble in threats, approached
The opening of his mouth ; but suddenly,
Seeing Orlando, it unlinked itself,
And with indented glides did slip away
Into a bush ; under which bush's shade
A lioness, with udders all drawn dry,
Lay couching, head on ground, with cat-like watch,
When that the sleeping man should stir ; for 't is
The royal disposition of that beast
To prey on nothing that doth seem as dead.
This seen, Orlando did approach the man,
And found it was his brother, his elder brother.
   Celia. O, I have heard him speak of that same brother ;
And he [reported] him the most unnatural
That lived 'mongst men.
   Oliver.   And well he might so do,
For well I know he was unnatural.
   Rosalind. But, to Orlando. — Did he leave him there,
Food to the sucked and hungry lioness?

Oliver. Twice did he turn his back, and purposed so;
But kindness, nobler ever than revenge,
Made him give battle to the lioness,
Who quickly fell before him : in which [battling]
From miserable slumber I awaked.
   Celia. Are you his brother?
   Rosalind.   Was it you he rescued?
   Celia. Was 't you that did so oft contrive to kill him?
   Oliver. 'T was I; but 't is not I. I do not shame
To tell you what I was, since my conversion
So sweetly tastes, being the thing I am.
   Rosalind. But, for the bloody napkin? —
   Oliver.   By-and-by.
When from the first to last, betwixt us two,
Tears our recountments had most kindly bathed,
As, how I came into that desert place; —
In brief, he led me to the gentle Duke,
Who gave me fresh array and entertainment,
Committing me unto my brother's love;
Who led me instantly unto his cave,
There stripped himself; and here, upon his arm,
The lioness had torn some flesh away,
Which all this while had bled; and now he fainted,
And cried, in fainting, upon Rosalind.
Brief, I recovered him: bound up his wound;
And, after some small space, being strong at heart,
He sent me hither, stranger as I am,
To tell this story, that you might excuse
His broken promise; and to give this napkin,
Dyed in his blood, unto the shepherd youth
That he in sport doth call his Rosalind.

Rosalind had listened eagerly to Oliver's story. The thought of poor Orlando, wounded and bleeding, was too much for her woman's heart, and at the sight of the napkin, stained, as she now knew, with his blood, in spite of her man's dress and her boasted courage, she fainted, and would have fallen, had not Celia caught her in her loving arms, exclaiming, " Why, how now, Ganymede ! sweet Ganymede !"

" Many will swoon when they do look on blood," said Oliver.

" There is more in it," cried Celia in terror. — " Cousin ! — Ganymede !"

At the sound of Celia's voice Rosalind stirred and opened her eyes, whispering faintly, " I would I were at home."

" We 'll lead you thither," answered Celia tenderly; and turning to Oliver she said, " I pray you, will you take him by the arm?"

As they went, Oliver tried to arouse Ganymede's spirit with a little good-humored raillery. Said he, —

Be of good cheer, youth. — You a man ! — You lack a man's heart.

Rosalind. I do so, I confess it. Ah, sir ! a body would think this was well counterfeited. I pray you, tell your brother how well I, counterfeited. Heigho ! [*With a deep sigh.*]

Oliver. This was not counterfeit : there is too great testimony in your complexion, that it was a [feeling] of earnest.

Rosalind. Counterfeit, I assure you.

Oliver. Well then, take a good heart, and counterfeit to be a man.

Rosalind. So I do ; but, in faith, I should have been a woman by right.

Celia. Come, you look paler and paler : pray you, draw homewards. — Good sir, go with us.

Oliver. That will I, for I must bear answer back how you excuse my brother, Rosalind.

Rosalind. I shall devise something : but, I pray you, commend my counterfeiting to him. — Will you go ?

And Oliver accompanied them to their cottage before returning to report matters to Orlando.

XII.

HE last we saw of Touchstone and Audrey, they had started off in search of a chapel and a priest. They wandered a long time in vain, till Audrey's patience was nearly exhausted. As they were dragging rather wearily along, a young country fellow, named William, joined them. This gave Touchstone a chance to show off his wit and wisdom at the expense of the country clown, who fancied he had some claim upon Audrey. That young woman had no eyes for him, however, now that she had so fine a gentleman for a lover as Touchstone appeared to be.

As William approached, and stood grinning and bowing, with his hat in his hand, the Court Fool assumed an air of superiority, and said : —

It is meat and drink to me to see a clown : by my troth, we that have good wits have much to answer for; we [have to be mocking]; we cannot hold [in]. — Good evening, gentle friend. [*To* WILLIAM.] Cover thy head, cover thy head; nay, pr'ythee, be covered. How old are you, friend?

William. Five-and-twenty, sir.

Touchstone. A ripe age. Is thy name William?

William. William, sir.

Touchstone. A fair name. Wast born i' the forest here?

William. Ay, sir, I thank God.

Touchstone. Thank God : — a good answer. [*With lofty condescension.*] Art rich?

William. Faith, sir, so-so.

Touchstone. So-so is good, very good, very excellent good : — and yet it is not; it is but so-so. Art thou wise?

William. Ay, sir, I have a pretty wit.*

Touchstone. Why, thou say'st well. I do now remember a saying, *The fool*

---

* *Wit* and *wisdom* were nearly the same in our author's time.

doth think he is wise; but the wise man knows himself to be a fool. The heathen philosopher, when he had a desire to eat a grape, would open his lips when he put it into his mouth; meaning thereby, that grapes were made to eat, and lips to open. You do love this maid?

William. I do, sir.

Touchstone. Give me your hand. Art thou learned?

William. No, sir.

Touchstone. Then learn this of me: To have, is to have; for it is a figure in rhetoric, that drink, being poured out of a cup into a glass, by filling the one doth empty the other; for all your writers do consent that *ipse* is he: now, you are not *ipse*, for I am he.

William [very much puzzled]. Which he, sir?

Touchstone. He, sir, that must marry this woman. Therefore, you clown, aban-don — which is in the vulgar leave — the society — which in the boorish is company — of this female, — which in the common is woman; which together is, abandon the society of this female; or [*advancing upon him with louder and louder voice*], clown, thou perishest; or, to thy better understanding, diest; to wit, I kill thee, make thee away, translate thy life into death, thy liberty into bondage. I will deal in poison with thee, or in bastinado, or in steel; I will [fight against thee with conspiracy]; I will [confound thee with cunning]; I will kill thee a hundred and fifty ways: therefore tremble, and depart.

Poor Audrey shook in her shoes at these terrible and mysterious words, and she begged her former sweetheart to retire. He, poor fellow, was nothing loth; and, staying but a moment to recover from the bucketful of words which had been emptied on him, he shut up his wondering mouth, put on his hat, and hastily retreated.

In still another part of the forest the two now happily reconciled brothers were walking and talking together, and Oliver was telling Orlando about his visit to the cottage, and all that had happened there when he told the story of Orlando's mishap. There must have been something good and lovable about Oliver, in spite of his former unkindness to Orlando; for, as it appeared from his story, he not only had fallen in love with the charming young shepherdess (as he believed Celia to be), but also in that single interview had won her love in return. Orlando was much interested in it all, though it seemed almost incredible.

Orlando. Is it possible, that on so little acquaintance you should like her? that, but seeing, you should love her? and, loving, woo? and, wooing, she should grant? and will you persevere [and marry] her?

Oliver. Neither call the giddiness of it in question, the poverty of her, the small acquaintance, my sudden wooing, nor her sudden consenting; but say with me, I love Aliena; say with her, that she loves me; consent with both, that we may [have] each other: it shall be to your good: for my father's house, and all the revenue that was old Sir Rowland's, will I [settle] upon you, and here live and die a shepherd.

Orlando. You have my consent. Let your wedding be to-morrow: thither will I invite the Duke, and all his contented followers. Go you, and prepare Aliena; for, look you, here comes my Rosalind.

And Orlando advanced gladly to meet Ganymede, who, nevertheless, spoke first to the man she cared least for, and cheerily said to Oliver, "God save you, brother."

" And you, fair sister," answered Oliver, as he went away to find his Aliena, — for he addressed Ganymede as a woman, either to carry out his brother's little play, or because he had been privately informed by Celia that the youth was indeed to be his sister. Then Ganymede turned to Orlando, and exclaimed, —

O, my dear Orlando, how it grieves me to see thee wear thy heart in a scarf.

Orlando. It is my arm.

Rosalind. I thought thy heart had been wounded with the claws of a lion.

Orlando. Wounded it is, but with the eyes of a lady.

Rosalind. Did your brother tell you how I counterfeited to swoon, when he showed me your handkerchief?

Orlando. Ay, and greater wonders than that.

Rosalind. O, I know [what you mean]. -- Nay, 't is true: there was never anything so sudden, but Cæsar's brag of — " I came, saw, and overcame : " * for your brother and my sister no sooner met, but they looked ; no sooner looked, but they loved ; no sooner loved, but they sighed ; no sooner sighed, but they asked one another the reason ; no sooner knew the reason, but they sought the remedy : and in these degrees have they made a pair of stairs to marriage, which they will climb [immediately].

Orlando. They shall be married to-morrow, and I will bid the Duke to the nuptial. But, O, how bitter a thing it is to look into happiness through another man's eyes ! By so much the more shall I to-morrow be at the height of heart-heaviness, by how much I shall think my brother happy in having what he wishes for.

Rosalind. Why then, to-morrow I cannot serve your turn for Rosalind ?

Orlando. I can live no longer by thinking.

Rosalind. I will weary you then no longer with idle talking. Know of me then (for now I speak to some purpose), that I can do strange things. I have, since I was three years old, [been familiar] with a magician, most profound in his art. If you do love Rosalind so near the heart as your [action seems to show], when your brother marries Aliena, you shall marry her. I know into what straits of fortune she is driven ; and it is not impossible to me to set her [very self] before your eyes to-morrow.

Orlando. Speak'st thou in sober meaning ?

Rosalind. By my life, I do. Therefore, put you in your best array, bid your friends ; for, if you will be married to-morrow, you shall; and to Rosalind, if you will. Look, here comes a lover of mine, and a lover of hers.

This referred to the cruel Phebe and her devoted slave Silvius. Phebe came to reproach Ganymede with having shown the letter she had written and sent by Silvius ; but Ganymede made light of that, and said it had been done purposely to anger her and turn her love to Silvius, who deserved it. Said Ganymede, "You are there followed by a faithful shepherd : look upon him, love him ; he

---

* These were the words with which Cæsar described the rapidity of one of his victories.
In Latin, *Veni, vidi, vici.*

worships you." "Good shepherd," said Phebe to Silvius, "tell this youth what 't is to love." This Silvius undertook to do : whereupon the whole company began to echo his words with their own experiences of the tender passion, until Ganymede-Rosalind broke in impatiently, for she had a little mysterious plan to please them all.

"Pray you, no more of this," said she ; "it is like the howling of wolves against the moon. — Silvius, I will help you, if I can : — Phebe, I would love you, if I could ; I will marry you, if ever I marry woman, and I 'll be married to-mor-

row : — Orlando, I will satisfy you, if ever I satisfied man, and you shall be married
to-morrow : — Silvius, I will content you, if what pleases you contents you, and
you shall be married to-morrow. — In the name of all your loves, I command you
to meet me. — So, fare you well."

> *Silvius.* I 'll not fail, if I live.
> *Phebe.* Nor I.
> *Orlando.* Nor I.

The next day the Duke, with the lord Amiens and the melancholy Jaques,
was talking over the strange promises of Ganymede to Orlando, while Oliver
and Celia stood by. Just as the Duke was expressing his doubts, and Orlando
his hopes and fears, young Ganymede appeared, accompanied by Silvius and
Phebe, and, walking to the centre of the group, asked them all to have patience
while the agreement she had made with the different parties was once more clearly
stated. Then, turning to the Duke, she asked, —

> You say, if I bring in your Rosalind,
> You will bestow her on Orlando here?
> *Duke Senior.* That would I, had I kingdoms to give with her.
> *Rosalind.* And you [*to* ORLANDO] say you will have her when I bring her ?
> *Orlando.* That would I, were I of all kingdoms king.
> *Rosalind.* You [*to* PHEBE] say you 'll marry me, if I be willing?
> *Phebe.* That will I, should I die the hour after.
> *Rosalind.* But if you do refuse to marry me.
> You 'll give yourself to this most faithful shepherd ?
> *Phebe.* So is the bargain.
> *Rosalind.* And you [*to* SILVIUS] say that you 'll have Phebe, if she will ?
> *Silvius.* Though to have her and death were both one thing.
> *Rosalind.* I 've promised to make all this matter even.
> Keep you your word, O Duke. to give your daughter : —
> You yours, Orlando. to receive his daughter; —
> Keep your word, Phebe, that you 'll marry me,
> Or else. refusing me, to wed this shepherd : —
> Keep your word, Silvius, that you 'll marry her,
> If she refuse me : — and from hence I go,
> To make these doubts all even.

After thus thoroughly puzzling them all, Rosalind went away with Celia. The
Duke, turning to Orlando, said, "This shepherd boy reminds me of my daughter
Rosalind."

"My lord," answered Orlando, "the first time that I ever saw him I thought
he might be brother to your daughter ; but, my good lord, this boy is forest-born,
though highly educated by his uncle, a great magician living in this forest."

All this pairing was very amusing to Jaques, and he said, with a little good-
natured contempt, "There is surely another flood coming, and these couples are

coming to the ark." Then raising his eyes, he espied another two approaching, and he added, "Here comes a pair of very strange beasts, which in all tongues are called fools." These, of course, proved to be our friend Touchstone, with Audrey on his arm. In another moment he entered the circle, and, with a magnificent bow, said, in the highest style of Court manners, "Salutation and greeting to you all!" Then Jaques told the Duke that this was the motley-minded gentleman that he had so often met in the forest, and who swore that he had been a courtier.

At this Touchstone spoke up with spirit, and said, —

If any man doubt that, let him put me to my [proof]. I have trod a measure ;* I have flattered a lady ; I have been politic with my friend, smooth with mine enemy ; I have undone three tailors ; I have had four quarrels, and like to have fought one.

Jaques. And how was that [made] up?

Touchstone. Faith, we met, and found the quarrel was upon the Seventh Cause.

Jaques. How — Seventh Cause? — Good my lord* [*to the* DUKE], like this fellow.

Duke Senior. I like him very well.

Touchstone. God [reward] you, sir; I desire you of the like.* I press in here, sir, amongst the rest of the country [couples]. — A poor virgin, sir, an ill-favored thing, sir, but mine own : a poor humor of mine, sir, to take what no man else will. Rich honesty dwells like a miser, sir, in a poor house, as your pearl in your foul oyster.

Jaques. But, for the Seventh Cause, how did you find the quarrel on the Seventh Cause?

Touchstone. Upon a lie seven times removed. — (Bear your body more seeming, Audrey.) — As thus, sir. I did dislike the cut of a certain courtier's beard : he sent me word, if I said his beard was not cut well, he was in the mind it was : this is called the "retort courteous." If I sent him word again it was not well cut, he would send me word he cut it to please himself: this is called the "quip modest." If again, it was not well cut, he [dispraised] my judgment: this is called the "reply churlish." If again, it was not well cut, he would answer, I spake not true : this is called the "reproof valiant." If again, it was not well cut, he would say, I lied: this is called the "countercheck quarrelsome: " and so to the "lie circumstantial," and the "lie direct."

Jaques. And how often did you say, his beard was not well cut?

Touchstone. I durst go no further than the "lie circumstantial," nor he durst not give me the "lie direct ; " and so we measured swords, and parted.

Jaques. Can you nominate in order now the degrees of the lie?

Touchstone. O sir, we quarrel in print;* by the book, as you have books for good

---

* A stately, solemn dance, comporting with the dignity of the Court.
* For *my good lord ;* like the French *cher monsieur.*
* An affectation of ceremonious language.
* In all this Touchstone ridicules the nice distinctions of the law of duelling — sometimes called the Code of Honor — which, in Shakespeare's day, was just beginning to take form, and appear in books.

manners : I will name you the degrees. The first, the Retort Courteous ; the second, the Quip Modest ; the third, the Reply Churlish ; the fourth, the Reproof Valiant ; the fifth, the Countercheck Quarrelsome ; the sixth, the Lie with Circumstance ; the seventh, the Lie Direct. All these you may avoid but the Lie Direct ; and you may avoid that too, with an *if.* I knew when seven justices could not [make] up a quarrel ; but when the parties were met themselves, one of them thought but of an *if,* as *if you said so, then I said so ;* and they shook hands and swore brothers. Your *if* is the only peacemaker ; much virtue in *if.*

Jaques. Is not this a rare fellow, my lord ? he 's as good at anything, and yet a fool.

Duke Senior. He uses his folly like a stalking-horse,[a] and under the presentation of that, he shoots his wit.

While they were thus amusing themselves with the wise nonsense of the fool, Celia and Rosalind returned, both dressed as befitted young princesses. Rosalind came forward to her father, the Duke, who was too much surprised to speak, and bending dutifully before him, said, "To you I give myself, for I am yours ; " and then turning with a loving look to Orlando, she added, "To you I give myself, for I am yours."

In great amazement the Duke cried, " If there be truth in sight, you are my daughter."

And Orlando, equally astonished, exclaimed, " If there be truth in sight, you are my Rosalind."

Poor Phebe, seeing her handsome Ganymede changed to a lovely girl, cried dolefully, " If sight and shape be true, why then, — *my* love, adieu ! "

And Rosalind, smiling with pleasure and dimpling with fun, turned in succession to the Duke, to Orlando, and to Phebe, with a speech in one sentence for each : " I 'll have no father if you be not he : I 'll have no husband if you be not he : nor e'er wed woman, if you be not she."

The Duke welcomed his dear niece Celia and her lover Oliver as warmly as he did his daughter and Orlando ; and even silly Phebe made the best of her faithful Silvius, declaring that she really liked him after all, and would marry him for his devotion.

In the midst of the surprises and the happy congratulations, a new-comer entered in the person of young Jaques de Bois, the brother of Orlando and Oliver, who brought tidings which added yet more to the happiness of all. Duke Frederick, he said, while on his way to the forest with a large army, had met an old hermit, whose conversation had so changed his heart that he resolved to embrace the same life and retire from the world, restoring the crown to his banished brother, and with it all the property and lands taken from those that were exiled with him.

[a] A horse, or something formed like a horse, behind which the hunter hides himself so as not to be seen by the game.

This was joyous news to all. The banished Duke heartily welcomed young De Bois, and congratulated his companions on their good fortune. He begged them, however, to delay a little, that all might fully enjoy the rustic revelry, and have a merry dance with the happy brides and bridegrooms. Jaques, the melancholy philosopher, was the only one who objected to the Duke's idea. He said he preferred to seek out the recent convert, that he might, if possible, learn something new from him. In spite of the Duke's entreaties he bade them all goodby with the kindliest wishes; for his own part, he said he had decided to take possession of the Duke's abandoned cave, and make it his future home.

The rest we leave dancing blithely in the Forest of Arden. The weddings took place in the merry greenwood, and then all the parties betook themselves to their several places, — the shepherds to their pastoral life, and the lords and ladies to the palaces where they were most at home, and which they were well fitted to adorn.

And now, in looking back over our finished story, and seeing how bright and fresh and *out-of-doors* it has been; how the pleasant people who have suffered, have not suffered so very much, while out of their suffering happiness has come; how all the good have been rewarded, and all the bad have become good, and then been rewarded too; how everybody who ought to get married has got married, and to just the right person; and how the queer folk who could not well be fitted in to the new order of things have been snugly provided for in forest-caves and such out-of-the-way corners, — are you not ready to say that the whole is rightly named, and everything exactly AS YOU LIKE IT?

JULIUS CÆSAR.

INTRODUCTION.

ESIDES the exquisite comedies — two of which we have given in this volume — Shakespeare wrote some tragedies, or dramatic poems, presenting scenes from life with mournful ending ; and also some histories, or passages taken directly from historical chronicles, and put into dramatic form. "JULIUS CÆSAR," a play written not more than a year or two from the time when "As You Like It" was produced, is both a tragedy and a history.

It deals with characters and events belonging to a period in Roman history perhaps better known and more interesting to us as American republicans than any other epoch in the life of the world ; because it shows us how a true and pure republican, so many centuries ago, was wrought upon to commit a great crime to save the liberties of his country, and teaches us, by the disastrous result of his effort, the vanity of expecting to do good by evil means. The only source from which the poet could draw materials for his work was the *Lives of Illustrious Greeks and Romans*, written in Greek, in the first Christian century, by a man named Plutarch, and translated by Sir Thomas North out of a French version.

The fidelity with which Shakespeare has followed his copy, taken together with the life and spirit which he has imparted to the dull page, making the formal characters of the history stand out as living, breathing Romans, has been much admired. It has been a matter of wonder with some that the play should have taken its name from Julius Cæsar, when that person has so small a part in it ; being presented only in a few comparatively unimportant scenes, and being assassinated in the third act. It has been said that Brutus is the true hero of the play, which should have been called by his name. To which it is replied, that the life and character of Cæsar are the pivot on which the whole action of the drama turns, and that the spirit of Cæsar, strong and terrible, is present, as a controlling and an avenging power, to the very end. Brutus himself exclaims, amid the disasters of the closing day, —

> " O Julius Cæsar, thou art mighty yet !
> Thy spirit walks abroad, and turns our swords
> Into our own proper entrails."

Others object that the very slight representation here given of the great Julius is untrue to history : that he was simple and modest, as became a soldier and a man of prompt and energetic action ; while here he appears pompous and pretentious. To this it is sometimes replied, that Shakespeare was, in this play, intent on showing the motives that prompted the extreme course of the republicans, and Cæsar was to be presented in the light in which he appeared to them. It is said also that, according to Plutarch, the character of Cæsar, just before his death, did change for the worse in these very respects. He had been spoiled by success and power ; he was transformed by his ambition, — "the covetous desire to be called king," as Plutarch says. It is this that made him assume the air and manner of a sovereign, and lend an ear to flatterers, and take counsel of the superstitions he had before despised. Thus he presented to the republican plotters his most offensive side, and thus Shakespeare has chosen to depict him.

We, on the other hand, have reason to rejoice in the picture here given us of the Ideal Republican, — upright and faithful. That Brutus was too good a man to be successful, that his very virtues were the cause of his failure, does not impair, but increase, our gratitude for this lovely model of domestic and civic virtue. We enter with full sympathy into his claim when about to die, —

> " I shall have glory by this losing day
> More than Octavius and Mark Antony
> By their vile conquest shall attain unto."

Well says a recent writer: " Of true failure he suffered none. Octavius and Mark Antony remained victors at Philippi. Yet the purest wreath of victory rests on the forehead of the defeated conspirator."

JULIUS CÆSAR.

I.

 WO thousand years ago, the Empire of Rome was the greatest the world had ever known. It comprised a vast number both of powerful nations and small states within its limits. All the civilized world paid allegiance to this mighty Mistress.

At its first foundation, about seven hundred and fifty years before the birth of Christ, while yet a very small state, it was ruled by kings, and so continued to be for about two centuries and a half, when the sixth monarch, Sextus Tarquinius, was driven out of the city by the people for his tyranny and many crimes. The leader of this revolution was one Lucius Junius, who, while waiting an opportunity to strike the blow, concealed his purpose by pretending to be an idiot. It was during this time that he received the nickname of *Brutus*. After this, for more than five hundred years Rome continued to be a republic; and so deep had been the impression made upon the Roman people, that during all that time the very word *king*, in connection with their government, was enough to rouse their jealousy and rage. The name of " Brutus," first given as a reproach, became of course a badge of honor to all who could claim it by descent.

But the Roman republic, which remained for a number of centuries pure, became, for that reason, powerful; and its very power, with the wealth that came from its many conquests, caused its ruin. At the period when our story begins, luxury had sapped the foundations of morality, and all classes of society were thoroughly corrupt. There had been from the beginning an order of nobility, established by Romulus himself; and so there had always existed two powerful parties, the patricians (or nobles) and the plebeians (or common people), whose struggles for the supreme power kept the country in perpetual turmoil. According to the Constitution, the Romans were really very free. All laws were made in the Comitia, or assembly of the whole people ; but then the Senate had by degrees encroached upon this power, and now no act could be submitted to the people until the Senate had first discussed it. On the other hand, the plebeians had their triumphs also. The Senate, at first confined to the patricians, was at last open to all ranks. An order of *Tribunes of the People* was established, with special powers, to watch over and protect the people's rights. The supreme power was vested in two *Consuls*, chosen by the people, and these too, at first taken only from the higher order, came at last to be selected from the plebeians also.

In short, the liberties of the Roman people were not in any great danger, except from their own vices. From the plundered countries and cities of the conquered world, the patrician families became very wealthy, and then, as luxury brought the most fearful corruption into the higher classes, they in turn debased the common people in every way with bribes ; so that virtue, either in private or in public life, was rare indeed. The republic seemed ripe for destruction. Men looked nervously about, as if in momentary expectation that some successful general would take advantage of his influence with a powerful army to seize the reins of government, and declare himself King or Emperor of Rome.

For when a people get into this condition, military glory comes to be held in high esteem among them. They worship power, and always want to be on the stronger side. The Roman people were no exception to this rule. Among them a successful general was always sure of a cordial welcome. Two of the most famous generals in the world's history were Romans, born in this first century before Christ, within a few years of each other. They were Pompey, sometimes surnamed *the Great*, and Julius Cæsar, whom all the world admits to be great, with or without a surname.

Pompey won great applause while yet a young man by extensive conquests in Asia, and by ridding the Mediterranean of hordes of pirates who had rendered the passage of that sea a terror to all who were compelled to undertake it. On his return to Rome, laden with spoils, trophies, and captives, he was received with the wildest joy and the most extravagant praises. A Triumph was decreed him by the Senate. This was a brilliant military procession, including everything in the way of display that could do honor to the favorite of the people. Triumphal arches were erected in the streets through which he rode in his chariot. The houses were gayly decorated. The multitude, every one in his best attire, thronged the streets and squares, bearing banners and flags, and shouting for Great Pompey. We get some idea of the magnitude of the show in this case, when we are told that the procession was two days in passing a particular point. One would think, from their enthusiasm on this occasion, that Pompey never could be forgotten by the Roman people; but now another hero was arising, who was destined to prove his superior, and to eclipse his glory forever.

Caius Julius Cæsar was born just one hundred years before what is called the Christian Era, from which we reckon our time. He was a patrician by birth; but by his brilliant military exploits, varied talents, and personal attractions, he had endeared himself to the lower classes also. He too had distinguished himself at an early age in the Asiatic wars; and afterward, having been educated in law and oratory by celebrated masters, he filled many important stations in civil life by the choice of the people, and at last rose to be Consul, the highest officer in the republic. As the consuls could not be at once re-elected, Cæsar went with an army into Gaul, — now France, — from which country Rome was in perpetual danger, because the passes of the Alps offered but a slight barrier to the incursions of its fierce and warlike inhabitants. Here Cæsar remained nine years. He entirely subjugated the Gauls, yet used his triumph so wisely that they became his unfailing friends. He conquered the Belgians also, and certain German tribes, and twice subdued the savage but intrepid Britons.

But by this time the fame of his exploits had struck terror into the hearts of the selfish and luxurious patricians of Rome. Cæsar had received the promise that on his return from Gaul, he should be permitted to stand as candidate for a second term of the consulship. But they remembered him to have been a vigorous reformer before he went to Gaul, and they trembled at the thought of his return, and his sure accession to power. Pompey was now consul, and, at his instigation, the Senate commanded Cæsar to resign his government of the province, to abandon his army, and come home. Cæsar answered by marching his army into Italy. Pompey fled from Rome, with the consuls, senators, and magistrates, and levied an army in the East; but Cæsar followed him, and inflicted upon him a disastrous defeat at Pharsalia, a place in Greece. After Pompey had escaped to Egypt, where he was treacherously slain, other generals took up the cause, but were all beaten by Cæsar, until, at last, having conquered the sons of Pompey, who had raised the last standard of revolt in the Roman province of Spain, this wonderful soldier returned to Rome, the master of the world.

All now were eager to recognize him as the destined ruler of the republic. The Senate made him Dictator (or absolute ruler) for life, and gave him the title of Imperator, with all the powers of sovereignty. His wisdom as a legislator proved

equal to his skill in military affairs.   He declared to the people his determination
to use his power for the good of the state ; he passed many useful laws ; he gen-
erously rewarded his friends, and conciliated his enemies by his clemency.   But
the patricians hated and feared him all the more ; while undoubtedly there were
some true and pure republicans — like Brutus, Cato, and Cicero — who shrank
with dread from that approaching shadow of kingly power, whose substance was
already upon them.

II.

THIS was the condition of matters in Rome when, one fine, bright day, the appearance in the streets of swarms of people, dressed in their best attire, showed that it was a holiday in the great city, and that the populace were waiting for some grand pageant or procession.

Now this Roman populace was composed of very different material from what we are accustomed to see on similar occasions. In the first place, they were very ignorant. There were then no printed books, no newspapers or periodicals, no reading-rooms, where the common people might learn about public affairs. Education was confined to the higher classes; and the crowds who gathered in the Forum, or great square, heard the news either by report and gossip, or else directly from the orators, who addressed them in set speeches, and swayed them with the power of eloquence in one direction or another. All great crowds are excitable and fickle; but these Romans, because of their ignorance, were especially so, and sometimes, under the temporary influence of their orators, became a terrible and almost resistless power. And this was too often without regard to right or reason; yet they had a deep respect for Roman law, and a kind of vague love for Roman liberty; and any man who had their personal regard, by a shrewd use of well-chosen words about such things, could lead them at his will.

It was such a crowd that now thronged the streets of Rome. In that day every man of the people was a mechanic, and was compelled by law to wear the badge or sign of his trade, except on legal holidays. These were evidently working-men ; yet they wore not the badges of their several callings, but were arrayed in their best apparel, and had a cheerful, merry-making air, and a look of expectancy, as though something of great interest was shortly to make its appearance. In short, they "made holiday." Cæsar was presently to enter the city, returning in triumph from Spain, where he had defeated the sons of Pompey, and the Great Dictator was the idol of the hour.

But not all faces wore the same contented, pleasure-seeking expression. There were some scowling brows and muttered curses among those who watched the merriment of the thoughtless artisans. At length two tribunes, — a kind of civic officers elected by the people, — who belonged to that large party that, some from patriotic and some from envious motives, hated Cæsar, and dreaded the rapid growth of his power, confronted one of these laughing crowds, and addressed them sharply. Their names were Flavius and Marullus, and thus they berated the multitude, who finally shrank away before them : —

Flavius. Hence ! home, you idle creatures, get you home.
         Is this a holiday ?   What ! know you not,
         Being [mechanics, that you should] not walk

Upon a laboring-day without the sign
Of your profession ? — [*To one.*] Speak, what trade art thou ?
1 *Citizen.* Why, sir, a carpenter.
Marullus. Where is thy leather apron, and thy rule ?
What dost thou with thy best apparel on ? —
[*To another.*] You, sir ; what trade are you ?
2 *Citizen.* Truly, sir, [compared with] a fine workman, I am but, as you would say, a cobbler.*
Marullus. But what trade art thou ? Answer me [correctly].
2 *Citizen.* A trade, sir, that I hope I may use with a safe conscience ; which is indeed, sir, a mender of bad soles. — I am indeed, sir, a surgeon to old shoes ; when they are in great danger, I re-cover them. As [goodly] men as ever trod upon [calf's-skin] have gone upon my handywork.
Flavius. But wherefore art not in thy shop to-day ?
Why dost thou lead these men about the streets ?
2 *Citizen.* Truly, sir, to wear out their shoes, to get myself into more work. But, indeed, sir, we make holiday, to see Cæsar, and to rejoice in his triumph.
Marullus. Wherefore rejoice ? What conquest brings he home ?
What tributaries follow him to Rome,
To grace in captive bonds his chariot wheels ?
You blocks, you stones, you worse than senseless things !
O you hard hearts, you cruel men of Rome,
Knew you not Pompey ? Many a time and oft
Have you climbed up to walls and battlements,
To towers and windows, yea, to chimney-tops,
Your infants in your arms, and there have sat
The live-long day, with patient expectation,
To see great Pompey pass the streets of Rome :
And when you saw his chariot but appear,
Have you not made an universal shout,
That Tiber trembled underneath her banks ?
And do you now put on your best attire ?
And do you now [choose] out a holiday ?
And do you now strew flowers in his way,
That comes in triumph over Pompey's blood ?
Be gone !
Run to your houses, fall upon your knees,
Pray to the gods to [turn away] the plague
That needs must light on this ingratitude.
Flavius. Go, go, good countrymen ; and for this fault
Assemble all the poor men of your sort :
Draw them to Tiber banks, and weep your tears

* *Cobbler*, in Shakespeare's time, meant *botcher* — any kind of coarse workman, and not *shoemaker* alone, as now ; so that the word did not convey an answer to the tribune's question.

Into the channel, till the lowest stream
Do kiss the most exalted shores of all.[a]

The citizens, as if shamed by the reproaches of the tribunes, silently dispersed.
Then said Flavius, turning to Marullus, —

Go you down that way towards the Capitol ;
This way will I.   Disrobe the images,
If you do find them decked with [ornaments].
Marullus.   May we do so ?
You know it is the feast of Lupercal.
Flavius.   It is no matter ; let no images
Be hung with Cæsar's trophies.   I 'll about,
And drive away the [people] from the streets :
So do you too, where you perceive them thick.
These growing feathers plucked from Cæsar's wing,
Will make him fly an ordinary [height],
Who else would soar above the view of men,
And keep us all in servile fearfulness.

To understand this, we must know that among the statues of kings and famous
men which adorned the public places in Rome, Cæsar had set up a statue of himself.   This pleased his particular friends, but to many it gave deep offence.   In
anticipation of the great triumphal procession, these statues were adorned with
trophies brought home from the war by Cæsar.   Some one, hoping thus to please
the Dictator, had placed a laurel crown, tied with white ribbon, on his statue.   The
white ribbon was a badge of royalty, and seemed to say, "Cæsar, too, will one day
be king."

Now, among the Romans, there was a profound hatred of the very name of
king.   For five hundred years, no matter what might have been done in the
countries which they ruled abroad, at home their government had been called a
republic, and no one among their great statesmen and generals had ever dared to
dream of wearing a crown.   Many things, like the crowning of the statue and the
fact that Cæsar had had a chair like a throne made for his use at the theatre and
in the Senate-chamber, seemed to show the secret ambition of his heart.   He had
already the power of a king, and it seemed but a short step from the real thing
to the name of the thing.   There were many who were jealous of this increasing
dignity and state of Cæsar, and they made his ambition an excuse for trying to
destroy him.   The two tribunes, who, as we have seen, were secret enemies to
Cæsar, under pretence of obeying the ancient laws of Rome, stripped the orna-
ments from the statues, took the ribbon and wreath from Cæsar's brow, and sent
to prison the man who had placed them there.

---

[a] That is, till the lowest tide do reach the extreme high-water mark.

When Cæsar afterwards learned what had been done, he was very angry, and moved the Senate to dismiss the meddlesome tribunes from their office, declaring that it was his place, not theirs, to disavow such claims. But meanwhile they went about, before the triumphal ceremonies, and had the statues stripped of their adornments.

III.

HE feast of the Lupercalia was celebrated every year at Rome in honor of Lupercus, a Roman deity corresponding to the god whom the Greeks called Pan. Among other ceremonies at this festival, the priests of the order, among whom were some young men of the highest rank, ran, half naked, through the streets, bearing whips made of leathern thongs, with which they struck freely all whom they met. These blows were supposed to confer great blessings on those who chanced to receive them.

Connected with the festivities, there was at this time a grand procession. First came Julius Cæsar and his wife Calphurnia, attended by Mark Antony, a near friend of Cæsar's, while Cicero, Brutus, Cassius, Casca, and many more of the leading citizens followed, and an immense crowd of the common people had gathered to look on. The procession moved, accompanied by music, amid great popular excitement. Antony, although at this time one of the consuls (the highest officers in the government), appeared among the youths, whip in hand, prepared for the race, as he was the chief of one of the bands of Lupercalian priests. He was censured by many for his want of dignity; but it seemed to please Julius Cæsar, who commanded his wife to stand directly in the way of the young priest as he ran, and ordered Antony not to forget to touch her in "the holy chase."

Antony replied, "I shall remember : when Cæsar says, 'Do this,' it is performed."

In the midst of the excitement and above the din of the music, a voice was suddenly heard from the throng, calling "Cæsar !" in a tone so loud and clear that Cæsar turned to listen, exclaiming, —

> Ha ! who calls ?
> *Casca.* Bid every noise be still. — Peace yet again ! [*Music ceases.*
> *Cæsar.* Who is it in the press that calls on me ?

I hear a tongue, shriller than all the music,
Cry, Cæsar! Speak: Cæsar is turned to hear.
Soothsayer. Beware the ides * of March.
Cæsar. What man is that?
Brutus. A soothsayer bids you beware the ides of March.
Cæsar. Set him before me ; let me see his face.
Casca. Fellow, come from the throng : look upon Cæsar.
       [*They place him face to face with* CÆSAR.
Cæsar. What say'st thou to me now ? Speak once again.
Soothsayer. Beware the ides of March.
Cæsar. He is a dreamer ; let us leave him. — Pass.

With flourish of trumpets, the sound of martial music, and the waving of banners, the gorgeous pageant moves on. When the last chariot has disappeared, and only the distant shouts of the crowd are heard, there still linger in the public square two men, who are to make the "dream" of that soothsayer a reality. These are Brutus and Cassius, — the one a patriot, the other a politician.

Brutus was a nephew of the celebrated philosopher and statesman, Marcus Cato, by whom he had in great part been educated. His character was full of beauty and sweetness. He was upright, gentle, and pure. Everybody esteemed him, and he was revered and trusted by the people. He loved his country, and sincerely desired for her the best and largest liberty. But he was a mere student, an enthusiastic lover of books, and knew little of the hearts and ways of men. In the wars between Pompey and Cæsar, Brutus had sided with the former ; but after the overthrow of Pompey, Cæsar had forgiven him and taken him to his bosom, and afterwards placed him in offices of power and trust : so that there was at this time much love and intimacy between the two.

Cassius was the brother-in-law of Brutus, but there had been lately some coolness between them, arising from the jealousy of Cassius, because some of his personal ambitions had been thwarted through Cæsar's preference for Brutus. But Cassius was a shrewd, practical man, with a perfect knowledge of the workings of the human heart. Although not without certain manly qualities, such as courage and energy, much valued by the Romans of that day, he would never, like Brutus, be hampered by virtuous scruples, but if he had an object in view, would think any means right by which it might be gained. Cassius had already begun to study ways of making an end at once of Cæsar, whom he hated ; and had plotted with many other rich and powerful Romans, who desired the same thing, not because they wished for the liberty of the people, but because the power of this one great man overshadowed and belittled their own. But there were many things about this soldierly "tyrant" which interested the Roman populace, while these aristocratic and selfish patricians were themselves far from

---

* The 15th of the month.

popular. There was therefore not a little danger connected with their enterprise.
So it became a matter of importance to them to obtain some one who "sat
high in all the people's hearts," to lead their cause, and to stand between them
and the judgment of the multitude. It was for this that Cassius fixed his keen
eye on Brutus, — standing moody and lost in thought, — as a man who should by
all means be won over to the conspiracy; and he now drew near, and began with
words of friendly complaint.

"Brutus," he said, "you are changed of late. I have not from you that gentleness and show of love that I was wont to have. You are too cold and distant
to your friend who loves you."

"It is not, Cassius, that I love you less," answered the noble Brutus. "Some
troubles I have, some anxious thoughts, which belong only to myself. If these
have seemed to change my outward behavior, think only, I pray you, that poor
Brutus, with himself at war, forgets to show his love to other men."

"O Brutus, would that you had some mirror which might reflect your real
worth unto yourself. I have often heard it wished by some of the greatest men
in Rome, groaning under the burdens of this age, that the noble Brutus could but
see himself as others see him."

"Into what dangers would you lead me, Cassius, that you would have me look
into myself for that which is not in me?"

"Well, good Brutus, hear me. I will be your mirror, and will show you to
yourself. And do not view me with suspicion, gentle friend; but, remember, I
am serious-minded, like yourself, and not one of those fickle, boasting revellers
whom you might fear to trust."

Just at this moment a great shout is heard from the feast of the Lupercalia,
whither the procession and the crowd have gone, and the patriot Brutus, now
thoroughly aroused, betrays the nature of his secret anxiety by exclaiming, —

> What means this shouting? I do fear the people
> Choose Cæsar for their king!

This is the tempter's opportunity, and he seizes it : —

> Ay, do you fear it?
> Then must I think you would not have it so.

Then Cassius breaks forth into a thoroughly hearty strain of hatred and contempt, thinly disguised as patriotism : —

> I cannot tell what you and other men
> Think of this life ; but, for my single self,
> I had as lief not be as live to be
> In awe of such a thing as I myself.
> I was born free as Cæsar ; so were you:

We both have fed as well; and we can both
Endure the winter's cold as well as he:
For once, upon a raw and gusty day,
The troubled Tiber chafing with her shores,
Cæsar said to me, "Darest thou, Cassius, now
Leap in with me into this angry flood,
And swim to yonder point?"— Upon the word,
Accoutred as I was, I plungèd in,
And bade him follow: so, indeed, he did.
The torrent roared, and we did buffet it
With lusty sinews, throwing it aside,
And stemming it with hearts of controversy,[a]
But ere we could arrive[b] the point proposed,
Cæsar cried, "Help me, Cassius, or I sink."
I, as Æneas, our great ancestor,
Did from the flames of Troy upon his shoulder
The old Anchises bear, so from the waves of Tiber
Did I the tired Cæsar.   And this man
Is now become a god; and Cassius is
A wretched creature, and must bend his body,
If Cæsar carelessly but nod on him.
He had a fever when he was in Spain,
And, when the fit was on him, I did mark
How he did shake: 't is true, this god did shake:
His coward lips did from their color fly;
And that same eye, whose bend[1] doth awe the world,
Did lose its lustre.   I did hear him groan;
Ay, and that tongue of his, that bade the Romans
Mark him, and write his speeches in their books,
Alas! it cried, "Give me some drink, Titinius,"
As a sick girl.   Ye gods, it doth amaze me,
A man of such a feeble temper[2] should
So get the start of the majestic world,
And bear the palm alone.

Here the conversation was interrupted by another burst of tremendous shouting, followed by a triumphant flourish of trumpets, from the games of the Lupercalia.   Brutus listened anxiously for a moment, then frowned, and said, —

Another general shout!
I do believe that these applauses are
For some new honors that are heaped on Cæsar.

---

[1] Glance.   [2] Temperament, disposition.
    [a] That is, with contending, or courageous hearts.
    [b] Old form for arrive at, etc.

Cassius. Why, man, he doth bestride the narrow world,
Like a Colossus ; * and we petty men
Walk under his huge legs, and peep about
To find ourselves dishonorable graves.
Men at some time are masters of their fates :
The fault, dear Brutus, is not in our stars,[b]
But in ourselves, that we are underlings.
Brutus and *Cæsar :* what should be in that *Cæsar ?*
Why should that name be sounded more than yours ?
Write them together, yours is as fair a name :
Sound them, it doth become the mouth as well ;
Weigh them, it is as heavy ; conjure with them,
Brutus will start a spirit as soon as *Cæsar.*
Now, in the names of all the gods at once,
Upon what meat doth this our Cæsar feed,
That he is grown so great ?   Age, thou art shamed :
Rome, thou hast lost the breed of noble bloods !
When went there by an age, since the great flood,
But it was famed with more than with one man ?
When could they say, till now, that talked of Rome,
That her wide walls encompassed but one man ?
O, you and I have heard our fathers say
There was a Brutus once, that would have brooked [1]
The eternal devil to keep his state in Rome,
As easily as a king.

This was a master stroke on the part of Cassius.   The Brutus here alluded to
was Lucius Junius Brutus, who had headed the revolution that drove the first
kings out of Rome more than five hundred years before.   This Brutus considered
himself a descendant of that one ; and such a man would desire to be worthy of
a noble ancestry.   After a few moments of troubled silence, he replied, —

What you have said,
I will consider ; what you have to say,
I will with patience hear, and find a time
Both meet to hear and answer such high things.
Till then, my noble friend, [reflect on] this :
Brutus had rather be a villager
Than to repute himself a son of Rome

---

[1] Endured.

* The Colossus was one of the Seven Wonders of the World.   It was a bronze statue,
a hundred and twenty feet high, bestriding the harbor at Rhodes, so that ships passed under
its legs.

[b] *Our stars* — Astrology, in the olden time, taught that the stars had an influence on the
fortunes of men.

Under such hard conditions as this time
Is like to lay upon us.
  Cassius.   I am glad that my weak words
Have struck but thus much show óf fire from Brutus.
  Brutus. The games are done, and Cæsar is returning.
  Cassius. As they pass by, pluck Casca by the sleeve;
And he will, after his sour fashion, tell you
What hath proceeded worthy note to-day.

        Re-enter CÆSAR *and his Train.*

  Brutus. I will do so. — But, look you, Cassius;
The angry spot doth glow on Cæsar's brow,
And all the rest look like a [scolded] train.
Calphurnia's cheek is pale; and Cicero
Looks with such ferret ª and such fiery eyes,
As we have seen him in the Capitol,
[When] crossed in conference by some senator.
  Cassius. Casca will tell us what the matter is.

The procession now passed through the square, at a little distance from where
the two citizens stood conversing. Cæsar appeared for some reason discontented,
and presently, as his eye fell upon the spare form and lowering looks of Cassius,
he called Mark Antony to his side.

          Cæsar. Antonius!
          Antony. Cæsar?
          Cæsar. Let me have men about me that are fat;
Sleek-headed men, and such as sleep o' nights.
Yond Cassius has a lean and hungry look;
He thinks too much: such men are dangerous.ᵇ
          Antony. Fear him not, Cæsar, he 's not dangerous.
He is a noble Roman, and well given.[1]
          Cæsar. Would he were fatter! but I fear him not:
Yet, if my name were liable to fear,
I do not know the man I should avoid
So soon as that spare Cassius. He reads much;
He is a great observer, and he looks
Quite through the deeds of men: he loves no plays,
As thou dost, Antony; he hears no music:
Seldom he smiles, and smiles in such a sort,

---

[1] Disposed.
  ª The ferret is a ferocious little animal of the weasel kind, noted for its fire-red eyes.
  ᵇ According to *Plutarch*, Cæsar actually made use of this language. He said, in answer
to some friends, who warned him against Antony and Dolabella as dangerous, "As for those
fat men and smooth-combed heads, I never reckon of them; but these pale-visaged and car-
rion-lean people, I fear them most," — *meaning Brutus and Cassius*, adds the historian.

As if he mocked himself, and scorned his spirit
That could be moved to smile at anything.
Such men as he be never at heart's ease,
While they behold a greater than themselves,
And therefore are they very dangerous.
I rather tell thee what is to be feared,
Than what I fear, for always I am Cæsar.
Come on my right hand, for this ear is deaf,
And tell me truly what thou think'st of him.

So the train passed on; but Casca, an enemy of Cæsar, and one who concealed under a rude and careless manner a deeply dangerous disposition, in obedience to a sign from Brutus remained behind.

Casca.   You pulled me by the cloak: would you speak with me?
Brutus.   Ay, Casca; tell us what hath chanced to-day,
    That Cæsar looks so [grave].

Casca.   Why, you were with him, were you not?
Brutus.   I should not then ask Casca what hath chanced.
Casca.   Why, there was a crown offered him: and, being offered him, he put it by
with the back of his hand, thus; and then the people fell a shouting.

Brutus. What was the second noise for ?

Casca. Why, for that too.

Cassius. They shouted thrice : what was the last cry for ?

Casca. Why, for that too.

Brutus. Was the crown offered him thrice ?

Casca. Ay, marry, was it, and he put it by thrice, every time gentler than the other ; and at every putting-by mine honest neighbors shouted.

Cassius. Who offered him the crown ?

Casca. Why, Antony.

Brutus. Tell us the manner of it, gentle Casca.

Casca. I can as well be hanged, as tell the manner of it : it was mere foolery ; I did not mark it. I saw Mark Antony offer him a crown : — yet 't was not a crown neither, 't was one of these coronets,[a] — and, as I told you, he put it by once: but, for all that, to my thinking, he would fain have had it. Then he offered it to him again ; then he put it by again : but, to my thinking, he was very loth to lay his fingers off it. And then he offered it the third time : he put it the third time by ; and still, as he refused it, the rabblement shouted, and clapped their chopped hands, and threw up their [dirty] caps, and uttered such a deal of [bad] breath, because Cæsar refused the crown, that it had almost choked Cæsar ; for he swooned, and fell down at it. And for mine own part I durst not laugh, for fear of opening my lips, and receiving the bad air.

Cassius. What ! did Cæsar swoon ?

Casca. He fell down in the market-place, and foamed at mouth, and was speechless.

Brutus. 'T is very like ; he hath the falling-sickness.[b]

Cassius. No, Cæsar hath it not ; but you, and I,
         And honest Casca, *we* have the falling-sickness.[c]

Casca. I know not what you mean by that ; but, I am sure, Cæsar fell down.

Brutus. What said he, when he came unto himself ?

Casca. When he came to himself again, he said, if he had done or said anything amiss, he desired their worships to think it was his infirmity. Three or four wenches, where I stood, cried, " Alas, good soul ! " — and forgave him with all their hearts. But there 's no heed to be taken of them : if Cæsar had stabbed their mothers, they would have done no less.

Brutus. And after that, he came thus sad away ?

Casca. Ay. — I could tell you more news, too : Marullus and Flavius, for pulling scarfs off Cæsar's images, are put to silence.[d] Fare you well : there was more foolery yet, if I could remember it.

Cassius. Will you sup with me to-night, Casca ?

Casca. No, I am [engaged].

Cassius. Will you dine with me to-morrow ?

---

[a] It has been suggested that Cæsar allowed this offer to be made, to test the people.

[b] Epilepsy; a disease which causes those who suffer from it to fall suddenly to the ground. Cæsar was subject to it in his later years.

[c] Meaning the disease of prostrating themselves before Cæsar.

[d] Deprived of their offices.

Casca. Ay, if I be alive, and your mind hold, and your dinner worth the eating
Cassius. Good ; I will expect you.
Casca. Do so.   Farewell, both.

After Casca had left, Brutus said with a smile, —

> What a [dull] fellow is this grown to be !
> He was quick [witted] when he went to school.
>   *Cassius.* So is he now, in execution
> Of any bold or noble enterprise.
> This rudeness is a sauce to his good wit.
>   *Brutus.* And so it is.   For this time I will leave you.
> To-morrow, if you please to speak with me,
> I will come home to you ; or, if you will,
> Come home to me, and I will wait for you.
>   *Cassius.* I will do so : — till then, think of the world.

Brutus went away, thinking of the Roman world, which seemed to him to be
resting under a dark cloud, and left the brooding Cassius to himself. Cassius smiled
grimly, as he thought how easily he was moulding this noble Roman to his wish
by simply playing on his better nature, — his love of country and of liberty, — and
on his weaknesses of personal vanity and pride of ancestry.   Still, it was needful
to be cautious, because of the great love Brutus was known to bear to Cæsar ; but
if the patriot could be made to feel that Cæsar was wronging Rome, it might be
possible to win him.   Musing on this, Cassius said, —

> I will this night   •
> In at his windows throw (in several hands,
> As if they came from several citizens)
> Writings, all tending to the great opinion
> That Rome holds of his name ; wherein obscurely
> Cæsar's ambition shall be glancèd at :
> And, after this, let Cæsar seat him sure,
> For we will shake him, or worse days endure.

IV.

T HAT night a terrible tempest of thunder and lightning swept over the city. The whole earth seemed shaken, and the heavens were dropping fire, as if the gods, angry with the world, were threatening its destruction. Those who by chance were in the streets told each other of wonderful sights. Casca, with a drawn sword, breathless, as if just escaped from some great danger, and staring wildly as if in dread of some new peril, rushed into the public square at the same moment that Cicero, one of the Roman senators, entered it from the other side. Casca has laid aside his affected indifference now.

"O Cicero," he exclaimed, "I have seen tempests when the winds split knotty oaks; I have seen the ocean swell, and rage, and foam, until it reached the sky; but never such a night as this till now. The very skies rain fire! I met a slave whose hands did flame and burn like twenty torches, and yet re- mained unscorched! I drew my sword against a lion that I met near the Capitol; but he only glared at  me, and then went by, without offering to harm me. A hundred women, pale with terror, drawn together in a crowd, swore they saw men on fire walking through the streets. Yesterday, at noon, an owl sat hooting and shrieking in the market-place! These are fearful omens!"

"They are indeed wonderful," rejoined Cicero, "but yet may not mean evil. Men are very apt to misinterpret such things. — Does Cæsar come to the Capitol to-morrow?"

"He does; and he bade Mark Antony send word to you to meet him there."

"Good night, then, Casca : this is no night for men to walk in."

After the departure of Cicero, Casca was joined by Cassius. They talked about the strange events of the night, and their possible meaning. To the mind of Cassius, all events conspired to feed his burning hate of Cæsar. Though the night was terrible with its fires and ghosts, strange birds and beasts, yet there was one man more to be dreaded than even these tokens of the wrath of the gods; the thunder, the lightning, and the lion in the Capitol, all betokened only *Cæsar*.

"O Casca," he cried, "though Romans still have limbs and sinews like their ancestors, our fathers' minds are dead, and we are governed by our mothers' spirits; else would we never suffer underneath this yoke!"

"They say, indeed," replied Casca, "that the senators to-morrow mean to establish Cæsar as a king; and he shall wear his crown by sea and land, in every place, save here in Italy!"

> *Cassius.* I know where I will wear this dagger then;
> Cassius from bondage will deliver Cassius.
> That part of tyranny that I do bear
> I can shake off at pleasure.
> *Casca.*   So can I:
> So every bondman in his own hand bears
> The power to cancel his captivity.
> *Cassius.* And why should Cæsar be a tyrant then?
> Poor man! I know he would not be a wolf,
> But that he sees the Romans are but sheep:
> He were no lion, were not Romans hinds.
> — But, O grief!
> Where hast thou led me? I perhaps speak this
> Before a willing bondman: then I know
> My answer must be made; but I am armed,
> And dangers are to me indifferent.
> *Casca.* You speak to Casca ; and to such a man
> That is no [fawning] tell-tale. [Here 's] my hand:
> Be [active] for redress of all these griefs,
> And I will set this foot of mine as far,
> As who goes farthest.
> *Cassius.*   There 's a bargain made.
> Now know you, Casca, I have moved already
> Some certain of the noblest-minded Romans,
> To [undertake] with me an enterprise
> Of honorable-dangerous consequence ;

And I do know, by this, they stay for me
In Pompey's porch.[a]

While they are thus talking, another footstep is heard approaching in the
darkness. " Stand close awhile," said Casca, " for here comes one in haste."

Cassius. 'T is Cinna, I do know him by his gait :
He is a friend. — Cinna, where haste you so ?
Cinna. To find out you. Who 's that ? Metellus Cimber ?
Cassius. No, it is Casca ; one [who joins with us
In] our attempt.
Cinna. I am glad on 't. What a fearful night is this !
There 's two or three of us have seen strange sights.
Cassius. Am I not stayed for ? Tell me.
Cinna.   Yes, you are.
O Cassius ! if you could but win the noble Brutus
To our party, —
Cassius. Be you content. Good Cinna, take this paper,
                                     [*Producing several slips of paper.*

And look you lay it in the prætor's [b] chair,
Where Brutus may but find it ; and throw this
In at his window ; set this up with wax
Upon old Brutus' [c] statue : all this done,
Repair to Pompey's porch, where you shall find us.
Is Decius Brutus, and Trebonius, there ?
Cinna. All but Metellus Cimber, and he 's gone
To seek you at your house. Well, I will [haste],
And so bestow these papers as you bade me.
Cassius. That done, repair to Pompey's theatre.
                                     [CINNA *goes out.*
Come, Casca, you and I will yet, ere day,
See Brutus at his house : three parts of him
Is ours already ; and the man entire,
Upon the next encounter, yields him ours.
Casca. O, he sits high in all the people's hearts ;
And that which would appear offence in us,
His countenance, like richest alchemy,[d]
Will change to virtue, and to worthiness.

---

[a] *Pompey's Porch* — A large building connected with the theatre built by Pompey.

[b] Brutus was at this time prætor, or magistrate, in Rome.

[c] This was the statue of Lucius Junius Brutus, who drove the Tarquins out of Rome.
Plutarch tells us that one of these papers read, *Would that thou wert now alive !* and that the
prætor's chair was full of these bills, with *Brutus, thou art asleep !* and *Thou art not Brutus,
indeed,* written on them.

[d] *Alchemy* was the art by which the philosophers of old hoped to turn base metals into
gold. It was the source of the truer science of Chemistry.

Cassius. Him, and his worth, and our great need of him
You have right well [conceivèd].   Let us go,
For it is after midnight : and, ere day,
We will awake him, and be sure of him.

. Then they made their way through the tempestuous night to the house of Brutus.

BRUTUS IN HIS GARDEN.

V.

ACT II. SCENE 1.

WHEN Brutus went home, after his interview with Cassius, he had little inclination to sleep. Instead, therefore, of going to bed, he walked in his garden, wrapped in deep thought, and striving to reconcile his love for the man Julius with his duty to check the strides of the great Dictator towards royal power.

At length he called to his page, —

> What, Lucius, ho ! —
> I cannot, by the progress of the stars,
> Give guess how near to day. — Lucius, I say ! —
> I would it were *my* fault to sleep so soundly. —
> Lucius, awake ! [Why,] Lucius !

The lad entered, rubbing his eyes, and drowsily replying, —

> Called you, my lord ?
> *Brutus.* Get me a taper in my study, Lucius.
> When it is lighted, come and call me here.

While the lad sought the taper, the thoughts of Brutus returned to Cæsar, the danger that threatened Rome through his ambition, and the ways in which the evil might be remedied. At last he broke out thus : " It *must* be by his death. I cannot see how it may be avoided. Personally, I have no complaint to make of him ; but, in view of the general good, it is impossible to spare him. It is not what he is, but what he might become. He wants to be crowned, and that might change his nature. It is the bright day that brings forth the adder : so the sunshine of royalty might reveal the serpent of tyranny in Cæsar. Then, lest it may, we must treat him as the serpent's egg, and kill him in the shell."

While he was thus arguing with himself, the boy returned, bearing a sealed paper in his hand, and said, —

> The taper burneth in your closet, sir.
> Searching the window for a flint, I found
> This paper, thus sealed up ; and I am sure
> It did not lie there when I went to bed.   [*Giving him the paper.*
> *Brutus.* Get you to bed again ; it is not day.
> Is not to-morrow, boy, the ides of March ?
> *Lucius.* I know not, sir.
> *Brutus.* Look in the calendar, and bring me word.
> *Lucius.* I will, sir.   [*Exit.*
> *Brutus.* [These fiery meteors], whizzing in the air,
> Give so much light that I may read by them.
>   [*Opens the paper, and reads.*
> *Brutus, thou sleep'st : awake, and see thyself.*
> *Shall Rome,* et cetera. *Speak, strike, redress !* —
> " Brutus, thou sleep'st : awake ! " —
> Such instigations have been often dropped
> Where I have took them up.
> " Shall Rome, *et cetera.*" Thus must I piece it out :
> Shall Rome stand under one man's awe ? What ! Rome ?
> My ancestors did from the streets of Rome
> The Tarquin drive, when he was called a king.

"Speak, strike, redress!" — Am I entreated
To speak, and strike ?   O Rome ! I make thee promise,
If the redress will follow, thou receivest
Thy full petition at the hand of Brutus !

By this time Lucius, having consulted the calendar, returns and reports to
Brutus : " Sir, March is wasted fourteen days."
" 'T is good," answered the master ; and then, hearing a knocking outside,
he added, " Go to the gate ; somebody knocks." Lucius goes to the outer door,
and Brutus continues his soliloquy.

> Since Cassius first did whet me against Cæsar,
> I have not slept.
> Between the acting of a dreadful thing
> And the first [impulse], all the interim is
> Like a [dark] phantasm, or a hideous dream.
> The genius and the mortal instruments [a]
> Are then in council ; and the state of man,
> Like to a little kingdom, suffers then
> The nature of an insurrection.
>   *Lucius* [*returning from the gate*]. Sir, 't is your brother Cassius at the door,
> Who doth desire to see you.
>   *Brutus.*   Is he alone ?
>   *Lucius.* No, sir, there are more with him.
>   *Brutus.*   Do you know them?
>   *Lucius.* No, sir ; their hats are plucked about their ears,
> And half their faces buried in their cloaks,
> That by no means I may discover them
> By any mark of favor.[1]
>   *Brutus.*   Let them enter.
> They are the faction.   O Conspiracy !
> Sham'st thou to show thy dangerous brow by night,
> When evils are most free ?   O, then, by day
> Where wilt thou find a cavern dark enough
> To mask thy monstrous visage ?

The conspirators, with their faces hidden, now enter cautiously. Cassius
names them as they draw near to Brutus : Trebonius, Decius Brutus, Casca,
Cinna, and Metellus Cimber.   Brutus greets them cordially, and, in token of
sympathy, takes them each by the hand.   Cassius proposes that they shall all
bind themselves by a solemn oath ; but to this Brutus refuses his consent.

" No, not an oath," he said ; " if neither shame, nor suffering, nor the condition of our country, is motive strong enough, let us break off betimes, and every
man hence to his idle bed.   But if these, as I am sure they do, bear fire enough

---

[1] Countenance.   [a] The soul and the deadly passions.

BRUTUS AND THE CONSPIRATORS.

to kindle cowards and to steel with valor the melting spirits of women, then, countrymen,

> What need we any spur but our own cause
> To prick us to redress ? What other bond
> Than secret Romans, that have spoke the word,
> And will not palter ? and what other oath
> Than honesty to honesty engaged
> That this shall be, or we will fall for it ?

Do not stain our courage or our cause with oaths, when every drop of blood in every Roman's heart is false, if he do break the smallest particle of any promise he hath given."

> *Decius.* Shall no man else be touched, but only Cæsar ?
> *Cassius.* Decius, well urged. — I think it is not meet,
> Mark Antony, so well beloved of Cæsar,
> Should outlive Cæsar: we shall find of him
> A shrewd contriver ; and, you know, his means,
> If he improve them, may well stretch so far
> As to [destroy] us all; which to prevent,
> Let Antony and Cæsar fall together.
> *Brutus.* Our course will seem too bloody, Caius Cassius,
> To cut the head off. and then hack the limbs,
> Like wrath in death, and [hatred] afterwards ;
> For Antony is but a limb of Cæsar.
> Let us be sacrificers, but not butchers, Caius.
> We all stand up against the *spirit* of Cæsar,
> And in the spirit of men there is no blood :
> O, that we then could come by Cæsar's spirit,
> And not dismember Cæsar ! But, alas !
> Cæsar must bleed for it. And, gentle friends,
> Let 's kill him boldly, but not wrathfully ;
> Let 's carve him as a dish fit for the gods,
> Not hew him as a carcass fit for hounds :
> And for Mark Antony, think not of him,
> For he can do no more than Cæsar's arm,
> When Cæsar's head is off.
> *Cassius.*   Yet I do fear him :
> For in the [fixèd] love he bears to Cæsar —
> *Brutus.* Alas ! good Cassius, do not think of him.
> If he love Cæsar, all that he can do
> Is to himself ; take thought and die * for Cæsar :
> And that were much he should ; for he is given
> To sports, to wildness, and much company.

---

* *Take thought and die* — An old expression for *grieve one's self to death.*

Trebonius. There is no fear[a] in him ; let him not die,
For he will live, and laugh at this hereafter.   [*Clock strikes.*
Brutus. Peace! count the clock.
Cassius.   The clock hath stricken three.
Trebonius. 'T is time to part.
Cassius.   But it is doubtful yet,
Whether Cæsar will come forth to-day, or no ;
For he is superstitious grown of late,
Quite [different from] the opinion he held once.
It may be, these apparent prodigies,
The unaccustomed terror of this night,
And the persuasion of his augurers,
May hold him from the Capitol to-day.
     Decius. Never fear that : if he be so resolved,
I can o'ersway him : let me work ;
For I can give his humor the true bent,
And I will bring him to the Capitol.
     Cassius. Nay. we will all of us be there to fetch him.
     Brutus. By the eighth hour : is that the uttermost ?
     Cinna. Be that the uttermost, and fail not then.
     Metellus. Caius Ligarius doth bear Cæsar hard,[b]
Who rated him for speaking well of Pompey :
I wonder none of you have thought of him.
     Brutus. Now, good Metellus, go along by him.[c]
He loves me well, and I have given him reasons ;
Send him but hither, and I 'll fashion him.
     Cassius. The morning comes upon us : we 'll leave you, Brutus. —
And, friends, disperse yourselves ; but all remember
What you have said, and show yourselves true Romans.
     Brutus. Good gentlemen, look fresh and merrily :
Let not our looks [betray] our purposes.
And so, good-morrow to you every one.

The conspirators went away as cautiously as they came, leaving Brutus once more alone, but for the sleeping Lucius. Brutus looks at him kindly, glad that there is one in the world whom care does not make wakeful. As he stands, silent and thoughtful, his beloved wife, the noble Portia, whose anxiety has kept her from sleeping, comes out with a light, anxiously seeking him. She reproaches him gently for leaving her, and begs him to tell her his secret trouble.

          It will not let you eat, nor talk, nor sleep ;
          And, could it work so much upon your shape,
          As it hath [done upon your disposition],

---

[a] That is, there is no *cause* of fear in him.
[b] Owes Cæsar a grudge.   [c] By *his house.*

I should not know you, Brutus. Dear my lord,
Make me acquainted with your cause of grief.
Brutus. I am not well in health, and that is all.
Portia. Brutus is wise, and were he not in health,
He would embrace the means to come by it.
Brutus. Why, so I do. — Good Portia, go to bed.

Portia entreated Brutus, by all the love he had vowed to her, by the beauty
he had so often praised, by the sacred name of wife, to share with her the burden
that weighed so heavily upon his mind. She kneeled to him in her entreaty,
begging him to tell her who were the men that had come to him that night with
their faces hidden.

"Kneel not, gentle Portia," he said, as he raised and lovingly embraced
her.

"I should not need to kneel, if you were gentle Brutus," Portia softly answered. "Tell me, my Brutus, am I not your true and faithful wife? Is not my
home deep down within your heart? and shall I not share its pain and grief as
well as its joys?"

> *Brutus.* You are my true and honorable wife;
> As dear to me as are the ruddy drops
> That visit my sad heart.
> *Portia.* If this were true, then should I know this secret.
> I grant I am a woman; but, withal,
> A woman that Lord Brutus took to wife:
> I grant I am a woman; but, withal,
> A woman well reputed, Cato's daughter.
> Think you I am no stronger than my sex,
> Being so fathered and so husbanded?
> Tell me your counsels, I will not disclose them.
> *Brutus.* O ye gods!
> Render me worthy of this noble wife. [*Knocking within.*

> Hark! [some] one knocks.   Portia, go in a while;
> And by and by thy bosom shall partake
> The secrets of my heart.   Leave me with haste.

Obedient to her husband's will, Portia withdrew as Lucius entered, ushering in a tottering form, with pale face and bandaged head.

"Here is a sick man who would speak with you," said the boy.

"Caius Ligarius, that Metellus spake of," exclaimed Brutus.   "O, what a time, brave Caius, have you chosen to be sick!"

"I am not sick, if Brutus have any honorable work in hand," replied Ligarius.

"I have indeed such work in hand, Ligarius, if you were well enough to hear of it."

"Then, by all the gods that Romans bow before, I here discard my sickness," cried the invalid, throwing away his bandage.   "Soul of Rome! thou hast called back my failing powers to life.   Now bid me run, and strive with things impossible.   What 's to be done?"

"A piece of work that will make sick men whole."

"But are there not some whole that we must make sick?" asked Ligarius, with a meaning glance.

"That must we also," answered Brutus.   "What it is, my Caius, I will unfold to thee as we walk."

"Go on!" said the other, "and with a heart new-fired I follow you — to do, I know not what.   But 't is enough that Brutus leads me on!"

And the two went forth to join the other conspirators.

VI.

 HROUGH all the long night the tempest had raged with unabated fury. Calphurnia, Cæsar's wife, had been disturbed with frightful dreams, and had cried out in her sleep that they were "murdering Cæsar." When she waked she entreated her husband to remain at home, and not to visit the Capitol that day. In vain Cæsar tried to comfort her and to calm her fears. He sent a servant to the priests to bid them offer sacrifice, and bring him word if the omens promised him good fortune. "Cæsar must go forth," he said ; "dangers that threaten me behind my back will vanish when they see my face."

"O Cæsar, there have been horrid sights seen by the watch. A lioness whelped in the street ; graves yawned and yielded up their dead ; there have been battles in the air, and dropping blood, and wailing ghosts, and comets blazing in the sky. My very heart stands still with fear ! "

Cæsar replied, —

> What can be avoided
> Whose end is purposed by the mighty gods ?
> Yet Cæsar shall go forth : for these predictions
> Are to the world in general, as to Cæsar.
> Cowards die many times before their deaths ;
> The valiant never taste of death but once.
> Of all the wonders that I yet have heard,
> It seems to me most strange that men should fear,
> Seeing that death, a necessary end,
> Will come, when it will come.

Here the servant, who had been sent to the priests, returned. "What say the ¬urers? " asked Cæsar.

Servant. They would not have you to stir forth to-day.
Plucking the entrails of an offering forth,
They could not find a heart within the beast.
    Cæsar. The gods do this in shame of cowardice :
Cæsar would be a beast without a heart,
If he should stay at home to-day for fear.
No, Cæsar shall not : Danger knows full well,
That Cæsar is more dangerous than he.
We are two lions littered in one day,
And I the elder and more terrible ;
And Cæsar shall go forth.
    Calphurnia.   Alas ! my lord,
Your wisdom is consumed in confidence.
Do not go forth to-day : call it my fear
That keeps you in the house, and not your own.
We 'll send Mark Antony to the Senate-house,
And he shall say you are not well to-day :
Let me, upon my knee, prevail in this.   [*Kneeling.*
    Cæsar. Mark Antony *shall* say I am not well :
And, [to indulge thee], I will stay at home.   [*Raising her.*

At this moment Decius Brutus entered, intent upon his purpose of persuading
Cæsar to the Senate-house. Cæsar continued, —

Here 's Decius Brutus, he shall tell them so.
    Decius. Cæsar, all hail ! Good morrow, worthy Cæsar :
I come to fetch you to the Senate-house.
    Cæsar. And you are come in very happy time
To bear my greeting to the senators,
And tell them that I will not come to-day.
Cannot is false ; and that I dare not, falser :
I *will* not come to-day. Tell them so, Decius.
    Calphurnia. Say, he is sick.
    Cæsar.   Shall Cæsar send a lie ?
Have I in conquest stretched mine arm so far,
To be afraid to tell gray-beards the truth ?
Decius, go tell them Cæsar will not come.
    Decius. Most mighty Cæsar, let me know some cause,
Lest I be laughed at when I tell them so.
    Cæsar. The cause is in my will ; I will not come :
That is enough to satisfy the senate ;
But, for your private satisfaction,
Because I love you, I will let you know.
Calphurnia here, my wife, stays me at home :
She dreamed [last] night she saw my statue,
Which, like a fountain with a hundred spouts,
Did run pure blood ; and many [stalwart] Romans

Came smiling, and did bathe their hands in it.
And these does she apply [as] warnings, and portents
Of evils imminent; and on her knee
Hath begged that I will stay at home to-day.
    Decius. This dream is all amiss interpreted :
It was a vision fair and fortunate.
Your statue spouting blood in many pipes,
In which so many smiling Romans bathed,
[Betokens] that from you great Rome shall suck
Reviving blood.
This by Calphurnia's dream is signified.
    Cæsar. And this way have you well expounded it.
    Decius. I have, when you have heard what I can say :
And know it now. The senate have concluded
To give this day a crown to mighty Cæsar :
If you shall send them word you will not come,
Their minds may change. Besides, it were a mock
Apt to be rendered, for some one to say,
" Break up the senate till another time,
When Cæsar's wife shall meet with better dreams."
If Cæsar hide himself, shall they not whisper,
" Lo ! Cæsar is afraid " ?
Pardon me, Cæsar; for my [interest
In your advancement] bids me tell you this.
    Cæsar. How foolish do your fears seem now, Calphurnia!
I am ashamèd I did yield to them. —
Give me my robe, for I will go : —
And look where Publius is come to fetch me.

This Publius was not one of the conspirators. He had only happened in ; but while Cæsar spoke six of the league came, according to agreement, to join Decius Brutus, and they entered the palace together, as if to escort the great Dictator to the Capitol.

While they were exchanging courteous greetings, Mark Antony also entered. Little dreaming of the wicked thoughts that filled the hearts of all but Publius and Antony, Cæsar offered the party wine, thanked them for their kindness, and invited them to go with him to the Senate. Brutus alone seemed struggling between his love and that which he believed to be a higher duty ; but they all left Cæsar's house together, and went toward the Senate-house.

There was in Rome a teacher of oratory, named Artemidorus. This man, being on intimate terms with some of the young men of the city, had learned something of the plans of the conspirators, and he determined to warn Cæsar, if possible. It was difficult to obtain a personal interview with him, especially on so public an occasion. It was customary, however, for those who had petitions to present to stand by the wayside and give them into the hand of Cæsar as he passed.

So into the street, near the Capitol, came Artemidorus, with this letter which he had carefully prepared, making it as brief and alarming as possible, hoping thus to catch the eye of Cæsar, and perhaps avert the impending calamity.   He read it over aloud as he walked : —

Cæsar, beware of Brutus ; take heed of Cassius ; come not near Casca ; have an eye to Cinna ; trust not Trebonius ; mark well Metellus Cimber ; Decius Brutus loves thee not ; thou hast wronged Caius Ligarius.   There is but one mind in all these men, and it is bent against Cæsar.   If thou be'st not immortal, look about you : [over-confidence opens the way for] conspiracy.   The mighty gods defend thee !
Thy lover,[a]   ARTEMIDORUS.

> Here will I stand till Cæsar pass along,
> And as a suitor will I give him this.
> My heart laments that virtue cannot live
> Out of the teeth of [envious rivalry].
> If thou read this, O Cæsar ! thou mayst live ;
> If not, the fates with traitors do contrive.

In another part of the same street Brutus lived, and Portia, the noble Roman matron, now stood before her house, marking every little occurrence, and listening for every sound, her faithful heart racked with anxiety at what might befall her beloved husband.   Brutus had, since their interview in the garden, unbosomed all his secrets to her.   And now she discovers that, though a glorious woman, she is still only a woman, and her heart is not strong enough for the burden it is called to bear.   She knows that very nearly at this moment the great transaction is to take place.   Her nerves are wrought to the intensest pitch of anxiety and suspense. Every breeze brings to her ears the fancied sounds of turmoil and affray.   She sends Lucius on fruitless errands to the Senate-house, forgetting that she has not even told him why he is to go.

> *Portia.* I pr'ythee, boy, run to the Senate-house :
> Stay not to answer me, but get thee gone.
> Why dost thou stay ?
> *Lucius.*   To know my errand, madam.
> *Portia.* I would have had thee there, and here again,
> Ere I can tell thee what thou shouldst do there. —
> [*To herself.*] O constancy ! be strong upon my side :
> Set a huge mountain 'tween my heart and tongue !
> I have a man's mind, but a woman's might.
> How hard it is for women to keep counsel !
> [*To* LUCIUS.] Art thou here yet ?
> *Lucius.*   Madam, what should I do ?

---

[a] In the language of Shakespeare's time, the word *lover* applied alike to both sexes.

Run to the Capitol, and nothing else,
And so return to you, and nothing else ?
Portia. Yes, bring me word, boy, if thy lord look well,
For he went sickly forth: and take good note,
What Cæsar doth, what suitors press to him.
Hark, boy ! what noise is that?
Lucius. I hear none, madam.
Portia.   Pr'ythee, listen well :
I heard a bustling rumor, like a fray,
And the wind brings it from the Capitol.
Lucius. Sooth, madam, I hear nothing.

Presently Artemidorus passes along, and Portia immediately accosts him, asking, —
Is Cæsar yet gone to the Capitol ?
Artemidorus. Madam, not yet : I go to take my stand,
To see him pass on to the Capitol.
Portia. Thou hast some suit to Cæsar, hast thou not ?
Artemidorus. That I have, lady ; if it will please Cæsar
To be so good to Cæsar as to hear me,
I shall beseech him to befriend himself.
Portia. Why, know'st thou any harm 's intended towards him ?
Artemidorus. None that I know will be, much that I fear.
Good morrow to you. — Here the street is narrow :
The throng that follows Cæsar at the heels,
Of senators, of prætors, common suitors,
Will crowd a feeble man almost to death.
I 'll get me to a [wider] place, and there
Speak to great Cæsar as he comes along.
Portia. I must go in. — [*To herself.*] Ah me, how weak a thing
The heart of woman is ! — O Brutus,
The Heavens speed thee in thine enterprise ! —
Sure, the boy heard me. — [*Aloud to* Lucius.] Brutus hath a suit
That Cæsar will not grant. — O, I grow faint. —
Run, Lucius, and commend me to my lord.
Say, — I am [well ; then] come to me again,
And bring me word what he doth say to thee.

VII.

 NEW and splendid building had been erected by Pompey for the use of the Senate. It was to be occupied for the first time on the ides of March, — the very day about which the soothsayer had given warning to Julius Cæsar.

In the interior of the building was a statue of Pompey. The day before the ides of March a tiny wren flew into the hall, with a spray of laurel in its beak; it was followed by several birds of prey, who tore the wren to pieces, the laurel falling from its beak to the foot of Pompey's statue. As the laurel was a favorite with Cæsar, many thought this incident boded ill for him.

Influenced by his ambition and the skillful arguments of the conspirators, Cæsar had dismissed his caution, and, in spite of his wife's entreaties, went, with Brutus, Cassius, and the rest, through the broad, open street to the Capitol. Crowds of people thronged the way. Among them were Artemidorus, with his letter, and the soothsayer who had warned Cæsar to beware of the ides of March. Bands of music were playing, and the trumpets gave a great flourish as Cæsar appeared.

Seeing the old soothsayer in the crowd, and remembering at once the warning he had given, Cæsar looked at him with a meaning glance as he passed, and said, " The ides of March are come ! " as if to show how false a prophet he considered the man to be.

" Ay, Cæsar," the soothsayer replied, " *but not gone !* "

Artemidorus now drew near with his letter, crying, " Hail, Cæsar ! read this paper." He knew it was the only opportunity he should have, and, thinking thus to influence Cæsar, he further urged that the matter of the letter nearly concerned the man to whom it was addressed. He could not have made a greater mistake, for Cæsar immediately replied, with a magnanimity worthy of his lofty name and station, "What touches us ourself shall be last served. Bring your petition to the Capitol." And before the friendly Artemidorus could return to the charge, he was hustled away in the crowd, and the procession moved on.

Popilius Lena, who knew nothing of the plans of the conspirators, parted from them at the entrance to the Capitol, saying he wished success to their enterprises. He referred to the petitions he supposed they were about to present; but their guilty consciences made them believe his words pointed to the conspiracy. " I fear," said Casca, " our purpose is discovered."

> *Brutus.* Look, how he makes to Cæsar: mark him.
> *Cassius.* Casca, be sudden, for we fear prevention. —
> Brutus, what shall be done ? If this be known,
> Cassius or Cæsar never shall [return],
> For I will slay myself.
> *Brutus.*   Cassius, be constant :
> Popilius Lena speaks not of our purposes ;
> For. look, he smiles, and Cæsar doth not change.
> *Cassius.* Trebonius knows his time ; for look you, Brutus,
> He draws Mark Antony out of the way.

The conspirators had a wholesome fear of the courage and energy of Antony, the faithful friend of Cæsar. It was, therefore, in accordance with a previous arrangement that Trebonius drew him aside under pretence of having something important to say to him, while the senators took their seats, and Cæsar, from the

consul's chair, made ready to hear the petitions and complaints that might be presented to him.

It had been agreed that Metellus Cimber, whose brother Publius had been
banished by Cæsar, should be the first to draw near to Cæsar, and plead for the
pardon and restoration of the exile.   Decius was to follow, and urge Cæsar to
grant the pardon.   Then Cassius and Brutus were to come, pressing the same
request.   At a given signal Casca was to draw near and strike the first blow, and
then all the others, without delay, were to follow Casca's example.

The law did not allow arms to be brought into the Senate-house, but each
senator was furnished with an iron stylus, an instrument for writing upon tablets
of wax, and in the cases which contained these the conspirators concealed their
daggers.

At last all is ready, and Cæsar speaks from the consul's seat : —

> What is now amiss,
> That Cæsar and his senate must redress ?
> *Metellus* [*kneeling*]. Most high, most mighty, and most [powerful] Cæsar,
> Metellus Cimber throws before thy seat
> An humble heart, —
>   *Cæsar.*   I must prevent thee. Cimber.
> Thy brother by decree is banishèd :
> If thou dost bend, and pray, and fawn for him,
> I spurn thee like a cur out of my way.
> Know, Cæsar doth not wrong ; nor without cause
> Will he be satisfied.
> *Metellus.* Is there no voice more worthy than my own,
> To sound more sweetly in great Cæsar's ear,
> For the [recalling] of my banished brother ?
> *Brutus.* I kiss thy hand, but not in flattery, Cæsar ;
> Desiring thee that Publius Cimber may
> Have an immediate freedom of repeal.[a]
> *Cæsar.* What, Brutus !
> *Cassius.*   Pardon, Cæsar ; Cæsar, pardon ;
> As low as to thy foot doth Cassius fall,
> To beg enfranchisement[b] for Publius Cimber.
> *Cæsar.* I could be well moved, if I were as you ;
> If I could pray to move, prayers would move me ;
> But I am constant as the northern star,
> Of whose true, fixed, and resting quality,
> There is no fellow in the firmament.
> [For] I was constant Cimber should be banished,
> And constant do remain to keep him so.

---

[a] Recall from banishment by *repealing* the decree that banished him.
[b] Restoration to his rights as a citizen.

Cinna. O Cæsar ! —
Cæsar.   Hence ! Wilt thou lift up Olympus ? ⁱ
Decius. Great Cæsar, —
Cæsar.   Doth not Brutus bootless kneel ? ⁱ
Casca. Speak, hands, for me.

They had crowded around Cæsar, clamoring and insisting, until he grew angry
and thrust them away. This gave them a pretext for the signal. Cimber pulled
Cæsar's robe from his shoulders, and Casca, raising his dagger, struck the first
blow, stabbing Cæsar in the back of the neck.

All was now terror and confusion. Cæsar was unarmed, but, having in his
hand his iron stylus, he thrust it through the arm of one of the conspirators. The
others closed round him. In every direction in which he looked he saw murderous weapons and more murderous faces. The senators rose in confusion.
One after another of the men who had sworn to kill Cæsar, stabbed him. Resist-
ance was indeed in vain, and when Brutus also, the dear friend of Cæsar, thrust a
dagger into his bosom. Cæsar drew his mantle over his face and ceased to
struggle, uttering, in deep reproach, the memorable words, — " AND THOU, TOO,
BRUTUS? Then fall, Cæsar ! " As Cæsar, pierced by twenty-three wounds, fell
dead at the very foot of the statue of his great rival Pompey, and the senators
and people were retiring in confusion, Cinna shouted, —

> Liberty ! Freedom ! Tyranny is dead ! —
> Run hence, proclaim, cry it about the streets.
>   *Casca.* Some to the common pulpits,ᵇ and cry out,
> " Liberty, freedom, and enfranchisement ! "
>   *Brutus.* People, and senators ! be not affrighted.
> Fly not ; stand still : — ambition's debt is paid.
>   *Casca.* Go to the pulpit, Brutus.
>   *Decius.*   And Cassius too.
>   *Brutus.* Where 's Publius ?
>   *Cinna.* Here, quite confounded with this mutiny.
>   *Metellus.* Stand fast together, lest some friend of Cæsar's
> Should chance —
>   *Brutus.* Talk not of standing.ᶜ — Publius, good cheer :

ⁱ *Wilt thou lift up Olympus?* — That is, you may as well attempt to move that mountain
as me. *Doth not Brutus bootless kneel?* — If my dear friend pleads in vain, do you suppose
I will listen to *you ?*

ᵇ *Common pulpits* — These were permanent stands, built of brick or stone, in the public
squares, from which the orators might address the people. They were called *rostra* — the
Latin word for *beaks* — because the two front corners were made ornamentally to imitate the
beaks, or bows, of two ships ; or, sometimes, were adorned with the brazen prows of vessels
captured in war.

ᶜ Brutus means, talk not of standing together, as though we were expecting an attack
from the people ; we are the *friends* of the people, and they know it well.

There is no harm intended to your person,
Nor to no Roman else ; so tell them, Publius.
   Casca. And leave us, Publius ; lest that the people,
Rushing on us, should do your age some mischief.
   Brutus. Do so : — and let no man abide [1] this deed,
But we, the doers.

At this point Trebonius entered again. He it was who had led aside that dangerous Mark Antony, and Cassius rather anxiously inquired, —

Where 's Antony ?
   Trebonius.   Fled to his house amazed.
Men, wives, and children, stare, cry out, and run,
As it were doomsday.
   Brutus.   Fates, we [await] your pleasures. —   .
That we shall die, we know ; 't is but the time,
And drawing days out, that men [care about].
   Casca. Why, he that cuts off twenty years of life
Cuts off so many years of fearing death.
   Brutus. Grant that, and then is death a benefit :
So are we Cæsar's friends, that have abridged
His time of fearing death. -- Stoop, Romans, stoop,
And let us bathe our hands in Cæsar's blood
Up to the elbows, and besmear our swords ;
Then walk we forth, even to the market-place,
And, waving our red weapons o'er our heads,
Let 's all cry, Peace ! Freedom ! and Liberty !
   Cassius. Stoop, then, and wash.
                   [Then] every man away :
Brutus shall lead ; and we will [follow him]
With the most boldest and best hearts of Rome.

Here a servant of Antony's entered, and knelt at the feet of Brutus.

   Brutus. Soft ! who comes here ? A friend of Antony's.
   Servant. Thus, Brutus, did my master bid me kneel ;
Thus did Mark Antony bid me fall down,
And, being prostrate, thus he bade me say :
Brutus is noble, wise, valiant, and honest ;
Cæsar was mighty, bold, royal, and loving :
Say, I love Brutus, and I honor him ;
Say, I feared Cæsar, honored him, and loved him.
If Brutus will vouchsafe that Antony
May safely come to him, and be [informed]
How Cæsar hath deserved to lie in death,

---

[1] Answer for.

Mark Antony will not love Cæsar dead
So well as Brutus living ; but will follow
The fortunes and affairs of noble Brutus
With all true faith. So says my master Antony.   [*Rising.*
Brutus. Thy master is a wise and valiant Roman:
I never thought him worse.
Tell him, so please him come unto this place,
He shall be satisfied ; and, by my honor,
Depart untouched.

After the servant had gone to fetch his master, Brutus began to congratulate his friends on this conciliatory message of Antony's. " I know," said he, " that we shall have him among our warmest friends."   But the keen-eyed Cassius, who knew the crooked ways of men so much better than the guileless, unsuspicious Brutus, shook his head. " I wish we may," he replied, " but I doubt it much." This was the second time the friends had differed about Antony. There would be one more, and afterwards it would appear that the policy of Brutus was the more upright, but that of Antony the shrewder — for worldly success.

While they discussed this question, Antony entered. Brutus gave him kindly greeting : —

Welcome, Mark Antony.
Antony. O mighty Cæsar ! dost thou lie so low ?
                                                        [*Kneeling over the body.*
Are all thy conquests, glories, triumphs, spoils,
Shrunk to this little measure ? Fare thee well. —   [*Rising.*
I know not, gentlemen, what you intend,
Who else must be let blood, who else is rank : *
If I myself, there is no hour so fit

---

* *Who else must be let blood* — In old-fashioned phrase, *to be let blood* was just *to be bled.*
Who else is rank ? — Rank is a word implying overgrowth. We use it of weeds. The meaning
is : Who else must fall ? Who else has grown too tall (as you say Cæsar has) ?

As Cæsar's death hour ; nor no instrument
Of half that worth as those your swords, made rich
With the most noble blood of all this world.
I do beseech ye, if you [mean me ill],
Now, whilst your purpled hands do reek and smoke,
Fulfil your pleasure.   Live a thousand years,
I shall not find myself so [fit] to die ;
No place will please me so, no means of death,
As here by Cæsar, and by you ª cut off,
The choice and master spirits of this age.
    Brutus. O Antony ! beg not your death of us.
Though now we must appear bloody and cruel,
As, by our hands, and this our present act,
You see we do ; yet see you but our hands,
And this the bleeding business they have done.
Our hearts you see not : they are pitiful :
And pity to the general wrong of Rome
Hath done this deed on Cæsar.   For your part,
To you our swords have leaden points, Mark Antony :
Our arms, in strength of manhood, and our hearts.
Of brothers' temper, do receive you in
With all kind love, good thoughts, and reverence.

Here Cassius interrupted by calling out to Antony an inducement which he judged would be of far more importance to that gentleman than either " love " or " reverence."   He assured him of a large share in the new distribution of offices : —

Your voice shall be as strong as any man's
In the disposing of new dignities.
    Brutus. Only be patient till we have appeased
The multitude, beside themselves with fear,
And then we will [declare to] you the cause,
Why I, that did love Cæsar when I struck him,
Have thus proceeded.
    Antony.   I doubt not of your wisdom.
Let each man [reach to] me his bloody hand :
                [*Takes their hands, one after another.*
First, Marcus Brutus, will I shake with you : —
Next, Caius Cassius, do I take your hand ; —
Now, Decius Brutus, yours ; — now yours, Metellus ; —
Yours, Cinna ; — and, my valiant Casca, yours ; —
Though last, not least in love, yours, good Trebonius.
Gentlemen all, — alas ! what shall I say ?

ª *By Cæsar and by you* — that is, *by* Cæsar's side and *by* your hands ; playing on the different meanings of the word, — a sort of serious pun that Shakespeare was fond of.

My credit now stands on such slippery ground,
That one of two bad ways you must [construe] me,
Either a coward or a flatterer. —
That I did love thee, Cæsar! O, 'tis true :   [*Turning to the body.*
If, then, thy spirit look upon us now,
Shall it not grieve thee dearer [1] than thy death,
To see thy Antony making his peace,
Shaking the bloody fingers of thy foes, —
Most noble ! — in the presence of thy corse ?
Had I as many eyes as thou hast wounds,
Weeping as fast as they stream forth thy blood,
It would become me better than to close
In terms of friendship with thine enemies.
Pardon me, Julius !   Here wast thou bayed, brave hart ;
Here didst thou fall ; and here thy hunters stand.
How like a deer, stricken by many princes,
Dost thou here lie !
    Cassius [impatiently]. Mark Antony, —
    Antony.   Pardon me, Caius Cassius :
The enemies [a] of Cæsar shall say this ;
Then, in a friend, it is cold modesty.
    Cassius. I blame you not for praising Cæsar so,
But what compáct mean you to have with us ?
Will you be [marked] in number of our friends,
Or shall we on, and not depend on you ?
    Antony. [For that] I took your hands ; but was, indeed,
Swayed from the point by looking down on Cæsar.
Friends am I with you all, and love you all,
Upon this hope, that you shall give me reasons
Why and wherein Cæsar was dangerous.
    Brutus. [Else would this be] a savage spectacle.
Our reasons are so full of good regard,
That were you, Antony, the son of Cæsar,
You should be satisfied.
    Antony.   That's all I seek :
And am moreover suitor, that I may
[Convey] his body to the market-place ; [b]
And in the pulpit, as becomes a friend,
Speak in the order of his funeral.
    Brutus. You shall, Mark Antony.
    Cassius.   Brutus, a word with you. —
[*Aside to* BRUTUS.] You know not what you do : do not consent

---

             [1] Worse.
    [a] That is, *even* the enemies of Cæsar, etc.
    [b] This was the Forum, the principal public square in Rome.

That Antony speak [at] his funeral.
Know you how much the people may be moved
By that which he will utter ?
   Brutus [aside to CASSIUS]. By your pardon ;
I will myself into the pulpit first,
And show the reason of our Cæsar's death :
What Antony shall speak, I will protest
He speaks by leave and by permission :
And that we are contented Cæsar shall
Have all due rites and lawful ceremonies.
It shall advantage more than do us wrong.
   Cassius [aside to BRUTUS]. I know not what may [chance] : I like
     it not.
   Brutus. Mark Antony, here, take you Cæsar's body.
You shall not in your funeral speech blame us,
But speak all good you can devise of Cæsar ;
And say, you do 't by our permission ;
Else shall you not have any hand at all
About his funeral : and you shall speak
In the same pulpit whereto I am going,
After my speech is ended.
   Antony.   Be it so ;
I do desire no more.
   Brutus. Prepare the body, then, and follow us.

Brutus and Cassius went away, leaving Antony with dead Cæsar. Then Antony's deep feeling and purpose were shown, as he turned to the cold body, pierced with so many wounds, — all that remained of one he had so loved and honored, — and, kneeling by its side, exclaimed, —

O, pardon me, thou bleeding piece of earth,
That I am meek and gentle with these butchers !
Thou art the ruins of the noblest man
That ever livèd in the tide of times.
Woe to the hand that shed this costly blood !
Over thy wounds now do I prophesy,
(Which, like dumb mouths, do ope their ruby lips,
To beg the voice and utterance of my tongue,)
A curse shall light upon the limbs of men ;
Domestic fury and fierce civil strife
Shall cumber all the parts of Italy :
Blood and destruction shall be so in use,
And dreadful objects so familiar,
That mothers shall but smile when they behold
Their infants quartered [by] the hands of war ;
And Cæsar's spirit, ranging for revenge,

Shall in these [regions], with a monarch's voice,
Cry " Havoc ! "[a] and let slip the dogs of war.
[So] this foul deed shall smell above the earth
With carrion men, groaning for burial.

While Antony, overwhelmed with grief, thus called down the vengeance of
the gods on the murderers of Cæsar, a servant entered with a message for Antony
from Octavius, the nephew of Julius Cæsar, who was already within seven leagues
of Rome. The terrible sight that met this servant's gaze drove his master's message from his mind : he could only stare, and weep, and cry, " O Cæsar ! "

Antony bade him post back with speed and tell Octavius what had chanced,
warning him that Rome was not yet safe for any relative of Cæsar's. Meanwhile
Antony prepared to move the bloody corse to the Forum, where he determined to
try in his funeral oration the real feeling of the people toward the men who had
wrought this cruel deed.

---

[a] *Havoc* was, in ancient times, the word used in battle as the signal for *no quarter.*

VIII.

RUTUS and Cassius and their confederates went from the Senate-chamber to the Forum with their bloody daggers naked in their hands. They did not try to hide their part in the dreadful deed, which they looked upon as necessary and glorious.

All the public squares were called forums, but one larger and more magnificent than the others was called The Forum. This noble square was surrounded by stately buildings, and adorned with statues and every style of ornamental sculpture. Among other features was the Rostra, a sort of pulpit, so named (as already explained) because it was adorned with brazen beaks of ships taken in battle.

Here Cæsar, who was a skillful and eloquent orator, had often addressed the people, and here Brutus went to speak to the excited crowd that thronged the squares and all the streets that centred toward this great gathering-place of Rome. The immense area seemed like a surging sea, composed of wild and eager faces, in which suppressed mischief was mingled with eager curiosity. The whole city was thunder-struck by the bloody deed, of which, in the first shock of its surprise, it hardly knew *what* to think. But Brutus was to explain, and " render reasons," — Brutus, the honest and simple-hearted, — and if Cæsar had been an idol of the people, so, in another way, had Brutus. Now it appeared how well the conspirators had calculated the value of the alliance, when they entangled his virtue in their scheme.

But still the noisy crowd demanded the explanation, and shouted tumultuously, —

We will be satisfied: Let us be satisfied.

Brutus. Then follow me, and give me audience, friends. —
Cassius, go you into the other street,

And part the numbers. —
Those that will hear me speak, let them stay here ;
Those that will follow Cassius, go with him ;
And public reasons shall be rendered
Of Cæsar's death.

So Cassius, followed by a throng of the citizens, went to another public place, and Brutus ascended the rostra. For a time the noise and confusion prevented his being heard, but at last silence was obtained, and in the clear, calm tones of reason the orator began : —

Romans, countrymen, and lovers ! hear me for my cause, and be silent that you may hear : believe me for mine honor, and have respect[a] to mine honor, that you may believe ; censure[1] me in your wisdom, and awake your senses that you may the better judge. If there be any in this assembly, [even] any dear friend of Cæsar's, to him I say, that Brutus' love to Cæsar was no less than his. If, then, that friend demand, why Brutus rose against Cæsar ? this is my answer, — not that I loved Cæsar less, but that I loved Rome more [than he]. Had you rather Cæsar were living, and die all slaves, than that Cæsar were dead, to live all free men ? As Cæsar loved me, I weep for him ; as he was fortunate, I rejoice at it ; as he was valiant, I honor him ; but, as he was ambitious, I slew him. There is tears for his love ; joy for his fortune ; honor for his valor ; and death for his ambition. Who is here so base, that would be a bondman ? If any, speak ; for him have I offended. Who is here so rude,[b] that would not be a Roman ? If any, speak ; for him have I offended. Who is here so vile, that will not love his country ? If any, speak ; for him have I offended. I pause for a reply.

Then the whole multitude shouted, " None, Brutus, none ! "

Brutus. Then, none have I offended. I have done no more to Cæsar, than you shall do to Brutus. The [reason] of his death is enrolled in the Capitol ; his glory not extenuated,[2] wherein he was worthy, nor his offences enforced,[3] for which he suffered death. Here comes his body, mourned by Mark Antony : who, though he had no hand in his death, shall receive the benefit of his dying, a place in the commonwealth[e] ; as which of you shall not? With this I depart ; that, as I slew my best lover for the good of Rome, I have the same dagger for myself, when it shall please my country to need my death.

Now this brief address, with its cold, short sentences, was all reasoning : Brutus disdained to arouse the passions of the crowd. He really excited very

---

¹ Judge.   ² Belittled.   ³ Insisted upon.
ᵃ That is, have *reference* to, or *consider*, mine honor.
ᵇ That is, Who of you is such a barbarian as not to be proud of his Roman citizenship?
ᵉ Brutus meant that, while the tyrant lived, no citizen had really a place in the commonwealth, but in his death they all alike received the benefit of a restoration of their privileges as freemen.

little enthusiasm among them for his ideal Justice and Liberty ; but there he stood himself, and that, at first, was satisfactory. The people must have a Cæsar ; and if the old Cæsar was dead, let Brutus be a new one. So they burst out with various cries : —

" Bring him in triumph home unto his house," shouted one.

" Give him a statue with his ancestors ! " exclaimed another.

" Let *him* be Cæsar ! " cried a third.

And so they went on shouting and demanding that Brutus should take the place of the murdered Dictator, until at last Brutus with great difficulty got them quieted to listen to the funeral oration of Mark Antony.   He said, —

> Good countrymen, let me depart alone ;
> And, for my sake, stay here with Antony :
> Do grace to Cæsar's corpse, and grace his speech
> Tending to Cæsar's glories, which Mark Antony,
> By our permission, is allowed to make.
> I do entreat you, not a man depart,
> Save I alone, till Antony have spoke.

And then, satisfied that he had settled the question with his countrymen once for all, the honest Brutus delicately withdrew, that he might not embarrass Antony.

The sombre group — a few bearers, among whom were Antony himself and the servant of Octavius, carrying upon a bier a prostrate and rigid form, covered with a blood-stained pall — entered the Forum, the people silently making way for the poor procession to pass.   They set down their gloomy burden directly before the rostra, and Antony ascended, and stood before the mighty multitude. A tremendous task was his, but he was equal to it.   O, if Brutus had only per- mitted Cassius to make short work of this shrewd and brilliant politician, and lay him beside his imperial master ; or if he had refused him this golden oppor- tunity, as Cassius had counselled, how different might have been the result !   But it is better so : a revolution failed which ought never to have succeeded, especially by such means, and Brutus remains — a noble picture — the just, magnanimous, but unskillful patriot that history and Shakespeare have presented to us.

But now Antony addressed himself to his work.   His audience were all against him ; impatient at the very idea of any praise of Cæsar, and ready to tear him to pieces if he should speak a word in dispraise of Brutus.   But then he knew what sort of stuff crowds were made of, and he had the advantage of speaking last. Another of poor Brutus's mistakes : Antony might speak, but Brutus must have the advantage and the honor of speaking *first !*   Any American boy in a school debating-society could have taught him better than that.   But to separate, in the people's minds, the scheming Cassius, the bitter Casca, the ungrateful Decius, the proud Metellus, and the other conspirators — all rich patricians, and naturally more or less unpopular — from the beloved Brutus, whom they had set up in front as a shield, and so deprive them of the advantage of their cunning, — how was this to be done? He did not try to do it: on the contrary, he put them all in together. When he praised Brutus, he praised the others also. If he said "Brutus is an honorable man," he always added, "and so is Cassius, and so is Casca; so are they all, all honorable men;" till at last the crowd, not fancying this general praise, began to suspect they were all *dis*honorable men together, and Brutus, like another "dog 'Tray," was made to suffer for the company he was in.

Antony stood silent before the multitude, and waited for the tumult to cease. At length he got an opportunity to express a word of thanks to Brutus for his courtesy. This was the signal for another uproar. The crowd had caught the name, and they broke out on all sides with, "What's that?" and "What is he saying about Brutus?" But the explanation was passed along from one to another, until at last they settled down again, but not without many a growl of "'T were best he speak no harm of Brutus here," and "This Cæsar was a tyrant, and Rome is well rid of him; *that*'s·clear enough."

Again Antony pleaded for order and attention. "Friends, Romans, countrymen, pray give me a hearing." Then they were quiet, and he went on : —

> I come to bury Cæsar, not to praise him.
> The evil that men do lives after them,
> The good is oft interrèd with their bones :
> So let it be with Cæsar. The noble Brutus
> Hath told you, Cæsar was ambitious ;
> If it were so, it was a grievous fault,
> And grievously hath Cæsar answered it.
> Here, under leave of Brutus and the rest,
> (For Brutus is an honorable man ;
> So are they all, all honorable men,)
> Come I to speak [at] Cæsar's funeral.
> He was my friend, faithful and just to me :
> But Brutus says, he was ambitious :
> And Brutus is an honorable man.
> He hath brought many captives home to Rome,
> Whose ransoms did the general coffers fill.
> Did this in Cæsar seem ambitious ?
> When that the poor have cried, Cæsar hath wept;
> Ambition should be made of sterner stuff :
> Yet Brutus says, he was ambitious ;
> And Brutus is an honorable man.
> You all did see, that on the Lupercal
> I thrice presented him a kingly crown,
> Which he did thrice refuse. Was this ambition ?
> Yet Brutus says, he was ambitious ;

> And, sure, he is an honorable man.
> I speak not to disprove what Brutus spoke,
> But here I am to speak what *I* do know.
> You all did love him once, not without cause :
> What cause withholds you, then, to mourn for him ?
> O judgment ! thou art fled to brutish beasts,
> And men have lost their reason.

Here, partly to try the effect of what he had already said, and partly from real feeling, he paused as if overcome, and turned aside, saying,—

> Bear with me ;
> My heart is in the coffin there with Cæsar,
> And I must pause till it come back to me.

Already a change begins to appear in the spirit of his hearers.

"Methinks there is much reason in what he says," remarks one.

"When you come to think it over," says another, "Cæsar has n't been treated exactly right."

"Any way," added a third, "it is certain he was not ambitious, because you see he would n't take the crown."

"Well, if it turns out so," growled a sturdy fellow, "*some* folks will catch it."

"Poor Antony ! see how bad he feels. There 's not a nobler man in Rome than Antony."

But upon this there was a cry on every side of "Hush ! hush ! he 's beginning again." And Antony resumed : —

> But yesterday the word of Cæsar might
> Have stood against the world : now lies he there,
> And none so poor to do him reverence.
> O masters ! if I were disposed to stir
> Your hearts and minds to mutiny and rage,
> I should do Brutus wrong, and Cassius wrong,
> Who, you all know, are honorable men.
> I will not do them wrong : I rather choose
> To wrong the dead, to wrong myself, and you,
> Than I will wrong such honorable men.
> But here 's a parchment with the seal of Cæsar :
> I found it in his closet, — 't is his will :
> Let but the [people] hear this testament,
> (Which, pardon me, I do not mean to read,)
> And they would go and kiss dead Cæsar's wounds,
> And dip their napkins[1] in his sacred blood :

---

[1] Handkerchiefs.

Yea, beg a hair of him for memory,
And, dying, mention it within their wills,
Bequeathing it, as a rich legacy,
Unto their issue.

Here a single clear voice rang out in the crowd : " We 'll hear that will. Read
it, Mark Antony ! " and at once the vast assembly broke out in response, " The
will, the will ! we will hear Cæsar's will ! "

> *Antony.* Have patience, gentle friends ; I must not read it :
> It is not meet you know how Cæsar loved you.
> You are not wood, you are not stones. but men,
> And, being men, hearing the will of Cæsar,
> It will inflame you, it will make you mad.
> 'T is good you know not that you are his heirs ;
> For if you should, O, what would come of it ?

Of course they shouted all the more, " Read the will ! we 'll hear it, Antony ;
you *shall* read us the will : Cæsar's will ! "

> *Antony.* Will you be patient ? Will you stay awhile ?
> I have o'ershot myself to tell you of it.
> I fear I wrong the honorable men
> Whose daggers have stabbed Cæsar : I do fear it.

But now the fury of the people knew no bounds : " They were traitors : honorable men, indeed ! " they fairly yelled. " The will ! the testament ! " " They
were villains, murderers ! The will ! read the will ! "

> *Antony.* You will compel me, then, to read the will ?
> Then, make a ring about the corpse of Cæsar,
> And let me show you him that made the will.
> Shall I descend ? and will you give me leave ?

" Come down ! You shall have leave ! " burst forth the excited voices.
" Stand from the hearse ; stand from the body." " Room for Antony ; — most
noble Antony ! " " Stand back ! room ! bear back ! " When they were again
quiet, Antony exposed to view the very mantle (or toga) Cæsar had on when he
was killed, and which now served for a pall. It was all cut and torn in the
scuffle, and stained with blood ; and after a skillful allusion to one of Cæsar's
most famous victories, he began to point out the cuts made by the several daggers. He said, —

> If you have tears, prepare to shed them now.
> You all do know this mantle : I remember
> The first time ever Cæsar put it on ;

'T was on a summer's evening, in his tent,
That day he overcame the Nervii.
Look ! in this place, ran Cassius' dagger through :
See, what a rent the envious Casca made :
Through this the well-belovèd Brutus stabbed ;
And as he plucked his cursèd steel away,
Mark how the blood of Cæsar followed it.
For Brutus, as you know, was Cæsar's angel :
Judge, O you gods, how dearly Cæsar loved him !
This was the most unkindest cut of all ;
For when the noble Cæsar saw him stab,
Ingratitude, more strong than traitors' arms.
Quite vanquished him : then burst his mighty heart :
And in his mantle muffling up his face,
Even at the base of Pompey's statue,
Which all the while ran blood, great Cæsar fell.
O, what a fall was there. my countrymen !
Then I, and you, and all of us fell down,

Whilst bloody treason flourished over us.
O, now you weep ; and. I perceive, you feel
The dint of pity : these are gracious drops.
Kind souls ! what, weep you, when you but behold
Our Cæsar's vesture wounded ? Look you here,
Here is himself, marred, as you see, [by] traitors.

At this point he tore the mantle from the prostrate form before him, and there lay the body of Cæsar, all mangled and bleeding, its three-and-twenty wounds gaping as if dumbly to ask for pity and for vengeance. Then broke from the great crowd a tempest of wailing cries and sobs, which gradually grew to yells of fury. " O piteous spectacle ! "   " O most bloody sight ! "   " O noble Cæsar ! " " O traitors ! villains ! " " We will be revenged ! Revenge ! — about, — seek, — burn, — fire, — kill ! Let not a traitor live ! "

They were rushing forth in all directions to their work of destruction, when Antony called out, " Stay, countrymen ! "   A voice cried, " Hear the most noble Antony ! " They all responded, " We 'll hear him — we 'll follow him — we 'll die with him ! " Then resumed the orator, —

> Good friends, sweet friends, let me not stir you up
> To such a sudden flood of mutiny.
> They that have done this deed are honorable :
> What private griefs they have, alas ! I know not,
> That made them do it : they are wise and honorable,
> And will, no doubt, with reasons answer you.
> I come not, friends, to steal away your hearts :
> I am no orator, as Brutus is,²
> But, as you know me all, a plain blunt man,
> That love my friend ; and that they know full well
> That gave me public leave to speak of him.
> For I have neither wit,¹ nor words, nor worth,
> Action, nor utterance, nor the power of speech,
> To stir men's blood : I only speak right on ;
> I tell you that which you yourselves do know,
> Show you sweet Cæsar's wounds, poor, poor dumb mouths,
> And bid them speak for me : but were I Brutus,
> And Brutus Antony, *there* were an Antony
> Would ruffle up your spirits, and put a tongue
> In every wound of Cæsar, that should move
> The stones of Rome to rise and mutiny.

They shouted in reply, " We 'll mutiny. We 'll burn the house of Brutus." " Away then ! " cried a voice ; " come, seek the conspirators."

---

¹ Wisdom.
² This was simply false : Antony *was* an orator, and Brutus was only a reasoner.

Antony. Yet hear me, countrymen; yet hear me speak.
All. Peace, ho! Hear Antony ; most noble Antony.
Antony. Why, friends, you go to do you know not what.
Wherein hath Cæsar thus deserved your loves ?
Alas ! you know not : — I must tell you, then.
You have forgot the will I told you of.
All. Most true ; — the will : — let 's stay, and hear the will.
Antony. Here is the will, and under Cæsar's seal.
To every Roman citizen he gives,
To every [separate] man, seventy-five drachmas.*
Citizens. Most noble Cæsar ! — we 'll revenge his death.
Antony. Hear me with patience.
All. [Hush ! Silence there !]
Antony. Moreover, he hath left you all his walks,
His private arbors, and new-planted [gardens]
On this side Tiber : he hath left them you,
And to your heirs forever ; common pleasures,
To walk abroad, and recreate yourselves.
Here was a Cæsar! when comes such another ?
Citizens. Never, never. — Come, away, away !
We 'll burn his body in the holy place,
And with the brands fire the traitors' houses.
Take up the body.
    Voices. Go, fetch fire ! — Pluck down benches ! — Pluck down forms, windows,
anything !

The crowd, now grown to a mob, could be restrained no longer. They
caught up the bier with Cæsar's body, and in a whirlwind of rage swept yelling
through the Forum, and left the great square silent. Then Antony, with exultation
and triumph in his eyes, came down from the rostra, and as he listened to
the receding shouts of the infuriated multitude dispersing on their work of death,
exclaimed, —
        Now let it work. Mischief, thou art afoot:
        Take thou what course thou wilt!

The citizens hurried on with tears and curses, bearing the mangled body.
Some proposed to carry it to the Temple of Jupiter, on the Capitol Hill, and
burn it there before the very eyes of the assassins ; others, to use the Senate-house
itself as the funeral pyre of the people's friend. But as they were passing through
the square, two young, unknown soldiers (perhaps to spare the city a general
conflagration) rushed into the midst of the crowd with torches, set fire to the
trappings of the bier, and then immediately disappeared. The people remem-

---

* The *drachma* was a Greek coin worth about eighteen and a half cents. Cæsar left to
each Roman citizen about fourteen dollars, — a sum, however, worth a great deal more than
the same amount at the present day.

bered that Castor and Pollux, two deities, were said to have interfered more than once before to save the republic, and now they were more than ever sure they were right, because they had the approval of the gods.

The wildest excitement followed. A funeral pile was made on the spot, with everything that came to hand, — fagots, benches, window-frames, the banners and awnings, and general decorations. Everybody in the crowd rushed to add a chip or splinter. The soldiers threw in their spears and lances; the musicians, their instruments. The trappings of the horses, the clothing of the men, the necklaces and scarfs of the women, the very toys and playthings of the children, — everything, fit or unfit, was added to the pile, and increased the flame. On the pile so composed the body of Cæsar was reduced to ashes; and these were afterwards collected with affection and reverence, and placed in the tomb of the Cæsars, in the Field of Mars.

The populace, roused to a frenzy against all who had taken part in the conspiracy, endeavored to fire the houses of Brutus and Cassius, but were finally restrained, though with great difficulty, by the civil authorities. How completely the Roman people had lost their reason may appear from a single incident. In the square they met an unfortunate poet, named Cinna, whose worst crime was the making of bad verses. He certainly had had nothing to do with the conspiracy; but because he had the same name as another man who was a conspirator, the furious mob cut off his head, and carried it through the streets on a pike.

IX.

HEN the people were in such a mood, Rome was no place for the conspirators. Antony, passing from the Forum after his triumph, was met by the servant of Octavius, and informed that that young gentleman and Lepidus, the commander of the Roman cavalry, were already in the city, at the house of Cæsar, and that Brutus, Cassius, and the other conspirators had ridden like madmen through the gates of Rome.

Then these three men (the Triumvirate, as they were afterwards called) — Octavius Cæsar, the grand-nephew, adopted son, and heir of the great Julius ; Mark Antony, the dissolute but brilliant soldier, true friend and lover of Cæsar ; and Lepidus, the master of Cæsar's horse, who was to have succeeded him as governor of Gaul — met together to divide between them the empire of the world. Antony at first underrated Octavius, on account of his youth ; but he soon discovered the power and influence of the young man who was to become the Emperor Augustus. Lepidus he always despised as being, though a good soldier, a man of small abilities, " fit to be sent on errands," or to share the odium of the bloody deeds of the Triumvirate. " We lay these honors on the man," he said, " as we load an ass with gold,

> And, having brought our treasure where we will,
> Then take we down his load, and turn him off,
> Like to the empty ass, to shake his ears,
> And graze on commons.

Do not talk of him but as a property."

But these men had none of the scruples that had prevented Brutus from spilling a drop of blood more than was necessary to free Rome from a dreaded danger. They made a list of all that were even suspected of opposition to Cæsar, all of any rank or position who had even been lukewarm in his cause, and killed them wherever they could be found. This was done in a way as cold-blooded as the deed itself was cruel. They met at the house of Antony, and there determined upon the names of those who it was decided should die ; and even their desire to avenge the death of Cæsar was swallowed up in their eagerness to be rid of their own personal enemies. To reach this end, they arranged with one another : Octavius consented to give up to Antony's revenge the great orator Cicero, who was his enemy, and had written and spoken bitterly against him, on condition that Antony should sacrifice his uncle Lucius Cæsar, who was the enemy of Octavius ; while Lepidus consented to the death of his own brother Paulus, at the demand of the other two. They seemed to vie with each other in eagerness to "prick," or mark for slaughter, their relatives and friends.

Antony. These many then shall die ; their names are pricked.
Octavius. Your brother too must die : consent you, Lepidus ?
Lepidus. I do consent —
Octavius.   Prick him down, Antony.
Lepidus. Upon condition Publius shall not live,
Who is your sister's son, Mark Antony.
Antony. He shall not live : look, with a spot I damn him.

More than three hundred of the leading citizens of Rome fell by this bloody proscription.

The fugitive conspirators were scattered over the empire. Brutus and Cassius, however, had bent all their energies to the raising of an army, and it was needful for the Triumvirate to form a strong alliance, if they hoped to hold securely all they had won at such a fearful cost. By their abuse of power they soon made themselves very odious at Rome, and were not at peace among themselves. Each was jealous and envious of the others. Some sort of division, however, was at last made of the army and treasure. Lepidus remained at Rome to take care of public affairs, while Antony and Octavius Cæsar went to Macedonia to meet the two leading tyrant-killers (as they would fain be called), and the force they had amassed.

These two had fled from Italy secretly and alone, without money, without arms, without a ship, a soldier, or a place of refuge ; but the ability of Cassius and the virtue of Brutus had drawn many to their standards, and they were now in condition to contend for the empire of Italy. Cassius was more grasping in his nature than Brutus, who seemed to care little for wealth, save to advance the cause and pay his soldiers, to whom he was always kind and generous. Cassius demanded heavy ransoms for his prisoners, and laid heavy fines on conquered cities, while Brutus released thousands without ransom or condition. This course greatly increased the popularity of Brutus, and city after city surrendered to him without a struggle.

Cassius had gotten vast treasure, some of which Brutus wished to borrow in order to pay his soldiers. Cassius sent him a small amount, but so reluctantly that, to the sensitive nature of Brutus, the consent differed little from a denial. Brutus had also condemned and disgraced an officer of Cassius's command for taking bribes. From these causes a coolness had arisen between the two friends which Brutus felt keenly. The very courtesies which Cassius used toward him, in place of the old familiar ways, were in his eyes evidence of cooling friendship.

> " When love begins to sicken and decay,
> It useth an enforcèd ceremony."

Brutus, however, was unwilling to have the soldiers suspect a quarrel between their generals ; and when, on a certain occasion, Cassius came to the camp of Brutus, and began to complain, —

> " Most noble brother, you have done me wrong, — "

he commanded the soldiers and servants to withdraw. " Cassius," he said, " let us not wrangle here before the eyes of our armies, which should perceive nothing but love between us ; here in my tent you shall speak freely all your griefs, and I will give you audience."

Then the forces of both generals were removed to a distance, and guards were set to prevent all approach to the tent of Brutus ; and Cassius thus freely poured out his feelings : —

> That you have wronged me doth appear in this :
> You have condemned and noted [1] Lucius Pella
> For taking bribes here of the Sardians ;
> Wherein my letters, praying on his side,
> Because I knew the man, were slighted off.

---

[1] Marked, disgraced.

Brutus. You wronged yourself to write in such a case.

Cassius. In such a time as this, it is not meet

That every nice [1] offence should bear its comment.

Brutus. Let me tell you, Cassius, you yourself

Are much condemned to have an itching palm ;

To sell and mart [2] your offices for gold

To undeservers.

Cassius.　　　I an itching palm ?

You know that you are Brutus that speak this,

Or, by the gods, this speech were else your last.

Brutus. The name of Cassius honors this corruption.

And chastisement does therefore hide its head.

Cassius. Chastisement !

Brutus. Remember March, the ides of March remember.

Did not great Julius bleed for justice' sake ?

What villain [a] touched his body, that did stab,

And not for justice ?　What! shall one of us,

That struck the foremost man of all this world,

But for supporting robbers, [b] shall we now

Contaminate our fingers with base bribes,

And sell the mighty space of our large honors

For so much trash as may be graspèd thus ?

I had rather be a dog, and bay [3] the moon,

Than such a Roman.

Cassius.　　　Brutus, bay not me,

I 'll not endure it : you forget yourself,

To hedge me in.　I am a soldier, I,

Older in practice, abler than yourself

To make conditions. [c]

Brutus.　　　[Come, come] ; you are not, Cassius.

Cassius. I am.

Brutus. I say, you are not.

Cassius. Urge me no more, I shall forget myself :

Have mind upon your health ; tempt me no farther.

Brutus. Away, slight man !

Cassius. Is 't possible ?

Brutus.　　　Hear me, for I will speak.

Must I give way and room to your rash choler ?

Shall I be frighted, when a madman stares ?

---

[1] Petty.　　　　　[2] Trade.　　　　　[3] Bark at.

　[a] That is, Who of all those who touched his body was such a villain as to stab for anything else than justice ?

　[b] The Roman empire was full of office-holders who in various ways robbed and despoiled the people of the provinces they were sent to govern.　Cæsar did not soil his own fingers with such crimes, but it was charged that he sustained and favored those who did.

　[c] *To make conditions* — That is, settlements of all kinds, involving questions of money.

Cassius. O ye gods ! ye gods ! Must I endure all this ?
Brutus. All this ? ay, more. Fret, till your proud heart break ;
Go, show your slaves how choleric you are,
And make your bondmen tremble. Must I budge ? ᵃ
Must I observe ᵃ you ? Must I stand and crouch
Under your testy humor ? By the gods,
You shall digest the venom of your spleen,ᵇ
Though it do split you ; for, from this day forth,
I 'll use you for my mirth, yea, for my laughter,
When you are waspish.
    Cassius.   Is it come to this ?
Brutus. You say, you are a better soldier :
Let it appear so ; make your vaunting true,
And it shall please me well. For mine own part,
I shall be glad to learn of abler men.
    Cassius. You wrong me every way ; you wrong me, Brutus ;
I said, an older soldier, not a better :
Did I say *better ?*
    Brutus.   If you did, I care not.
Cassius. When Cæsar lived, he durst not thus have moved me.
Brutus. Peace. peace ! you durst not so have tempted him.
Cassius. I durst not ?
Brutus. No.
Cassius. What ! durst not tempt him ?
    Brutus.   For your life you durst not.
Cassius. Do not presume too much upon my love ;
I may do that I shall be sorry for.
    Brutus. You *have* done that you *should* be sorry for.
There is no terror. Cassius, in your threats,
For I am armed so strong in honesty,
That they pass by me as the idle wind,
Which I [regard] not. I did send to you
For certain sums of gold, which you denied me ;
For I can raise no money by vile means :
By heaven, I had rather coin my heart,
And drop my blood for drachmas, than to wring
From the hard hands of peasants their vile trash,
By any indirection.¹ I did send
To you for gold to pay my legions,
Which you denied me : was that done like Cassius ?
Should I have answered Caius Cassius so ?
When Marcus Brutus grows so covetous,

---

¹ Dishonest practice.
ᵃ That is, Must I give way to *you ?* Must I pay you reverential attention?
ᵇ The *spleen* used to be regarded as the seat of every sudden passion. This means, You
shall swallow the poison of your own anger.

To lock such rascal counters [a] from his friends,
Be ready, gods, with all your thunderbolts
Dash him to pieces !
 Cassius.   I denied you not.
 Brutus. You did.
 Cassius..   I did not : he was but a fool,
That brought my answer back. — Brutus hath [broke] my heart :
A friend should bear his friend's infirmities,
But Brutus makes mine greater than they are.
 Brutus. I do not, till you practise them on me.
 Cassius. You love me not.
 Brutus.   I do not like your. faults.
 Cassius. A friendly eye could never see such faults.
 Brutus. A flatterer's would not, though they did appear
As huge as high Olympus.
 Cassius. Come, Antony, and young Octavius, come,
Revenge yourselves alone on Cassius,
For Cassius is aweary of the world :
Hated by one he loves : braved by his brother ;
Checked like a bondman ; all his faults observed,
Set in a note-book, learned, and conned by rote,
To cast into my teeth. O, I could weep
My spirit from mine eyes ! — There is my dagger,
And here my naked breast ; within, a heart
Dearer than Plutus'[b] mine, richer than gold :
If that thou be'st a Roman. take it forth ;
I, that denied thee gold. will give my heart.
Strike, as thou didst at Cæsar : for I know,
When thou didst hate him worst, thou lovedst him better
Than ever thou lovedst Cassius.
 Brutus.   Sheathe your dagger.
Be angry when you will, it shall have scope :
Do what you will, dishonor shall be humor.[c]
O Cassius ! you are yokèd with a lamb,
That carries anger as the flint bears fire,[d]
Who, much enforcèd, shows a hasty spark,
And straight is cold again.
 Cassius.   Hath Cassius lived

---

 [a] *Rascal counters* — It is about the same as if Brutus had said "dirty money "; though counters were not money at all, but only round pieces of metal used in calculating.
 [b] Plutus was the god of riches.
 [c] That is, Whatever indignity you may hereafter offer me I will regard but as the whim of the moment.
 [d] In Shakespeare's time, the fire that was produced by the striking of the steel against the flint was supposed to be *struck out of the stone*, instead of from the metal, as we now know it to be.

To be but mirth and laughter to his Brutus,
When grief and blood ill-tempered vexeth him?
Brutus. When I spoke that, I was ill-tempered too.
Cassius. Do you confess so much? Give me your hand.
Brutus. And my heart too.
Cassius.   O Brutus ! —
Brutus.   What 's the matter?
Cassius. Have you not love enough to bear with me,
When that rash [temper] which my mother gave me
Makes me forgetful?
Brutus.   Yes, Cassius ; and henceforth,
When you are over-earnest with your Brutus,
He 'll think your mother chides, and leave you so.

After having given orders for the army to be encamped for the night, and for a council of officers to come to his tent, Brutus called to Lucius to bring a bowl of wine. Then Cassius said, —

I did not think you could have been so angry.
Brutus. O Cassius, I am sick of many griefs.
Cassius. Of your philosophy you make no use
If you give [way] to accidental evils.[a]
Brutus. No man bears sorrow better. Portia is dead.
Cassius. Ha ! Portia !
Brutus. She is dead.
Cassius. How 'scaped I killing. when I crossed you so ?
O insupportable and touching loss ! —
Upon what sickness?
Brutus.   Impatience of my absence,
And grief that young Octavius with Mark Antony
Have made themselves so strong ; — for with her death
That tidings came ; — with this she fell distract,[b]
And, her attendants absent, swallowed fire.
Cassius. And died so ?
Brutus. Even so.
Cassius. O ye immortal gods !
Brutus. Speak no more of her.

Then Brutus took a bowl of wine, and, drinking, said, —

In this I bury all unkindness, Cassius.
Cassius. My heart is thirsty for that noble pledge. —

---

[a] That is, to evils that cannot be avoided.
[b] Distracted ; that is, became crazed.

Fill, Lucius, till the wine o'erswell the cup ;
I cannot drink too much of Brutus' love.

Titinius and Messala, two officers of the army, now entered the tent to attend the council of war.   Letters from Rome, received by various persons, were compared, and found to confirm the rumors of Portia's death and the troubled state of affairs at home.   Cicero had been put to death, and many senators beside, by the arbitrary command of the Triumvirate.   Octavius and Antony with a mighty army — the very army with which Cæsar conquered Gaul — were marching down toward Philippi to avenge their murdered general.   Brutus was for going at once to meet them.   He inquired of Cassius, —

What do you think
Of marching to Philippi presently?
Cassius. I do not think it good.
Brutus.   Your reason?
Cassius.   This it is.
'T is better that the enemy seek us :
So shall he waste his means, weary his soldiers,
Doing himself [a harm] ; whilst we, lying still,
Are full of rest, defence, and nimbleness.
    Brutus. Good reasons must, of force, give place to better.
The people 'twixt Philippi and this ground
Do stand but in a forced affection,
For they have grudged us contribution :
The enemy, marching along by* them,
By* them shall make a fuller number up,
Come on refreshed, new-hearted, and encouraged ;

---

* *By* is here used in two senses. The meaning of the passage is clear enough : The enemy, marching *alongside of* these towns, *by means of* their inhabitants shall become stronger in numbers. See note on page 188 ("*By* Cæsar and *by* you cut off ").

From which advantage we shall cut him off,
If at Philippi we do face him there,
These people at our back.
  Cassius.   Hear me, good brother.
  Brutus. Under your pardon.ᵃ — You must note beside,
That we have tried the utmost of our friends.
Our legions are brimfull, our cause is ripe :
The enemy increaseth every day ;
We, at the height, are ready to decline.
There is a tide in the affairs of men,
Which, taken at the flood, leads on to fortune.
On such a full sea are we now afloat,
And we must take the current when it serves,
Or lose our ventures.ᵇ
  Cassius.   Then, with your will,ᶜ go on :
We will ourselves [march on], and meet them at Philippi.

Thus once again, under the strong personal influence of Brutus, Cassius yields his better judgment ; and the generals part, to take some rest before the dawning of that morrow on whose events the fate of the world depends. They parted in friendship. The old confidence and love had returned in more than its original force, and they were happy.

" Noble, noble Cassius," said Brutus, " good night, and good repose."

  Cassius.   O my dear brother !
This was an ill beginning of the night.
Never come such division 'tween our souls !
Let it not, Brutus.
  Brutus.   Everything is well.
  Cassius. Good night, my lord.
  Brutus.   Good night, good brother.

The other officers bid " lord Brutus " farewell, and in another moment all is quiet. Then the general calls the drowsy Lucius to bring his dressing-gown. When the lad enters with the gown, Brutus asks him, —

  Where is thy instrument ?
  Lucius. Here in the tent.
  Brutus.   What ! thou speak'st drowsily ?
  Poor [boy], I blame thee not ; thou art o'er-watched.¹

---

¹ Worn out with watching.
ᵃ That is, *by your leave :* let *me* speak.
ᵇ *Ventures* is whatever is put on board ship in hope of profit.
ᶜ *With your will* — As you say.

Call Claudius, and some other of my men ;
I 'll have them sleep on cushions in my tent.
Lucius. Varro, and Claudius !

Enter VARRO *and* CLAUDIUS.

Varro. Calls my lord?
Brutus. I pray you, sirs, lie in my tent, and sleep :
It may be, I shall [call] you by and by.
On business to my brother Cassius.
Varro. So please you, we will stand, and watch your pleasure.
Brutus. I will not have it so ; lie down, good sirs :
It may be, I shall otherwise bethink me.   [*Servants lie down.*
Look, Lucius, here 's the book I sought for so :
I put it in the pocket of my gown.
Lucius. I was sure your lordship did not give it me.
Brutus. Bear with me, good boy, I am much forgetful.
Canst thou hold up thy heavy eyes awhile,
And touch thy instrument a strain or two ?
Lucius. Ay, my lord, if it please you.
Brutus.   It does, my boy.
I trouble thee too much, but thou art willing.
Lucius. It is my duty, sir.
Brutus. I should not urge thy duty past thy might :
I know, young [folk] look for a time of rest.
Lucius. I have slept, my lord, already.
Brutus. It was well done, and thou shalt sleep again ;
I will not [keep] thee long ; if I do live,
I will be good to thee.

Lucius sweeps his faltering hand over the strings of the lute, and begins to sing ; but nature is too strong for him, his words come more and more faintly, his eyes sink slowly, and at length he fairly drops asleep. Then gently his master rises, takes the lute from his loosening fingers, composes his limbs to sleep more comfortably, and turns — scholar and book-lover that he is — to read by the dim taper in his tent.

                          Gentle [lad], good night :
I will not do thee so much wrong to wake thee.
If thou dost nod, thou break'st thy instrument :
I 'll take it from thee ; and, good boy, good night. —
Let me see, let me see : is not the leaf turned down,
Where I left reading ? Here it is, I think.

                    [*He throws himself on a couch to read.*

Enter the Ghost of CÆSAR.

How ill this taper burns.* — Ha ! who comes here ?
I think it is the weakness of mine eyes

---

* In all properly told ghost stories the lights burn dimly as the spectre approaches.

That shapes this monstrous apparition.
It comes upon me. — Art thou anything?
Art thou some god, some angel, or some devil,
That mak'st my blood cold, and my hair to [stand].
Speak to me what thou art.
   Ghost. Thy evil spirit, Brutus.
   Brutus.   Why com'st thou?
   Ghost. To tell thee thou shalt see me at Philippi.
   Brutus. Well; then I shall see thee again?
   Ghost.   Ay, at Philippi.
                              [Ghost vanishes.

Brutus. Why, I will see thee at Philippi then. —
Now I have taken heart, thou vanishest :
Ill spirit, I would hold more talk with thee. —
Boy ! Lucius ! — Varro ! Claudius ! Sirs, awake ! —
Claudius !
    Lucius [half-waking]. The strings, my lord, are false.
    Brutus. He thinks he still is at his instrument. —
Lucius, awake !
    Lucius. My lord ?
    Brutus. Didst thou dream, Lucius, that thou so criedst out ?
    Lucius. My lord, I do not know that I did cry.
    Brutus. Yes, that thou didst. Didst thou see anything ?
    Lucius. Nothing, my lord.
    Brutus. Sleep again, Lucius. — Sirrah Claudius !
[*To* VARRO.] Fellow thou, awake !
    Varro. My lord ?
    Claudius. My lord ?
    Brutus. Why did you so cry out, sirs, in your sleep ?
    Varro, Claudius. Did we, my lord ?
    Brutus.   Ay : saw you anything ?
    Varro. No, my lord, I saw nothing.
    Claudius.   Nor I, my lord.
    Brutus. Go, and commend me to my brother Cassius :
Bid him [at earliest morn march on] before,
And we will follow.
    Varro, Claudius. It shall be done, my lord.

Brutus had made these inquiries of his servants probably to discover if the
vision had appeared to any other than himself. From their replies he might have
guessed that the fearful phantom was born in his own brain, overstrained with
cares, a heart weighted with grief for his dear Portia, and a conscience which could
not but upbraid him with having murdered his best friend. And yet, in a very
important sense, the spirit of Cæsar still really walked abroad. The Roman people
worshipped his memory. They said he was a god, and had gone back to heaven ;
and they fancied they could see his star ascending the skies. The legions that had
followed him alive to so many victories were still faithful to his eagle standards,
now that he was dead, and were hastening to avenge him. All the conspirators
died miserable deaths in exile : it was as though the spirit of their victim had
turned back their murderous swords into their own bowels. What happened to
the most illustrious of them, we are now to see.

X.

ROM Sardis the armies of Brutus and Cassius marched to Philippi. On one side of the plains of Philippi were encamped the armies of Octavius and Antony; the camp of Cassius was opposite Antony's, and that of Brutus was opposite the young Cæsar's. The hostile forces were nearly equal in numbers.

Brutus was anxious for immediate battle, that he might free his country, and put an end to the toils and expenses of war; besides, he felt that the patriot army was as powerful now as it would ever be, and that delays would weaken rather than strengthen it. Cassius, on account of many bad omens which had disheartened the soldiers, wished to postpone the contest till a more favorable moment; but the counsel of Brutus prevailed. The scarlet robes, the signal for battle, were hung out on the tents of Brutus and Cassius: the two friends gave each other the farewell embrace in the presence of the armies.

A brief parley was sounded, and out from the opposing camps came the generals to hold a conference. Brutus began rather sarcastically, —

> Words before blows : is it so, countrymen ?
> *Octavius.* Not that we love words better, as you do.
> *Brutus.* Good words are better than bad strokes, Octavius.
> *Antony.* In your bad strokes, Brutus, you give good words :
> Witness the hole you made in Cæsar's heart,
> Crying, " Long live ! hail, Cæsar ! "

This reproach aroused Cassius, who interposed, saying, " Antony, the place where *your* blows fall is yet to be known. As for your words," referring to the cunning speech Antony had made to the Romans in the Forum, "they have robbed the very honey from the bees."

" Yes," said Brutus, "and their noise besides ; " adding, —

For you have stolen their buzzing. Antony,
And very wisely threat before you sting.
  Antony. Villains, you did so when your vile daggers
Hacked one another in the sides of Cæsar:
You showed your teeth like apes, and fawned like hounds,
And bowed like bondmen, kissing Cæsar's feet;
Whilst damnèd Casca, like a cur, behind,
Struck Cæsar on the neck. O flatterers!
  Cassius. Flatterers! — Now, Brutus, thank yourself;
This tongue had not offended so to-day,
If Cassius might have ruled.

Here Octavius interrupted : "Come, come, instead of arguing our cause until
we sweat, let us do something for it that will bring forth redder drops." Then,
drawing his sword, he exclaimed, —

Look, —
I draw a sword against conspirators:
When think you that the sword goes up again?
Never, till Cæsar's three-and-twenty wounds
Be well avenged; or till another Cæsar
Have added slaughter to the sword of traitors.[*]
  Brutus. Cæsar, thou canst not die by traitors' hands
Unless thou bring'st them with thee.
  Octavius.   So I hope;
I was not born to die on Brutus' sword.
  Brutus. O, if thou wert the noblest of thy [race],
Young man, thou couldst not die more honorably.
  Cassius. A [foolish] schoolboy, worthless of such honor,
Joined with a masker and a reveller!
  Antony [*sneering*]. Old Cassius still!
  Octavius.   Come, Antony; away!
Defiance, traitors, hurl we in your teeth:
If you dare fight to-day, come to the field.

Here the generals ceased disputing, and repaired to their several camps, to
make ready for still warmer work.

Brutus and Cassius then reasoned together about what they would do in case
the worst should happen. Cassius said, —

If we do lose this battle, then is this
The very last time we shall speak together.
What are you then determinèd to do?

Brutus replied, "I shall arm myself with patience to await the providence of
some high powers that govern us below."

---

* Till another Cæsar (that is, himself) had been slaughtered by the same traitorous
swords that had slain the first.

Cassius. Then if we lose this battle,
You are contented to be led in triumph
Thorough [1] the streets of Rome?
 Brutus. No, Cassius, no : think not, thou noble Roman,
That ever Brutus will go bound to Rome;
He bears too great a mind.   But this same day
Must end that work the ides of March began.
And whether we shall meet again, I know not.
Therefore, our everlasting farewell take: —
Forever, and forever, farewell, Cassius.
If we do meet again, why, we shall smile ;
If not, why, then this parting was well made.
 Cassius. Forever, and forever, farewell, Brutus !
If we do meet again, we'll smile indeed ;
If not, 't is true this parting was well made.
 Brutus. Why, then lead on. — O, that a man might know
The end of this day's business ere it come!
But it sufficeth that the day will end,
And then the end is known. — Come, ho ! away !

 The command of the right wing had been given to Brutus at his request, though it properly belonged to Cassius, who was the older and more experienced soldier. Brutus, in his desire to bring the battle to a speedy close, and thinking, too, that he saw signs of weakness in Cæsar's camp, sent bills (or messages) by Messala to the different commanders, ordering an attack by all at once at a given signal : —

> Ride, ride, Messala, ride, and give these bills
> Unto the legions on the other side.[*]

---

[1] Through.
[*] That is, those commanded by Cassius; the left wing, in fact, of the army.

Let them [attack] at once ; for I perceive
But cold demeanor in Octavius' wing,
And sudden push gives them the overthrow.
Ride, ride, Messala : let them all come down.

Then the battalions of Brutus fell precipitately on Cæsar's camp, and, after some repulses, won a complete victory on that side of the field.

But, instead of pursuing their advantage, the soldiers fell to despoiling the tents of the opposite camp. Meanwhile Cassius, whose troops were opposed to those of Antony, was confused by the sudden movement of Brutus, and speedily found himself so hard pressed by Antony's forces that his horsemen broke and fled, and his footmen began to give way. Cassius did what he could to stem the tide of retreat. He even snatched a standard from a flying ensign, and slew the coward who was carrying it from the fight. But all was in vain, and, accompanied by Titinius, his trusted lieutenant, he withdrew to a little hill, from which he might look down upon the plain.

> *Cassius.* O, look, Titinius, look ! the villains fly.
> Myself have to mine own turned enemy :
> This ensign here of mine was turning back ;
> I slew the coward, and did take it from him.
> *Titinius.* O Cassius ! Brutus gave the word too early ;
> Who, having some advantage on Octavius,
> Took it too eagerly ; his soldiers fell to spoil, .
> Whilst we by Antony are all enclosed.

The noise of the battle seemed to be drawing nearer, and presently Pindarus, the bondman of Cassius, rushed in, crying, —

> Fly farther off, my lord, fly farther off :
> Mark Antony is in your tents, my lord :
> Fly, therefore, noble Cassius, fly far off.
> *Cassius.* This hill is far enough. Look, look, Titinius ;
> Are those my tents where I perceive the fire ?
> *Titinius.* They are, my lord.
> *Cassius.*   Titinius, if thou lov'st me.
> Mount thou my horse, and hide thy spurs in him,
> Till he have brought thee up to yonder troops,
> And here again ; that I may rest assured
> Whether yon troops are friend or enemy.
> *Titinius.* I will be here again, even with a thought.

Titinius sprang upon the horse, and spurred toward the troop of horsemen that were coming in the distance. Then Cassius sent Pindarus a little higher on the hill to follow Titinius with his eye, and report to his master what should take place.

PINDARUS REPORTING TO CASSIUS.

Pindarus. Titinius is enclosèd round about
With horsemen that make to him on the spur.

Now Brutus, seeing the discomfiture of Cassius, had sent a large detachment to his aid. Titinius, meeting this band, was received by them with shouts of joy. Those that knew him dismounted and embraced him as an old friend, while others rode round and round with songs of victory and the clashing of armor. All this Pindarus from his look-out mistook for the clamorous rejoicing of the enemy over the capture of Titinius, and so reported to his master below.

Believing that the day was lost, and that his own capture was certain, and smitten with grief and remorse that he had sent his dear friend to captivity, Cassius called back his bondman. When Pindarus had descended, Cassius thus addressed him : —

> Come hither, sirrah.
> In Parthia did I take thee prisoner :
> And then I swore thee, saving of thy life,
> That whatsoever I did bid thee do,
> Thou shouldst attempt it. Come now, keep thine oath.
>   [*Drawing his sword.*
> Now be a freeman : and with this good sword,
> That ran through Cæsar's bowels, search this bosom.
> Stand not to answer: here, take thou the hilt ;
> And when my face is covered, as 't is now,
> Guide thou the sword.

Pindarus did as he was bidden. Cassius pressed his breast upon the sword, and fell, saying with his parting breath, —

> Cæsar, thou art revenged,
> Even with the sword that killed thee.

Pindarus, knowing he was without witnesses that he had done this deed at his master's bidding, and having some fears of what might happen to him in consequence, gave one mournful glance at the prostrate body, then fled, and was never heard of more.

In a few moments the troop of horse, led by Messala, and bringing Titinius crowned with a garland which Brutus had given him for Cassius, came dashing up. Messala was saying, as they dismounted, —

> 'T is but [exchange], Titinius : for Octavius
> Is overthrown by noble Brutus' power,
> As Cassius' legions are by Antony.
> *Titinius.* These tidings will well comfort Cassius.
> *Messala.* Where did you leave him ?
> *Titinius.*   All disconsolate
> With Pindarus, his bondman, on this hill.
> *Messala.* Is not that he, that lies upon the ground ?
> *Titinius.* He lies not like the living. — O my heart !
> *Messala.* Is not that he ?
> *Titinius* [*bending over the body*]. No, this *was* he, Messala,

But Cassius is no more. — O setting sun !
As in thy red rays thou dost sink to-night,
So in his red blood Cassius' day is set :
The sun of Rome is set.   Our day is gone ;
Clouds, dews, and dangers come ; our deeds are done.
Mistrust of my success hath done this deed. —
What, Pindarus !   Where art thou, Pindarus ?
  Messala. Seek him, Titinius, whilst I go to meet
The noble Brutus, thrusting this report
Into his ears : I may say, thrusting it :
For piercing steel, and darts envenomèd,
Shall be as welcome to the ears of Brutus,
As tidings of this sight.
  Titinius.   Hie you, Messala,
And I will seek for Pindarus the while.

When Messala had gone Titinius cried in anguish, —

Why didst thou send me forth, brave Cassius ?
Did I not meet thy friends ? and did not they
Put on my brows this wreath of victory,
And bid me give it thee ?   Didst thou not hear their shouts ?
Alas! thou hast miscónstrued everything.
But hold thee ; take this garland on thy brow :
Thy Brutus bid me give it thee. and I
Will do his bidding. [*Puts the wreath on* CASSIUS' *head.*]—Brutus,
      come apace,
And see how I regarded Caius Cassius. —
By your leave, gods : — this is a Roman's part :
Come, Cassius' sword, and find Titinius' heart.

Refusing to live when his beloved general was no more, the brave Roman put
the point of Cassius' sword to his breast, fell on it, and died.

Soon after Messala returned, bringing with him Brutus, young Cato, Strato,
Volumnius, and Lucilius.   Brutus, looking for the form of Cassius, and failing in
the confusion to discover it, asked. —

Where, where, Messala, doth his body lie ?
  Messala. Lo ! yonder : and Titinius mourning it.
  Brutus. Titinius' face is upward.
  Cato.   He is slain !
  Brutus. O Julius Cæsar! thou art mighty yet :
Thy spirit walks abroad, and turns our swords
In our own proper * entrails.

---

* *Proper* here is the same as *own*, and the whole expression means our *own, own* — or
our *very own* — entrails.

Cato.   Brave Titinius!
Look, [if] he have not crowned dead Cassius!
Brutus. Are yet two Romans living such as these? —
The last of all the Romans, fare thee well!
It is impossible that ever Rome
Should breed thy fellow. — Friends, I owe more tears
To this dead man, than you shall see me pay. —
I shall find time. Cassius. I shall find time. —
Come, therefore, and to Thassos send his body :
His funeral shall not be in our camp,
Lest it [discourage] us. — Lucilius, come ; —
And come, young Cato ; let us to the field. —
Labeo, and Flavius, set our [legions] on ! —
'T is three o'clock : and, Romans, yet ere night
We shall try fortune in a second fight.

Again the battle raged, the soldiers fought hand to hand in desperate conflict,
and in their midst fought Brutus, Cato, Lucilius, and others. Brutus, to cheer his
soldiers, cried, —

Yet, countrymen, O, yet hold up your heads !
Cato. What [coward] doth not ? Who will go with me ?
I will proclaim my name about the field. —
I am the son of Marcus Cato, ho !
A foe to tyrants, and my country's friend.
I am the son of Marcus Cato, ho !   [*Rushes at the enemy.*
Brutus. And I am Brutus, Marcus Brutus, I ;
Brutus, my country's friend : know me for Brutus.

Brutus plunges into the thickest of the fight. Many noble men gather round
to defend his life by the sacrifice of their own. Cato is overpowered and falls.

Lucilius. O, young and noble Cato ! art thou down ?
Why, now thou diest as bravely as Titinius.
And may'st be honored, being Cato's son.

A soldier with drawn sword springs toward him, crying. —

Yield, or thou diest.
Lucilius.   I only yield to die.*
There is so much that thou wilt kill me straight.   [*Offering money.*
Kill Brutus, and be honored in his death.

Lucilius pretended to be Brutus, thus hoping to gain time for his chief. The
soldiers, believing him to be the real Brutus, and proud of their noble captive,
refused to kill him. "Tell Antony," they shouted, "Brutus is taken !" Antony
arrived.

---

* In Shakespeare it is, "Only I yield to die ; " meaning "I yield only that I may die."

Soldiers. Brutus is taken, Brutus is taken, my lord.
Antony. Where is he?
Lucilius. Safe, Antony: Brutus is safe enough.
I dare assure thee that no enemy
Shall ever take alive the noble Brutus :
The gods defend him from so great a shame!
When you do find him, or alive or dead,
He will be found like Brutus, like himself.
    Antony. This is not Brutus, friend; but, I assure you,
A prize no less in worth. Keep this man safe,
Give him all kindness : I had rather have
Such men my friends ' than enemies. Go on,
And see [if] Brutus be alive, or dead ;
And bring us word unto Octavius' tent
How everything is chanced.

When Brutus, after hard and desperate fighting, found that all hope of victory
was gone, he gathered the few friends that yet remained to him, and, withdrawing
a little from the fight, sat down with them upon a rock. Then, one by one, he
secretly entreated them to end a life that was now valueless to him. Clitus and
Dardanius both refused, though they were deeply touched by his great sorrow.
Brutus then called Volumnius aside.

Brutus. Come hither, good Volumnius : list a word.
Volumnius. What says my lord?
Brutus.   Why, this, Volumnius.
The ghost of Cæsar hath appeared to me
Two several times by night: at Sardis once ;
And, this last night,[a] here in Philippi fields.
I know my hour is come.
Volumnius.   Not so, my lord.
Brutus. Nay, I am sure it is, Volumnius.
Thou seest the world, Volumnius, how it goes :
Our enemies have beat us to the pit :   [*Sounds of battle drawing nearer.*
It is more worthy to leap in ourselves,
Than tarry till they push us. Good Volumnius,
Thou know'st that we two went to school together ;
Even for that our love of old, I pray thee,
Hold thou my sword-hilt whilst I run on it.
Volumnius. That 's not an office for a friend, my lord.
                              [*Sounds still approaching.*
Clitus. Fly, fly, my lord ! there is no tarrying here.
Brutus. Farewell to you ; — and you ; — and you, Volumnius. —
                    [*Shaking hands with each in turn.*

---

[a] Plutarch says : " The battle being at hand, the spirit appeared again unto him, but spake
never a word. Thereupon Brutus, knowing that he should die, did put himself to all hazard
in battle, but yet fighting could not be slain."

Strato, thou hast been all this while asleep ; [a]
Farewell to thee too, Strato. — Countrymen,
My heart doth joy, that yet in all my life
I found no man but he was true to me.
I shall have glory by this losing day,
More than Octavius and Mark Antony
By their vile conquest shall attain unto.
So, fare you well at once ; for Brutus' tongue
Hath almost ended his life's history.
Night hangs upon mine eyes ; my bones would rest,
That have but labored to attain this hour.

Brutus is naturally despondent, and feels that he has lived to no purpose but to die.

Still the sounds of alarm and confusion continue to draw nearer. Voices are heard without, exhorting all to escape for their lives. Clitus echoes the words : "Fly ! fly ! my lord, fly !" "Hence, and I will follow," answered Brutus. Clitus, Dardanius, and Volumnius hurried away. Only Strato remained with Brutus, who said to him, —

I pr'ythee, Strato, stay thou by thy lord.
Thou art a fellow of a good [repute] ;
Thy life hath had some [taste] of honor in it :
Hold, then, my sword, and turn away thy face,
While I do run upon it. Wilt thou, Strato ?
Strato. Give me your hand first : fare you well, my lord.
Brutus. Farewell, good Strato. — Cæsar, now be still :
I killed not thee with half so good a will. [*He runs on his sword, and dies.*

The trumpets were sounding a retreat, as Octavius and Antony and their army, with Messala and Lucilius as prisoners, entered that part of the field. Octavius, seeing Strato, asked of Messala, —

What man is that ?
Messala. My master's man. — Strato, where is thy master?
Strato. Free from the bondage you are in, Messala :
The conquerors can but make a fire of him ;
For Brutus only overcame himself,
And no man else hath honor by his death.
Lucilius. So Brutus should be found. — I thank thee, Brutus,
That thou hast proved Lucilius' saying true.
Octavius. All that served Brutus I will entertain them.
Fellow, wilt thou [take service under] me ?
Strato. Ay, if Messala will [transfer] me to you.
Octavius. Do so, good Messala.

---

[a] This little touch is very lifelike. They are so battle-worn and weary that Strato falls asleep on the hard rock, with the sounds of the conflict in his very ears.

Messala. How died my master, Strato ?

Strato. I held the sword, and he did run on it.

Messala. Octavius, then take him to follow thee
That did the latest service to my master.

Antony. This was the noblest Roman of them all :
All the conspirators, save only he,
Did that they did in envy of great Cæsar ;
He, only, in a general honest thought
Of common good to all, made one of them.
His life was gentle : and the elements
So mixed in him, that Nature might stand up,
And say to all the world, *This was a man !*

Octavius. According to his virtue let us use him,
With all respect and rites of burial.
Within my tent his bones to-night shall lie,
Most like a soldier, ordered honorably. —
So, call the [troops] to rest ; and let's away,
To [share] the glories of this happy day.

THE END.